THE EDGE OF TIME

THE EDGE OF TIME

Loula Grace Erdman

———

DODD, MEAD & COMPANY • NEW YORK

24,778

*The characters, places, incidents and situations in this
book are imaginary and have no relation to any person, place or actual happening*

Two groups of people have helped to build the Texas Panhandle.

The rancher came with his horse and his rope and his gun and built the cattle empire.

The nester came, too, with his wagon and his woman and a plow and built another kind of empire.

Much has been written about the romance of the range. It is of the homesteader that I choose to write, believing that the story of his stubborn courage has been overlooked in the greater glamor that is the ranch legend.

It is to the homesteader, then, that this book is dedicated.

THE EDGE OF TIME

Tʜᴇ *man rode ahead, not looking back, and the woman steered her course by him as a sailor would by a known star. Although she held the reins slack and easy, she was not unmindful of them.*

A cow followed the wagon. A rope, tied to the endgate, was around her neck. Two barrels were fixed to the wagon's side—one with water in it, the other empty. A rosebush in a box of dirt was on the side of the empty barrel. Packed in the wagon were many things—household goods, food, supplies.

The road the man and woman followed pointed like a slim forefinger, southward and westward. It had been years in the making. At first it was a single path, made by a solitary horseman. Others had followed, obliterating his faint markings and, paradoxically enough, at the same time making them more permanent. By now, the road did not need a sign saying, "To Texas."

It was the artery through which the commerce of the land flowed—freighters, bringing in supplies; dusty herds, plodding northward to market. On both sides of it the great ranches sprawled out miles upon endless miles. The business that went over it was cattle business.

And now, where great herds were wont to go, a single cow

I

walked; where groups of freighter wagons had left their deep cuts in the earth, a single wagon came.

This wagon was different from the others, with a difference that went beyond the household gear and the rosebush and the cow trailing behind. A woman was in it.

And a plow.

CHAPTER ONE

Bᴇᴛʜᴀɴʏ ꜰᴜʟᴛᴏɴ knew she shouldn't be letting her mind jump around the way it was doing. A bride ought to listen to her wedding ceremony, weighing every word of it, putting it away in her heart to remember and to cherish all the days of her life.

Wade was standing beside her, stiff and straight, and maybe a little scared, although nobody would suspect it for he was never the one to let on when he was frightened. Even as a boy, the thing he seemed to fear most was being afraid. A lock of black hair fell down across his forehead. He looked as if he wanted to push it back, but wasn't sure whether it was the right thing to do, what with everything being so dignified and all. Bethany knew that look of his. It was as much a part of him as were his blue eyes, fixed steadily on the preacher now, or the way one eyebrow was raised a little higher than the other so that he always seemed intent and questioning, as if he didn't mean to take anybody's word for a thing until he'd had a look at it himself.

Maybe Wade wasn't listening any more than she was. Maybe he, too, had his mind on the wagon waiting outside. She could see it, easy as not, through the lace curtains of the parlor window. The April breezes were ruffling its canvas a little, making it look eager and impatient, like a horse stamping its foot to be off. The wagon that was going to take them to Texas.

It might as well have been the moon they were going to, for all she knew about it first hand. She had only Wade's word for what it was like, and everyone said you couldn't trust a Cameron man when he got to talking about a new country. Everyone of the name had a feel for newness, a great wish to be out and seeing for himself what lay beyond the turn of the road.

"Dearly Beloved, we are gathered together—" Brother Metcalf intoned.

She could feel her heart beating hard and fast, knocking away against her breast so that she wondered if the force of it showed through the dove grey silk of her wedding dress. It was such a plain sedate wedding dress. Mama hadn't liked it at all. It had scarcely any bustle and a tight little basque with no trimming save some white ruching at neck and wrists. Her cousin Rosemary, sitting across the room in a rose and blue striped foulard, made with a fashionably large bustle and elaborate trimmings of lace and satin ribbon, looked much more bridelike than the bride herself.

"If there was time, we'd make you one like it," Mama had said. "Oh, dear, I wish we didn't have to hurry so—"

Bethany didn't mind the plainness of her dress. She liked it as it was, the front of it smoothing down neatly over the delicate curves of her breast, the modest bustle from which the grey drapes fell gracefully. The color showed off to an advantage the warm olive tones of her skin, her brown hair, her hazel eyes. The dress was exactly right to be taking into a new country where people had other things besides the latest styles to think of.

She could feel Rosemary's blue eyes fixed on her in a look

that was a mixture of light mockery, spoiled petulance, and something else that set Bethany to trembling a little. Wade must have sensed this, for he moved his shoulder a fraction closer to her in a pressure that was strong and sure.

"Do you take this man?" Brother Metcalf was asking her.

Haven't you any shame at all? Rosemary had said. Any shame at all? Falling into his arms like a spineless idiot when everyone knows he's taking you just to spite me. Do you think you can hold him, getting him like that!

Bethany tore her eyes away from Rosemary. She had no business looking at her in the first place.

"I do," she said steadily.

"I pronounce you man and wife," Brother Metcalf said.

Wade bent to kiss her, and then he brushed back the lock of hair that had been bothering him. Mama took Bethany in her arms. She was crying a little, but that didn't mean she was unhappy. Mama cried easily.

"Bethany, you looked sweet—" she said. "You were lovely—"

Papa's eyes were wet when he kissed her, and Bethany might have cried a little then herself, only Papa blew his nose hard, after the kiss was over, and turned to Wade.

"Well, well, my boy," he said, "she's yours now, and don't think just because she's a quiet little thing she'll always do what you tell her to!"

Everyone laughed then which was what he had meant them to do. After that, the good wishes came easy and natural—the preacher first and then Uncle Fred and Aunt Clara and, last of all, Rosemary.

"I'm sure I hope you'll be very happy," Aunt Clara said darkly, as if she hadn't the faintest notion she'd get her wish. Aunt Clara was given to dire predictions and always took it as a personal affront when things turned out better than she had feared.

5

Rosemary said something airy and light about wishing her the same. She kissed Bethany casually, a mere brush across the cheek, and looked as if she were considering kissing Wade too. He managed the moment very nicely, taking her hand and saying, "Thank you, Rosemary," as if her good wishes to Bethany had also included him.

The minister took the new Bible Papa handed him, and filled out the decorated pages labeled "Marriages." He signed his name at the bottom and had Bethany and Wade sign. He asked Uncle Fred and Aunt Clara to sign as witnesses. He blotted the page and handed the book to Wade, who stood uncertainly, not quite knowing what to do with it.

"Here," Mama said, "just lay it on the center table and then we'll go out into the dining room for something to eat."

The dining room table looked beautiful. There was a great bouquet of early jonquils in the center and at one end the tiered wedding cake, with little candy decorations all over it and, on the top, a bride and groom. The bride's dress was made from scraps of Bethany's own. All the best china and silver were there, and the silver coffee pot that had been Great-grandmother's pride. Matilda, her black face alight with excitement and well-wishing, came in with plates of hot biscuits and a dish of chicken salad. Never fear the neighbors wouldn't have all the details, and soon. Bethany Fulton and Wade Cameron may have had a quiet wedding, but it was a proper Star Hill one, with flowers and a big cake, and a reception afterwards. Chicken salad and hot biscuits and a tiered cake meant a reception, even if only a half dozen people were there to eat them.

Bethany cut the cake, and they all stood around talking and eating. Wade looked at her impatiently, as if to say, "Isn't it time we were off?"

"Excuse me," Bethany said, more to reassure him than for politeness, "I'm going upstairs to change."

6

"Want me to wait to dig up the rosebush until you come down, honey?" Papa asked.

She could not speak; she only nodded.

"I'll go with you," Mama said.

They went out into the hall, with its umbrella stand in the corner, up the stairs with the big clock on the landing just where the stairway turned. Bethany glanced at the clock—it was just ten. Not a half hour ago she had gone down those stairs as Bethany Fulton. She came up now, Bethany Cameron. Her heart started beating again, the way it had during the ceremony. They went into her own room, with its mahogany bureau and the bed with the white spread and all the other things she had looked at every night and morning since she could remember.

"Here," Mama said. "Let me unhook your dress for you."

Bethany could have done it herself, easy as not, but she let her mother do it.

"I feel bad," Mama said, busying herself with the fastenings of the dress, "sending you off with so few clothes. I'll try to have some stitched up for you, or at least send you some lengths for them, after you are gone."

"I have plenty," Bethany told her. "It isn't as if I were going to live in town."

They were hunting for things like that to say—anything to keep back the words that were really on their minds. Words like how far it was to Texas and how one short month ago none of them had dreamed she was going to need clothes in which to marry anyone, least of all Wade Cameron.

She put on her second best dress, a brown challis with little yellow flowers in it. It would be nice to start out that first day. Of course, after that she'd wear those pretty calicos Miss Tillie had made for her. At least she had several of those—new, and bright, and mighty pretty. But this first day was different. Mama packed the grey silk in a box, wrapping tissue paper in

7

the folds. Her mouth trembled as she worked, and her hands shook so that the dress went into the box all crooked. When she had tied the string, she turned to Bethany and took the girl in her arms.

"Bethany, honey," she whispered. "Bethany, my baby—"

"It's *all right*," Bethany said. Her own throat felt tight, as if an iron hand had clasped it hard. But at the same time she knew she was wiser than her mother, and stronger, and more sure. "You mustn't worry, Mama," she said. "*Everything* is going to be all right."

(She was going to make things all right. She had just as good as asked Wade Cameron to marry her, and the words might stand between them all their lives. But she wasn't sorry. She was married to him now, and she was going to Texas with him. She'd have to see that things came out right.)

"We must go, now, Mama," she said. "Wade is waiting for me."

"I know." Mrs. Fulton wiped her eyes. "I'm being silly. Wade's a good boy. I've known him all his life. But it *is* such a long way off."

"Yes," Bethany did not deny this. "Yes—that's why we must be starting."

She turned to look at herself in the little oval mirror atop the bureau, set her second best bonnet on her head and tied the strings under her chin, gathered up mittens and little purse and her coat.

"We'd better go now," she said gently.

She let Mama go out first, and then she turned to take one last look at the room she had known ever since she had been a child. She thought she had never seen the muslin curtains look so white, the low rocking chair so comfortable. Her hand closed tightly on the knob; she hesitated a moment. And then she heard Wade's voice in the hall down stairs.

"—oh, not so long," he was saying. "Six weeks maybe, unless something goes wrong."

Bethany closed the door, followed her mother down the steps, her feet light and sure. Wade saw her, came to meet her.

"Your Pa's gone out to dig up the rosebush," he said. "You're to come on out there."

He put his hand on her elbow with a gesture the like of which she had seen her father use hundreds of times, a sort of helpless male impatience with the slowness of women. It was as if he were saying, "Well, I don't suppose this woman would ever get started if I didn't hurry her a bit."

Mr. Fulton was waiting for them beside the rosebush, spade in hand. Now that Bethany was there, he dug deep into the ground. He lifted the shoot gently, leaving some of the dirt on the roots. Then he wrapped it in a sack and set it in a box of dirt.

"There, honey," he said, straightening up, "I guess it's ready to go to Texas. Ought to travel fine."

He saw Bethany standing there in her brown challis, with the little bonnet on her head.

"I reckon," he said gently, "you're *both* ready to go to Texas."

And then they all walked toward the wagon.

The canvas top looked very white against the greenness of the bed. Anyone would know this was a new wagon, bound upon a new adventure. It had a fresh, urgent look about it, as if it knew quite well it was undertaking an important journey. Two strong horses were hitched to it and by the side of one of these was tied Wade's riding horse, Rex. Behind the wagon trailed a good little Jersey cow, her calf only recently weaned.

The wagon was packed with supplies of Wade's selection, things bought with money left over from the sale of his mother's little house. After he had bought what he thought was needful, he still had some money left. He told Bethany about it.

"I'm packing it in the sack of seed in the bottom of the

9

wagon," he said. "Unless something unexpected happens, we won't be needing it until we get to Texas. But you remember where it is, in case we do."

It was the strangest thing—when Wade told her where the money was, she felt almost as much married to him as she did when the preacher said the words over them.

Her own family added to the wagon's store the sort of dowry they would have given her had she married a farm lad at home. A cow. (They would have given her a dozen hens, but Wade said they'd better not. The coyotes were pretty bad out there.) A rag carpet, hand woven. A feather bed and some home-made quilts and bed linens. A set of dishes from the Store. Fifty quarts of preserves and jelly and things like that. Two hams and three sides of bacon. Some seeds for the garden. And three books—the poems of Longfellow, *Pilgrim's Progress*, and the family Bible into which the marriage record had been written. Wade's gift had been a side saddle.

"You'll surely need it when we get to Texas," he told her.

The wagon was a magnet now that drew them all toward it. Wade untied the horses, and Rex looked at him with nervous questioning. What sort of foolishness is this? the horse seemed to ask.

"Well, I guess it's time we started," Wade said. He shook hands all around, even with Rosemary.

Bethany kissed her mother first, and then her father. Uncle Fred and Aunt Clara pressed forward to kiss her, and Rosemary, after a slight hesitation, kissed her too. Then Bethany went back to her mother's arms to cling, just for a moment. After that she turned to Wade.

"I'm ready," she told him.

He lifted her to the seat of the wagon and got in beside her. The neighbors came out on their front porches to wave—Mrs. Malone and Mrs. Sanders and old grandfather Clark, leaning on his cane, a sort of fierce yearning in his faded eyes.

"Good-by," they called. "Good luck—"

Wade sat very straight. He looked first at Bethany, and then at Mr. and Mrs. Fulton, standing together at the side of the wagon.

"It's not as far as it sounds," he told them. "Texas isn't. If you get sick, or need her, or anything, just let me know. I'll rush her up to Dodge City by stage and she can catch the train there and be home in less than a week."

He hesitated a moment, and then went on, knowing that the thing he had been saying was not what they really wanted to hear.

"Don't worry," he added. "I'll be good to her."

He tossed the black lock off his forehead, slapped the lines over the horses' backs.

"Get up," he said.

And headed the wagon west—toward Texas.

Bethany turned to wave, seeing them standing there and seeing at the same time the little village of Star Hill—the white houses, sitting close and companionably together, like friends who have just drawn chairs up into an intimate circle so that they may enjoy each other more. The churches with their white steeples. Main Street, with its stores and post office and Dr. Henson's little office. Trees, their leaves as yet small and palely green, their branches arching out across the street to touch one another. And in the front of every house beds of yellow and purple and pink flowers, blossoming into multicolored loveliness.

The street turned slightly so that, in order to see Mama and Papa, she must look back through the wagon. That was the last she saw of them, through the oval bow of the wagon. They were still waving, although it was doubtful that they could see her.

The road ahead stretched out wide and straight. It was as if it opened up to receive them, pushed aside its barriers to make room for them. Behind them, the road dwindled down, growing smaller and smaller, until at last it closed in on the town and the people they had left. And, like the road, Bethany's heart ran both forward and back, on a path whose beginning and end were strangely alike.

For she had grown up on talk of Texas. She had grown up loving Wade Cameron.

She was born in 1866, the year a quarter of a million Texas cattle were driven up the trail to be shipped from Kansas City or St. Joseph. Star Hill, the little Missouri town of her birth, was only a few miles from the trail, so that the sight of these cattle—lean as greyhounds and covered with dust and bearing faint resemblance to fat staid cattle in Missouri pastures—was a thing familiar to all. The men who drove them were a race apart as well. They too were lean and hard after months in the saddle—soft-spoken and straight-shooting. At their belts they wore six shooter guns, looking so much a part of them that you felt maybe they slept with them in place. They sat their saddles easy-like, and pushed their hats back on their heads with a nonchalance that was at once both arrogant and deprecating. And their talk, with its slow, drawling intonations, was big talk. They talked of ranches so that every man who listened yearned to be up and away to Texas.

The ranches were so big, they said, that beside them a section of land wasn't any more than a pocket handkerchief someone had dropped accidental-like; that you didn't have to buy your land—you just turned your cattle out to graze, free, on grass so rich it was all a cow-critter needed to live on. They said it was the only life for a real man—raising cattle in Texas was.

Small wonder that all the little boys of Star Hill played at being cowboys and said when they grew up they were going to Texas. Most of them forgot all about it later. Wade Cameron did not forget.

Bethany could remember him, a rope tied at his waist, a red handkerchief around his neck, out in the vacant lot practicing at lassoing tree stumps, going out to the pasture behind the houses to practice on Bossy, the gentle little Jersey. She and Rosemary would follow him about, their small legs aching with their efforts to keep up with him.

"Wait for us, Wade—" they would cry. "We're coming—"

"Oh, golly gee—can't a fellow go anywhere without you two kids following him?"

But mostly he waited.

Wade, mending their toys for them, making them slippery elm whistles in the spring, shooting rabbits and tanning hides for doll furs. He hunted a great deal, sighting down the barrel of his little rifle as if he thought he was a cowboy picking off a bad man. He could sell the rabbits in town, so it was a waste of time to stop and skin them, the way the girls begged him to.

"Silly—cutting up this stuff to stick on doll clothes—"

But he took great pains with the fur so that it was soft and pliable. Rosemary still had some of it, packed away with her doll things.

The three houses sat close together—Rosemary's and Bethany's and Wade's. First came Rosemary's, which was the nicest because Uncle Fred worked in the Bank for Mr. Brad Bishop and Aunt Clara said they had to keep up appearances. Next was Bethany's, which was nice too, because Papa had the store and could get things cheap. Then there was a vacant lot where the boys played, and after that, Wade's house. It was small because Mrs. Cameron was a widow who took in sewing. If Wade hadn't started helping out when he was quite young, she couldn't have managed at all. All the men in town liked to have him help.

"Get that Cameron kid," they'd say. "He's a good worker."

Mostly the children gathered at the Fulton house because Mama wasn't such a particular housekeeper as Aunt Clara was. The three of them played dominoes together on the kitchen table in winter, eating apples and popcorn and sometimes making pull taffy. In the summer they played out in the yard, Rosemary and Bethany making doll houses by the maiden blush rosebush, its pinky-white, velvet-soft petals falling over the playthings. Great-grandmother Allen had brought the first cutting of this bush when she came up from Virginia, years ago. Her daughters and her granddaughters had both made ceremonies of getting a cutting from it on their wedding day. Bethany never tired of hearing the story.

"When I marry, I'll get a cutting of it too, won't I?" she asked her mother.

"Sure you will, honey. But we won't have to think of that for a long time yet."

By now, few cattle were coming up the trail to Kansas City and St. Joe. They went, instead, to the new town, to Dodge City. But the home-keeping men of Star Hill still remembered the old days, and talked of them.

"If I were a young man, and family-free," Bethany's father said, "I'd go right to Texas."

"Oh, I don't know," Uncle Fred objected. "It sounds sort of faraway to me. Don't even have railroads out there, they tell me."

"You just try going off to Texas, Fred Neale," Aunt Clara sputtered, "and see if you don't go alone. Taking Rosemary way out there, to be scalped by the Indians, like as not."

"I didn't say I was going, Clara," Uncle Fred told her patiently. "I said I didn't think it sounded like a good idea."

"I should say not—" Aunt Clara sounded as if she still weren't sure he didn't have things all packed and ready to go.

Bethany and Rosemary sat on the bottom step of the porch, watching for the first star. Rosemary saw it. She closed her eyes, said the bit of doggerel that went with the wish.

"Know what I wished?" she asked, opening her eyes.

"You daresn't tell," Bethany protested. "It won't come true if you do."

"That's a lot of nonsense," Rosemary said. "Things come true if you make them. I wished I'd marry Wade Cameron when I grow up."

Bethany was only eleven, but something hot and rebellious welled up in her heart. Rosemary would do it. She did everything she wanted to. Maybe that came of being all pink and white and blue and gold, like a valentine. When you looked like that, you got everything you wanted.

"I wished it, but I'm not so sure I really want him," Rosemary went on airily. At twelve, she talked smoothly, like a woman. "Mother says he'll never amount to anything. The Cameron men never do. Wade's father could have made all sorts of money here in Star Hill, but he was bound to go to Kansas. And then the Bushwhackers killed him there."

Rosemary paused, as if to drive home the importance of her statement.

"Before that, his grandfather went off to California to look for gold and no one ever heard of him again," the girl continued. "Mother says all the Cameron men have been like that. And now here is Wade, saying he's going to Texas and be a cowboy."

"Maybe it's a good thing, being a cowboy is," Bethany said. She rarely argued with Rosemary, but this was different.

"Maybe it's *all right* for him to be a cowboy," she insisted stubbornly.

"Well," Rosemary said, "you needn't be so—so cross about it. I just said he was like all the rest of the Cameron men, wanting to run off somewhere different."

"A man ought to go where he wants to—" Bethany tapered off uncertainly.

It was silly to sit here quarreling over whether Wade should

15

go to Texas when he was only fourteen. It would be a long time before his mother would let him go off and leave her. She was not well and she needed him—both his presence and the money he earned helping in the lumber yard.

"He's a good boy, my Wade is," Mrs. Cameron would say, her adoration showing through her eyes like light shining through a window.

"Oh, Ma—" Wade would protest, pushing back his hair with an impatient gesture. His hair was always bothering him.

"I've a good mind to cut that lock off," he threatened.

"It would just grow back right away," Bethany reminded him sensibly.

"I guess you're right," he admitted. "Say—listen to this one—"

He had got a harmonica and was forever playing it, cradling it against his lips with his hands cupped around it. His first notes were always soft and wavering, as if he were feeling for the melody he wanted. But there was no uncertainty about them. He knew what he wanted to play and by and by he would get around to it; when the thing was right in his heart, then he would let it out. It might be something to dance to, like "Turkey in the Straw," or a sad thing that brought tears to your eyes, or an eerie, lonesome wail like the whistle of a train in the distance. It made his mother nervous when he played.

"His Pa used to play like that," she explained. "When Wade gets that harmonica in his mouth it just seems like he's gone from me entirely."

The girls were growing up now. Aunt Clara made them both new dresses.

"I declare, Bethany," the woman said, snipping away at bastings. "You're that skinny. I can't make a dress fit you right."

"You're like your great-grandma," Mama soothed her. "She

looked like a puff of wind would blow her away, and she was really as strong as a horse. Good thing, too, for Missouri wasn't easy when she came up here from Virginia. You have her coloring, too."

Of course, Bethany would have liked having fair skin and pink cheeks like Rosemary. But she was reconciled to her darker skin tones, knowing she had got them from Great-grandma. She could remember the old lady who, even to the last, retained a certain warm glow in lips and cheeks. Bethany had her eyes, too—hazel, with flecks of deeper color in them, like bits of leaves that had lain long in a forest pool.

"Say, Bethany," Wade said once, "your eyes are like marbles —only, well—sort of soft-like—"

They were, indeed, flecked like a boy's prize agate, but, as he had said, they gave no feeling of hardness. Rather, they seemed warm, as did her brown hair, her rich coloring. About her was a look of neat and compact strength, a quietness that was anchored in the spirit.

Rosemary was always full of light chatter, dimpling prettily as she talked.

"Why don't you get a job at the bank, Wade?" she asked. "Father said he knew Mr. Bishop would take you in."

"I have a job," Wade told her. "Besides, I don't want to work in the bank."

But Rosemary mentioned the matter to her father anyway, and came back to report success.

"Listen, Rosemary," Wade said. Never in all the years the girls had known him had they heard his voice so filled with dark coldness. "I *told* you I wasn't going to work in the bank. You had no business getting your father to ask. Mr. Bishop will think I was afraid to come myself."

"But it's such a good job—"

"Good job nothing. Cooped up inside all day—. Now you just quit talking about it. Hear me?"

For once, Rosemary was silenced. But later she told Bethany how foolish Wade was to turn down a job like that.

"There's Mr. Bishop, a widower with no children. Maybe he would have adopted Wade and left him some of that money. He's that rich!"

"Wade wouldn't want anyone to give him money," Bethany said.

"How do you *know* he wouldn't want it?" Rosemary asked. "Anyone would. Why sometimes I even think it might be fun to marry Brad Bishop, just to get all that money."

"Marry Brad Bishop!" Bethany was incredulous. "Why he's an old man—older than Papa."

"He's no such thing. He isn't much over thirty. He's awfully nice. I've been going down to the bank a lot lately, just to walk home with Father. Mr. Bishop always comes over and laughs and teases me. He doesn't seem old at all—"

"Well—" Bethany was still uncertain.

"But still, Wade is awfully nice. Oh dear—I wish it wasn't so much trouble making up my mind. If you were in my place, what would *you* want to do?"

"I—oh—" Bethany's voice came out thick and blurred because her heart got into her throat and would not push aside to let the words by. "I don't know—"

She did know. She was sixteen years old, and she knew she loved Wade Cameron better than anything else in the world. She was ashamed because she loved him maybe even better than she did Mama and Papa. She could see him coming a block away and her heart would lurch up sudden and quick, as if it wanted to run to meet him. Sometimes at evening when she heard the sound of his harmonica it seemed it was his voice calling to her. She wished she were still a little girl and could run after him crying, "Wait for me—I'm coming, Wade."

Rosemary could still say that. Not in those exact words, but in others that meant the same. And it began to look as if Wade listened to her. He spent a great deal of time at her house, cutting across Bethany's yard to get there.

"Hello, Bethany."

"Hello, Wade."

"Seen anything of Rosemary?"

"No—I guess she's around the house somewhere. How's your mother?"

"Not so well today. Tell your mother she said thank you for the cake."

He walked on, whistling a little as he went. He had grown tall, which was like all the Cameron men, so Mama said. His black hair still fell across his forehead whenever he got impatient or excited about something. That impatience came from the Cameron men, too. Mostly it was with himself, but sometimes it extended to others, even to Rosemary.

The girl was growing into even greater beauty than her childhood had promised—her eyes more blue, her skin clearer, her features more regular. She was completely aware of this beauty, acting upon the knowledge of it with a relaxed sureness as if she felt that the possession of it gave her the right to take whatever she wanted. She appropriated all the boys in town, playing one against the other.

"I should think you'd be ashamed," Bethany burst out. "Telling Wade you'd go to the church social with him and then going off with Don Emery at the last moment."

"I didn't really tell Wade I'd go with him," Rosemary said lazily. "I just said I *might*. And you know yourself you wouldn't turn down a chance to ride that new saddle horse of Don's. If he had asked *you*."

"But you *did* promise Wade. I heard you."

"Why Bethany Fulton," Rosemary opened her blue eyes wide. "I believe you're jealous. Either that, or you're stuck on Wade yourself—"

ı just think a person ought to keep her word," Bethany said lamely, feeling herself go all hot with blushes.

Wade thought so too. When he came for Rosemary, to find her already gone with Don Emery, his anger flared up quick and sharp. By the time he saw the girl, however, he had control of himself. He didn't mention the matter to her, which was something both intriguing and challenging to Rosemary. She herself had to bring it up, dimpling prettily.

"You really didn't understand that I was going with you, did you Wade?" she asked.

"No," he said. "Not after I got to your house and found you gone, I didn't. Now see here, Rosemary," he turned and faced her, looking at her quietly. "You've got a right to go with whoever you want to. But don't go telling me again you'll go with me and then not do it. You hear me?"

"Now Wade," she pouted, "I didn't think you'd be *cross* about it."

"I'm not cross. I'm just telling you what you'd better not do."

After that, Rosemary treated him with new respect; a sort of understanding seemed to exist between them. The town accepted this. They began to say "Wade and Rosemary" as if the two names belonged together. In Star Hill, that was a thing of import.

Wade's mother died the summer he was twenty-one. Her death came as no great surprise to anyone—she had been ill for a long time. Everyone did wonder, however, what Wade was going to do now that he was alone in the little house. It didn't take him long to tell them. He was going to sell the house and go to Texas.

Bethany, who was not at all surprised, got the word from Rosemary.

"Wade's going to Texas," she announced.

"I thought he would," Bethany said.

Rosemary looked at her sharply, as if she questioned Bethany's source of knowledge. And then she went on, more interested in other news, news Bethany could not know.

"Bethany—" she preened herself, pursing her lips so that they seemed to gather her face into a single shape of triumph, "Bethany—*he asked me to marry him*—when he comes back." She made a song of the words.

Bethany stood listening to her, knowing the thing Rosemary was telling her, knowing that foreknowledge made it no easier.

"Aren't you glad?" Rosemary asked.

"Yes—" Bethany told her simply. In a way, she was. If it had to come, better for it to be over. "Are you going to?"

"He *thinks* I am—" Rosemary laughed lightly. "And maybe I will—some of these years."

"I think—" Bethany burst out. But she was never to say what she thought, for just then Wade came walking up to them. There was a look of excitement about him, as if he had come alive all over, suddenly and completely.

"I guess Rosemary told you I was going to Texas," he said.

"Yes," Bethany answered steadily. "Yes—I think it's fine—"

Word came back from Wade in Texas. He had gone to Dodge City. He had got a job working with the freighters plying between Dodge City and Mobeetie. He had bought himself a horse.

"You'd think he'd bought the universe," Rosemary said, "the way he talks about that horse."

He had quit freighting and gone to work on a ranch, which was what he had really gone to Texas to do. Mail sent to Mobeetie would reach him—the ranch headquarters were only about thirty miles or so from there.

"Thirty miles to mail," Rosemary said. "Imagine that—"

In Star Hill, things went on much the same as they had always done. Nothing happened, and everything happened. Bethany celebrated her nineteenth birthday and Mr. Brad Bishop took to driving Rosemary and Uncle Fred home from the Bank in the afternoon, for the girl continued to go down to meet her father when he was finished for the day. Star Hill did not fail to notice and comment.

"Do you think you should?" Bethany asked uncertainly.

"Meet Father?" Rosemary opened her blue eyes wide. "I don't see why not. I've done it since I was a little girl."

"What do you hear from Wade?" Bethany asked, changing the subject.

"Oh, nothing much. He said something about filing on a claim, whatever that is. And buying a few cattle and an extra horse up in the Strip, wherever *that* is. I wouldn't be a bit surprised," she added carelessly, "if he didn't come home before long—"

"Yes," Aunt Clara broke in, attacking her sewing as if she would inflict upon it all her grievance against life. "He'll be coming home, of that I'm sure. I only wish I were as sure that you'd use a little sense. Just a *little* sense—"

Bethany was the first one to see Wade when he came home from Texas. He rode up to Rosemary's gate on a bay horse with a dark mane and a proud light way of putting its feet down. Bethany, watching from behind the parlor curtains, felt her heart stand still in her body, like a clock in a house that has been struck by lightning. He tied the horse to the hitching post, ran his hand across the animal's shining neck, as if to say farewell, and then went up to Rosemary's door. He did not stay long. Bethany knew why. Earlier in the afternoon Rosemary had gone driving with Brad Bishop.

And, just as if Wade had never been gone away, he came next to Bethany. Hearing his knock, the girl made herself walk sedately to the door, holding tight to herself to keep from rushing the way she wanted to. She opened the door and saw him standing there, and could scarcely bring her voice up past the lump of joy in her throat.

"Hello, Bethany," he said.

"Hello, Wade—come in—"

He stepped inside, looked around as if he wanted to check every detail of the house.

"It looks the same," he sighed contentedly. "It looks good."

He turned toward her. "You look good, too," he said. "Good enough to eat."

"Don't," she said. "Mama has some cookies—"

They both laughed at that, and then she led the way out to the kitchen and together they sat down at the table. Bethany got out cookies and milk.

"How was Texas?" she asked.

"Oh, fine—how about another glass of milk? I haven't had any to speak of since I left Missouri."

"I'd think you'd have all you wanted down there in Texas among all those cows—"

"You couldn't get a teacupful from all those range cattle," Wade told her. "And even if there were gallons of it, the cowboys wouldn't milk. That's woman's work. Say, did you see my horse?"

"Yes—"

"Isn't he a beauty? Name's Rex."

"He's awfully pretty. I noticed him when you rode up."

Wade had been gone a year. He seemed exactly the same as he was when he left, yet he was different. A great many things must have happened to him, the way they happened to any boy who went away from home for the first time. They probably weren't all easy things, or pretty things, but the sum of them had given him this new look. He had gone away a boy, and he had come back a man. Even Bethany could see that.

"Have any idea where Rosemary is?" he asked her.

"No—" She really hadn't the faintest notion of where Rosemary and Brad Bishop had been going. "But I imagine she'll be back before long."

"Say, why don't you come out and see Rex?"

It was while they were out admiring the horse that Brad Bishop and Rosemary drove up. The girl saw the two of them standing there, and for a moment the smile set on her face, like a ripple on a piece of ice.

"Why, Wade Cameron," she said. "Whenever did you get back?"

"Just now—"

Brad Bishop helped her out of the buggy, and the two of them came over to shake hands with Wade.

"How was Texas?" the older man asked.

"Fine, sir," Wade told him, never taking his eyes off Rosemary.

Brad Bishop stood there for a moment, as if he did not quite know what to do. Then he turned back to the buggy, got in and took up the lines.

"I'll see you later, Rosemary," he said. "Come down to the bank sometime, Wade, and we'll have a visit."

He touched his hat and drove away.

"Well," Rosemary said lightly, but still with a nervous undertone in her voice, "you did surprise me, Wade. Now come on in the house and tell me all about Texas—"

In the days that followed, Texas was practically all any of them heard about. Wade was full of it. And when he talked, Bethany was reminded of the pictures of men in her history book—tall men and lean with rifles on their shoulders, walking beside covered wagons headed West.

"Mr. Bishop says ranchers are as rich as anything," Rosemary said. "I bet you'll be rich in no time with that ranch you filed on."

"I didn't file on a ranch," Wade told her. "I'm just a home-steader. Except," he added thoughtfully, "out there they call us nesters."

"I've heard about homesteaders," Aunt Clara said. "Or nesters. Whatever you call them, it's all the same. They live in sod shanties, and grasshoppers eat their crops. Then the Missionary Society or their families send them barrels. I've helped pack a many a one."

"I filed on a section," Wade said. It was hard for him never to see Rosemary alone. What he told her must always be said before others—her parents, Bethany's parents, Bethany herself. Rosemary always seemed to manage to have others around when he came.

"A section is a good bit of land," Uncle Fred said, impressed.

"It's not as much out there as it is here," Wade admitted. "I mean, there's less rainfall, so we can't raise a lot of things like we do here. But it's good land, and I already have built a dug-out and a corral and a shed for the stock."

"I guess you sank all your mother's house money in the deal," Uncle Fred said, looking every bit the banker as he spoke.

"No, sir, I didn't. I paid two dollars an acre—part down, and thirty years to pay the balance. I earned most of the money out there."

He seemed to take it as Uncle Fred's right to inquire into his business.

"Two dollars an acre for good land," Papa broke in. "That sounds pretty fine. The way I see it, Texas now is just about like Missouri was when our folks came here from Virginia. A new country. Man's country. You don't know yet what you *can* do with it."

"You make me tired," Aunt Clara snapped. "You're just like all the men. Never was a man yet who didn't fancy himself running right alongside Daniel Boone and maybe even a step or two ahead of him. What I've always wanted to look at is *Mrs.* Daniel Boone's diary. Cooking over fireplaces and dodging Indians and living on squirrels and lye hominy. No new country in mine, thank you."

"Oh, goodness, Mother," Rosemary broke in lightly. "Texas isn't like that. It's 1885, and things are different now."

Wade took out a piece of paper, drew a rough sketch of the state of Texas. On the middle of the part that stuck up like a chimney on a house he drew an x.

"A lot of the state is settled, and pretty much like Missouri. But I'm up in what they call the Panhandle, where the x is. That's new country—not like the rest of the state. Still lots of land there, almost for the taking."

"And nobody there to take it except the Indians," Aunt Clara said. "And they'll get your scalps before you have a chance to get the land, I fancy."

"There aren't many people there yet," Wade admitted. "But the Indians don't bother anybody. I like the country the way it is. It will fill up in time."

He looked like the men in the history books again, and Bethany yearned over him, thinking she could not bear that he should lose his dream.

"I think it sounds lovely," she said staunchly.

He turned to regard her quietly, as if, for the first time since he came back, he was really seeing her.

"It is," he told her.

He told them more about his claim. In Texas, you got your land from the state, and not from the national government. Texas kept her own public lands when she came into the Union. Every other section was school land, so you couldn't get two sections right together. She got herself the prettiest state capitol you ever saw by trading Panhandle land to the company that built it.

"They have a way of getting things done down there,"

Wade said, grinning, as if he pretty much approved of the way.

"What'd you do with your stock while you're gone?" Uncle Fred asked.

"The cattle are running with the other herds—everybody's sort of run together. A friend of mine by the name of Newsome is looking after my other horse. Newsome filed on a section too. Just one between his and mine. Oh, I left things in pretty good shape. But I have to be getting back before long. Want to plant a crop." He looked at Rosemary as he said it.

"How do you get to that—that claim of yours?" she asked.

"You can take the train to Dodge City and go from there by stage to Mobeetie. My claim is about sixty miles farther on and we," he used the word unconsciously, he was so sure, "could get a wagon and go the rest of the way in it. But I figure it would be better to go by wagon from here, taking as much as we could carry with us. Things are awfully high in Dodge City, and Mobeetie, too."

"A covered wagon—like movers—" Rosemary shuddered.

"It isn't bad. You camp along the way and—well, I think you'd like it. I made the trip with the freighters and there was something sort of, well, sort of free about it. I *know* you'd like it."

It was the age-old cry of the pioneer man, trying to tell his woman about a new country. So Daniel Boone might have talked to his wife, explaining his dislike for the smoke from his neighbors' chimneys; so Lief Erickson; so Abram, urging Sarah on to Canaan. But the chances were they did not have to present their cases in front of witnesses.

"Well, maybe—" Rosemary was not entirely convinced. "Oh, my goodness," she cried jumping up quickly as a knock came at the front door, "I wonder who that can be!"

But she did not look at all surprised when her mother got up to admit Brad Bishop.

"Hello, Rosemary!" he said. "Hello, Wade!"

He spoke patronizingly as one might talk to a child who has forgotten himself and is trying to play grown-up. He laid his hat and gloves on the center table, moved over to take a chair as if he quite belonged here.

"What's this I hear about your going off to Texas?" he asked Rosemary. "Wade was down talking to me this morning about it. You, in a little sod shanty on the plains!"

"To Texas?" Rosemary drawled. "Whatever gave you the idea!"

Her words were an affirmation, not a denial.

"I've got to be going," Wade said absently. It was plain that he saw nothing of significance in Brad Bishop's visit. "I have some things to see about. I'll be back later."

When he came back, he found Rosemary gone. So he walked across the yard to Bethany.

"Mind if I stay here and wait for her?" he asked.

"No—come on in—"

"Why don't we sit on the porch? It's nice and warm today."

It was indeed warm for March. But that was not his reason for wanting to stay on the porch. He wanted to be there so that he could watch for Rosemary.

So they sat on the porch, and as usual he talked of Texas. He had been down today checking on supplies. Most of what he needed he could get here. Except a plow. He would have to try to buy one second hand from some homesteader down the trail in Kansas or the Territory. It took a special kind of plow to break up prairie sod.

"Couldn't you get it in Texas?" Bethany asked.

"No," Wade said. And then he added thoughtfully. "They don't like that word, out there—"

It was growing chilly. Bethany shivered a little, although she tried not to.

28

"Good Lord, Bethany," Wade said standing up quickly. "You're cold! Why didn't you say so!"

He was impatient with her for not mentioning the matter; he was impatient with himself for asking her to sit out here. He shook his hair back off his forehead, reached out his hand and pulled her to her feet.

"You little goose," he said, "sitting there and freezing to death and not saying anything about it."

He stood on the step below her, his face on a level with hers, so close that she wondered if he could hear the thudding of her heart. She had never been so close to him before—close enough so that she would have to move her lips only a few inches to touch his. His skin was darker than it used to be; that was Texas wind and sun showing up. She wanted to reach up and touch his hair, outline with her finger the lifted curve of his eyebrow.

Shame—shame—shame to think such things! To let herself think such things about the man who was going to marry her cousin. Her own cousin! Her eyes darkened with emotion.

"Why, Bethany," Wade's voice came to her from afar off. There was a quality of surprise in it, of something else she had never heard there before. "Bethany—I had forgotten how your eyes looked. Those little brown flecks—I used to say they were like my favorite marble—"

He was still holding her hand.

"I liked it better than any marble I ever had," he said. "Always carried it in my pocket for luck—"

At that moment Brad Bishop drove up with Rosemary. He helped her out of the buggy, the way he did it telling all that anyone needed to know about how things were between them. Seeing the gesture, Wade, dropping Bethany's hand, turned to walk toward Rosemary. Brad Bishop did not seem to notice him at all.

"I'll see your father tonight," he said to Rosemary, and drove off.

Rosemary turned to go into the house, saw Bethany and Wade still standing together, speechless, as if they had been caught in the web of the moment and could not struggle loose from it. She stopped to consider them, and then walked over to where they were. There was a kind of glittering excitement about her—the way she walked, the look on her face, the sound of her voice when she spoke.

"I guess I might as well tell you," she said. "*I'm going to marry Brad Bishop*—he asked me, and I am—"

She caught up her skirts and ran across the yard, up the steps of her own house and inside the door.

Wade watched her go, a look on his face Bethany could not bear to see. Hurt, unbelief and a blaze of anger that darkened his features so that she would not have known them for his. It frightened her, that look did. She tugged at his hand a little, to bring him back to himself.

"I'm sorry," she said, not knowing why she said it. She wasn't sorry. She was glad, with a deep exultant joy that swept through her like a wind through a forest—first a faint stirring, and then a force that shook her whole body with its intensity. A sort of inner light flooded her face, and her eyes shone from the midst of it, as if they were the source of that light. She tried to say, "I'm sorry," again, but this time the words would not come. Instead, she said other words, ones that surely could not be her own, although they seemed to fall easily from her lips.

"She's my own cousin, Wade," Bethany said, "and I shouldn't say this. But I think it's a terrible thing she has done. I don't see how she could. I think—I think it would be the most wonderful thing in the world to go to Texas."

She hesitated a moment and then went on, not dropping her eyes as she should have, but facing him frankly.

"—to go to Texas—with you—" she finished, scarcely above a whisper.

Well, she was going to Texas with him. The road behind them had closed in now, so that not even a small part of Star Hill was showing. This wagon was her world, suspended between past and present, each revolution of its wheels taking her farther away from all she had known. Wade held the lines loosely, facing straight ahead, in the direction they traveled.

"Are you comfortable?" he asked her.

"Yes," she answered stiffly.

How did a man and woman talk together, anyway, just after they were married? Oughtn't he tell her that she was wonderful, and that he had never thought he would be lucky enough to get her? Oughtn't he do something besides just watch the road ahead? Maybe *she* ought to say something—easy and light, so he wouldn't know she was embarrassed and even a little scared.

"Your Ma was right brave about letting you go away," he said, breaking the silence. "I thought there for a minute she might not be, but she was."

"She'll miss me," Bethany said a little thickly. She hoped she wasn't going to start crying: here, at the very beginning of her wedding journey.

Once more a constrained silence fell over them. Wade cleared his throat. "If you like," he said, "we can stay at the hotel at Elvon tonight instead of camping out. We'll get there about evening."

Bethany felt her face grow hot. She clasped her mittened hands tightly together in her lap.

"No," she said primly. "Let's just camp. We better get used to it."

Wade turned to face her. He grinned at her. "Good Lord, Bethany," he said. "*Relax.* If you sit that stiff your back will

31

be broken before you even get started to Texas!" He shifted the lines to one hand, put his other arm around her.

Funny thing—she hadn't cried at all when she left home, but now she was crying, the tears slipping down her cheeks to the front of the second-best challis.

Wade's arm tightened around her. He kissed her, not at all the way he had kissed her after the wedding ceremony, but hard and quick, bending her head back until the little bonnet fell off, dropping into the wagon bed behind her.

"Bethany, honey—" he whispered. "Don't cry, sugar. You know I'll be good to you. Darling—"

CHAPTER TWO

IT WAS, as Bethany said, the first of many campings. Day by day the ashes of their camp fires pushed forward, each one needling a little ahead of the one they had built the night before. It was as if the line of them was a thread that bound them to Missouri but, at the same time, went steadily on toward their destination.

Their world was this wagon, moving as they moved. The horses set their feet down rhythmically, drawing after them the weight of life itself—food, clothing, shelter. Rex walked along beside the team, not much liking the arrangement, but submitting to it.

"Wouldn't it be better to tie him behind?" Bethany asked. "He doesn't seem too happy where he is."

"He'd like it less in the back," Wade said. He raised his voice. "I wouldn't ask you to drag along behind the wagon with a cow, would I, Rex, old boy?"

The horse shook his head, as if he understood. They were very close, these two; almost they seemed to have a private language of their own.

The country was very beautiful now, green with the fresh bright innocence of a new-born spring. Dogwood hung white on roadside bushes and crabapple thickets were full of tight-budded promise. On every fence post meadow larks sat, their song a silvery sweetness in the air.

Bethany and Wade slept in the wagon on a bed made at the front. Unless it rained, they kept the canvas flap up and through that opening they could look out at a moon-washed or star-studded sky. Outside the stock was tied, so that Wade had only to lift his eyes in order to satisfy himself that everything was all right with them. On his side of the wagon bed, hung easy and safe on supporting pegs, was a shotgun. When Bethany first saw this, she looked at it with a sort of questioning fear and distaste.

"Just to scare off the coyotes," he told her easily. "I've got a rifle packed in the wagon, too. I'm going to teach you to use both of them, some of these days."

The first night they camped out the moon was a new delicate wedge of silver in a richly dark sky. Each night Bethany watched it grow until it was finally a luminous golden circle. It shone all night. She could wake up and see, through the open flap, a world white with beauty. She rose on one elbow to contemplate this loveliness. She had scarcely stirred; her movement was not much more than an intention to move, when Wade jerked straight up, his hands reaching for the gun at his side.

"What's the matter?" he said.

"Nothing— I was just looking at the moon."

"Oh— I thought maybe you heard something—"

"No," she repeated. "I was just looking at the moon—"

He lay back down.

It was a long time before she could go back to sleep. The moon might seem to make of the world a thing of innocent silver beauty, but that did not mean that danger was not in the midst of it. Even though they were still in settled country, Wade slept with one ear open. That shotgun wasn't there just to scare off the coyotes.

34

Bethany soon learned the pattern of these campings. Wade, who had been over the country before and therefore knew what lay ahead in the way of water and other favorable features, planned each day's journey, trying to make a certain number of miles, but stopping short of the goal if they came earlier to a place he liked. He built the campfire while Bethany got out skillet and coffee pot and supplies. Then he cared for the stock while she prepared the meal. At first he was unwilling to let her do the cooking alone.

"You might catch your dress on fire," he told her. "It's sort of dangerous, a woman around a campfire."

"The idea!" she exclaimed. "I'll be careful." She swept a look at him from under her lashes. "What did you bring me along for, anyway?"

"To cook, I reckon," he answered, grinning at her.

In the beginning she burned her hands and scorched her skin by getting too close to the fire or by trying to start while the fire was still too hot. Once it blazed up unexpectedly, singeing her hair and lashes. The acrid smell filled the little camp so that Wade, smelling it, rushed back to her, his face showing white beneath its tan. He snatched at her hair, although there was no sign of fire in it by now. And then he dropped his hands to her shoulders and shook her as a mother shakes a child who has escaped danger.

"You've got to be careful," he said roughly. "You could have burned yourself terribly. I *told* you to be careful."

(No shame, Rosemary had said. No shame at all! Don't you know he'll never love you?)

"I—I wasn't watching—" she said shakily, moved more by his fright than by any danger that might have been hers.

"You've got to watch out," he repeated. "Women have been burned to death over campfires."

He dropped his arms, and the color came slowly back into his face. Then he grinned at her, tossing back his hair.

35

"I can't have anything happening to you," he told her. "I promised your Ma I'd take care of you."

On Sundays they did not travel at all. They rested and let the stock rest. Wade saddled Rex and rode him around the camp—not far, but enough so that man and horse kept the feel of each other. It was a strange feeling—Sunday, and yet not Sunday. It was as if time were out of joint. Wade marked off the days on the calendar so that they would not lose track of them, and when he drew a cross through that first Sunday she felt strange and wrong inside. Sunday ought to be more than just another day on the calendar with an x marked through it.

"Don't you think we ought to—well, ought to read the Bible maybe?" she asked.

"Sure—" Wade was a little self-conscious, but he took the Bible she handed him. He cleared his throat, turned some pages and began to read.

"The Lord is my shepherd," he read. He finished the psalm, closed the book.

"Do you suppose you could sing something?" he asked.

"I guess so—I'm not sure I can get it pitched right, though."

"Wait a minute—"

He went to the wagon, came back with his old harmonica. He put it to his lips, cradling it in his hands, feeling for the notes.

"I'll play," he said. "You sing—"

He had the tune now, clear and distinct. She knew the words to that one, and began to sing,

"On Jordan's stormy banks I stand—"

The words floated out on the morning stillness. Wade was playing, with no hesitation at all. It didn't seem right, playing church songs on a harmonica. There was something sort of sacrilegious about it. No, there wasn't either. It was beautiful, like the harps of old, maybe even like the one the boy David had played upon.

"I'm bound for the promised land," she sang. Wade put down his harmonica and began to sing with her.

"Oh, who will come and go with me," they sang together. "For I'm bound for the promised land—"

It was well that Wade marked off the days on the calendar, for otherwise Bethany would have lost touch with them altogether, so much alike they were. And yet, for her, each one had a certain individual beauty, a quality that drew the two of them more closely into a private world of their own. They saw a house ahead of them a mile or so away, worked toward it until by and by they came to it, and left it behind as they had so many other houses on the road they had been traveling. It was as if time and the world stood still to let them pass.

Sitting by her side on the wagon seat, Wade talked much of Texas. She was not sure whether he did this because he liked talking about it, or because he wanted to prepare her for what was coming. They had to live on the claim three years, he told her, and make some improvements. That was part of the agreement. He had to pay interest on the money he still owed. He could manage that all right, though. He meant to plant a crop. That was why he was going to pick up a plow on the way out. He had to get back to plant that crop. Besides, if he stayed away too long, someone might jump his claim. It was a good one, not too far from water.

"You mean—you mean we don't have water at the *house!*" Bethany was incredulous.

"Good Lord, no." He tried to explain to her. There were scarcely any wells in the Panhandle—you had to go too deep to get water. Mostly what they had came from springs and creeks and lakes and rivers. He was lucky that he had only one section between him and water. Newsome—the friend who was looking after his other horse—had a section with a spring on it. Wade got land as close as he could to him.

"Is Newsome a—a nester, too?" Bethany asked.

"No—he works for the Boss of Triple T. When they passed the homesteading law down at Austin, the Boss had Newsome grab off the section with the spring on it. Fact is he got his cowboys to file on most of the good sections around—the ones with water on them. He'll buy from them after a while. Most of the ranchers did that."

"Why didn't they file on it themselves?" Bethany asked.

"Because the law says you can't file on more than one section of arable, or seven of grazing land. And one section of land—even seven sections—well, a rancher wouldn't think that was much more than a joke. Except one with water on it— that's a different thing again. Anyway, the Boss had Newsome grab that spring. But I've got my eye on it. I'm thinking Newsome won't be staying long. His wife doesn't like the country."

He told her about the dugout.

"It isn't like a soddie," he said. "It's really what you call a half-dugout. It's dug back into a rise of the land and has boards up above ground with sod for a roof. It's cooler in summer, warmer in winter, than a real house. And it has real glass windows."

Bethany didn't see anything so wonderful about that—all houses had real glass windows. But she didn't tell him that.

"Usually it's hard to get freighters to bring in stuff like glass and things they figure we could do without. But Hud Johnson—he's the freighter I worked with—did it for me. Told me I was crazy for wanting glass when I could make out with paper, but he brought it anyway."

38

"That's fine," Bethany said. "I have some pretty curtains in my box."

"It's good you have, because it isn't easy to buy things like that. You've got to sort of figure out a place, and get ready for it. Can't go off somewhere and expect the things you need to fall in your lap. That's why I want to pick up that plow. We're getting out where I'll begin looking."

He came upon his plow. Yes, the man was willing to sell. He had his sod broke up, and after that he'd use a different kind of plow. But where did Wade aim to take it, if it was any of his business?

"To the Texas Panhandle."

"I reckon it will be about the first one out there."

"There aren't many, and that's a fact."

"Well, I wish you luck. But from all I hear, that's not farming country."

"Nobody's tried it yet, to speak of."

Wade tied the plow under the wagon, and they drove on.

True to his promise, he taught Bethany to shoot, both the rifle and the shotgun.

"Now you just hold that shotgun tight against your shoulder, or it will kick like the devil," he warned her.

She did not hold it tight enough, and it kicked just as he said it would. But she kept on until she was able to handle it with little or no difficulty. Occasionally she would bring down some of the game so abundant around them—prairie chicken, quail, plover. At such times, Wade was as proud as she was of the exploit.

"Some woman I got," he said. "Goes out and shoots her own game and then cooks it this good! Say, pass the milk for the coffee."

"There isn't much," Bethany said. "You brought in scarcely any tonight, remember? She must be going dry."

"It's just traveling, and not enough good grass. You wait till

39

you get her on that Panhandle grass and you won't be able to find buckets enough to hold the milk."

"You're bragging—" she told him.

At night he got out the harmonica and played, one tune following another with a sweetness that went far beyond the bounds of the little camp. The firelight fell across his face, lighted up his hands as they cupped the instrument against his lips. He played "Old Zip Coon" and "Turkey in the Straw," and then "My Bonnie Lies Over the Ocean" and "Sweet Alice Ben Bolt."

"She didn't have much spunk, that one," he lowered his harmonica to say. "You aren't going to get much of anywhere trembling every time some one frowns at you."

He sat on the ground beside the campfire and she sat at his side. Close enough so that he could lay his hand on it was the gun. By now she scarcely noticed it.

Sometimes they camped with other people, which was an occasion for great visiting among both men and women. Then the men were quick to strike up acquaintances. Often Wade would take his rifle and, with some of the other men, would ride a little distance away to look for game—larger stuff now, because there would be more to share it. They would come back with an antelope, or occasionally a deer.

The women stayed behind to wash, to catch up on different chores and to visit. They were starved for companionship. Bethany got so that she could tell just by looking at people in which direction a wagon was going. The people headed West were full of hopes and high plans. Those going East were lost to hope, like ashes of the burnt-out campfires. Something had once flamed up in them, bright and sure and clear. But by now it had died down, and there was nothing to take its place.

"If yo're a-plannin' to go to Nebrasky," a man said, "you jest as well to turn around and hit back fur home. They ain't nothin' but drought and grasshoppers out there. I sez to the ole woman, 'we'll jest go back to yore folks in Arkansaw and leave Nebrasky to the 'hoppers, seein' as how they want it so bad.' "

"I'm going to Texas," Wade told him.

"The way I hear it, Texas ain't no better. Besides, that's ranch country and you won't be in nowise welcome."

"It's been opened for homesteading," Wade said. "Nobody said anything when I filed on my section."

"Where'd you file?" another man asked.

"In the Panhandle—on beyond Wolf Creek."

"A section—in that country. Good God, man—I guess nobody needed to say anything. You might as well try to build a house with one match stick as to make a living on one section out there."

"Mine's not like that," Wade said. "Mine's good land."

"Well, go ahead and try. Some men won't ever learn a fire is hot until they burns their fingers on it."

The women in the wagons were different, too. In the West-bound ones, many were young. Some had little children. Others, in the vernacular of the time, were just beginning "to show." They did not seem to be afraid of anything a new country had to offer, or if they were they did not say much about it, being still young and in love with their husbands and full of great dreams. The thing they minded most was going so far from doctors. In their hearts they were already praying for the greatest boon a pioneer woman could ask for— "an easy time and a well baby."

"Oh, you'll git along all right," the woman headed home from Nebraska told them. "Only trouble is, you jest as well to plan on givin' up a tooth for every young'un."

She grinned at them, pulling her lips down over snaggled-toothed gums, ducking her head sidewise like a bright bird.

"Some times I git to wonderin' if they are worth it," she added, still grinning.

41

The women listened to her, divided in their reactions, some vowing to themselves they would never be like her, some fearing they would.

Glad as Bethany was for a chance to be with other women and to talk with them, she was relieved to be away from people who bore so plainly the badge of failure.

As they went farther, they did not see so many other people. And it seemed to Bethany, looking out of the opened flap from her bed in the wagon, that she had not known stars could be so bright. She learned to watch for the Big Dipper, knowing that the North Star pointed toward home, or what had been home. She remembered that she and Rosemary used to watch for the first star of evening, and wish on it. But this she never told Wade. She never mentioned Rosemary to him. The name stood between them, a thin layer of reserve, like a pane of glass separating a room from the real world outside. You did not have to mention it in order to be aware of its presence.

Then came a night when there were no stars. Bethany awoke to see a sky black and thick, soft and menacing. It seemed to close down on her, squeezing her into the shape of nothingness. In the engulfing stillness, she reached out her hand toward Wade. He was not there.

She tried to scream, and no sound came. Her throat went through all the motions of sound, and yet there was only silence. She struggled until she brought her body to a sitting position, and then she felt the words rip from her throat.

"Wade—" she screamed. "Wade—Wade—"

Her voice was a rising crescendo of fear and horror that split through the dark menace of the night like a flash of lightning through a black sky.

He was there beside her. Out of the blackness he came, that terrible unfathomable blackness. He was breathing quickly, as if he had been running in great fright.

"Bethany," he cried. "What's wrong?"

"You weren't here," she whimpered, feeling all the embarrassment of an unreasonable child. "I woke up, and you weren't here."

"I had just gone to see about the horses," he said. "It's going to rain, and I wanted to be sure they were tied fast. Sometimes Rex gets nervous, just before a rain—"

"You weren't here—" she repeated, as if that explained everything.

"You little idiot," he said, but on his lips the words had no sting. "That was no reason to yell like that. You sounded like a snake had got in bed with you."

He got into the wagon and lowered the flap. There was no dividing the blackness he shut out from that which he shut in. But she felt as if in that single gesture he closed out all that menaced her, shut in all that was warm and safe and beautiful.

Suddenly she was crying. He reached out to touch her shoulder awkwardly.

"Stop crying, silly," he said. "I'm here now."

She clung to him, still sobbing, so that the very violence of her grief filled the wagon, reached out until it was a part of the dark vastness of the night.

"Why, Bethany," Wade whispered. "Don't take on like that. You know I wouldn't leave you. Bethany—honey—"

They drove on. They crossed the Arkansas, they crossed the Cimarron. The character of the country began to change. Trees and streams were left behind—gradually, as the days went by, there were fewer of them. It was as if the substance of them spread thinner and thinner in a process so gradual as to be indiscernible until finally one would be conscious of the fact that, where once they were, now they were not. With the thinning out of the trees, the settlements grew more scarce. In a curious sort of way the trees seemed to nourish the people.

So long as they were in tree country, wood for campfires was no problem. Even when the trees thinned out, in the bad lands, there were bushes and roots enough to cook with. But now they had come to a place where there were no trees, nor roots, nor bushes.

One evening Wade came up to build the campfire, carrying a small box of flat whitish disks. He began heaping them on the ground.

"What have you got there?" Bethany asked idly. And then suddenly, she knew. Not for nothing had she heard the stories of the plains pioneers. They ate jack rabbits and they burned—no, she would not!

"Cow chips," he told her. "I hoped we'd find some around this water hole."

"I won't," she cried. It was the first time she had protested any of his decisions. "They're—they're filthy—" She choked in her distaste and disgust.

He picked up one of the disks, handed it to her.

"Take it in your hand," he said, so quietly that she was afraid to disobey.

She took it, stood holding it. It was still warm from the sun, and it felt like dried punk, like the soft dead wood sometimes found at the side of an old tree stump back home.

"Now drop it," he said, "and look at your hands."

She looked at her hands, brown and travel-stained—but not dirty.

"Remember how they used to look after you had handled a piece of coal?" he asked.

She remembered, all right. The way coal dust ground into her knuckles, into the pores of her skin. The acrid taste of the smoke in her lungs, and the greasy film left on furniture and walls.

"Cow chips are nothing more than dried grass," he went on. "They've had a few things happen to them, but mostly, they are just dried grass—sort of second-hand. Just like coal used to be trees, they say. Just nature's way of using left-overs. This is a sight faster, and cleaner besides."

He bent over to light the fire and Bethany watched, fascinated, as it blazed up—a small, bright fire, clear and pure. Without another word she got out the skillet and the coffee pot and started supper.

They drove on. They crossed the North Canadian. They came to Camp Supply.

Long before this, they had established a pattern which they followed most of the time. Wade had never been too happy that Rex had to trail along always by the side of the team which pulled the wagon. He needed to be ridden more, just to keep him in shape. So Bethany had said, "Now, you go on and ride him part of every day and I'll drive the team and follow you."

Wade was riding ahead the day they came to the Dodge City Road, the day they met Hud Johnson and the freighters. Wade came riding up to the wagon with him. There was a kind of rough gallantry about the man. He took off his hat, and looked at Bethany with bold, though respectful, eyes.

"I'm right pleased to meet you, Ma'am," he said. "Heard ole Wade, the son-of-a-gun, talk about you. But I reckon you can't believe what a man in love says about his girl. Leastways, I never would have known you, Ma'am, from the things he told me about you."

Bethany tried to think of something to say, but no words came. She dared not look at Wade.

"It's good to have you, Ma'am," Hud Johnson went on. "We don't have near enough women in this country, and that's a fact. Anytime you want any little thing brought down from Dodge City, you just have ole Wade send me word."

Bethany said, "Oh, thank you. That's good of you."

"No trouble at all," he said. And went back to his wagon.

45

He cracked his whip over the mules' backs and the long line of wagons moved off. Their going made a jagged hole in the landscape.

They stopped at Sloan's Crossing—two houses and a little store. Sloan and his wife ran the store and the post office and a sort of inn. "You're going to come inside and sleep in a real bed," Sloan's wife told Bethany. "You ain't seen one since you left home, I venture."

"No," Bethany said. She thought—we've never slept in a real bed, Wade and I. Just in a wagon.

Wade decided they would stay for a few days, getting the wagon in shape, resting the horses. It was rough country they were coming to next, and from here on it would be a steady uphill pull. Bethany wanted to get some washing done. She wanted to sleep in that real bed.

The men at Sloan's Crossing knew Wade, had known him from the days when he worked with the freighters.

"So you're headed for your claim," they said. "Well, that's fine."

"Hope you get there without no trouble," one man said. "You ought to. Got the biggest part of the trip behind you."

"Hope you don't meet Poco and Indian Charlie down the way," Sloan told him.

"They on the loose again?" Wade asked.

"Sure are—robbed the mail hack a day or two ago."

They had much to say of those two, Poco and Indian Charlie. Poco was a little man; he got his name from a Spanish word meaning little. The Indian had his right ear notched.

"Like a steer that's been worked," the first man said. "Nobody knows for sure how he got it, but however he did it's sure given him a hate against the world. Team him up with Poco—well—"

"Now don't you be telling such things in front of Miz

46

Cameron," Sloan's wife protested. But Sloan was not to be side-tracked. Even with people coming through for mail and supplies and stuff, he still didn't get a proper chance to talk to folks.

"That Poco," he said. "The way he hates being little. Reckon he has to act cussed, just to prove he's a man. They say somewhere back he must have good stuff in him—can act as mannerly as if he was in a parlor."

"Yep—bow polite and ask permission to put a bullet through your heart. If he needed something you had, he would," the other man said. "Your horse or your stake—"

"Or your woman—" one of them added.

"No—" Sloan's wife put in, looking sidewise at Bethany, "you know he won't bother women. Good women, leastwise."

She turned to Bethany. "That's one thing about this country," she said. "We got so few women out here, they're a sort of curiosity. Hardly ever you come across a man bad enough to bother a woman. A good woman," she repeated, smoothing down her skirt with conscious virtue.

"That's right," Sloan admitted. "You got no cause to worry."

"They're probably in Dodge City by now," Wade said. "We got no cause to worry anyway."

Bethany wished she could be as sure as he was. When they started out the next day, she mentioned the pair to Wade.

"Do you suppose they've really gone to Dodge City?" she asked.

"Who?"

"Those two—Poco and Charlie."

"Now, Bethany," he said impatiently, "you stop worrying about them. They wouldn't fool with little stuff, like we got. They pick stage coaches and mail hacks and things like that."

"Oh—" she wanted to be convinced, but could not quite bring herself to it.

He grinned at her, sorry for his impatience, but unwilling to say so.

"Sometimes it's pretty good not to have much of anything," he told her. "That way, you don't have to be worried about robbers."

Wade had taken the stock to the water hole that evening while she cooked supper, the smoke of her campfire rising straight and lazy toward the blue sky. A smell of coffee, of meat frying, was in the air. She had just bent over to turn a flapjack when she heard men's voices. Their wagon was between her and the men, so she couldn't see who they were. She was not particularly interested—sometimes other travellers joined them in their camping.

"Good evening, friend," she heard a man say smoothly. "Nice evening, isn't it?"

"Good evening," Wade said.

There was something in his voice that brought her to instant attention. Like a man talking across a gun barrel, it sounded. She stood up straight, listening.

"Nice horse you got there," the stranger went on. "Now me, I'm not so lucky. My horse is limping. My pardner's isn't so good, either. I don't suppose you'd be willing to let us have a couple of yours, would you?"

"No—"

The sound of the single word sent Bethany around the wagon. She did not know how she went so fast, but she seemed not to have moved at all until she was clear of the wagon. She saw Wade then, standing with his hand on Rex's neck, facing the men on horseback. Even before she saw them, she knew what those men would look like.

One was a little man; scarcely more than a boy, he looked, from the size of him. He had a silk handkerchief knotted around his neck, a wide white hat pushed back on his head. He sat his horse with easy grace, holding the reins with one gloved hand. The man on the other horse was huge and dark and unkempt. Bethany's eyes flew to him.

"Oh, no—no—" she whispered.

The right ear lobe was notched.

Poco and Half-breed Charlie! All she had heard of them rushed back to her. Wade had said she needn't worry about them, but here they were. "He'll ask permission to put a bullet through your heart," the men at Sloan's Crossing had said.

Wade stood still, just facing them. He did not have a gun— thank God for that. Surely these men were not so low—no man was so low—as to shoot an unarmed man.

"We need two horses mighty bad," the small one said. "Of course, we'd feel a lot better about it if you'd give them to us—"

Yes, he'd shoot a man. If that man had what he wanted, he would, if the owner blocked the taking. He might shoot anyway, just for the sport of it. And what he would do to a woman—

What was it they had said, back at Sloan's Crossing?

"Funny thing, he won't bother a woman. A good woman, that is—"

She rolled down her sleeves, smoothed her hair. Then she walked away from the protection of the wagon, toward Wade and the men. She ignored Wade's desperate, though secret, signal to her to go back, walking straight toward him. Her knees were like jelly; there was a surging of blood in her ears. But she managed to put on a smile as she came, as one pulls on a tight glove. And then the look on Wade's face made them turn, and they saw her.

The small one regarded her carefully, sizing her up. He

wasn't a bit fooled by the smile on her face; he saw the terror that underlay it. He took off his hat and bowed to her.

"Good evening, Ma'am," he said.

Now that she saw his face, she knew he wasn't a boy, for all he had the size of one. He was a man, and he hated being boy-sized. It was as Mr. Sloan had said—he was always having to prove himself. He had to do things differently, so that stories would be told about him—stories that would make people forget how small he was. He was dangerous, that man. He *had* to be.

"Good evening," she said, walking past him.

She put herself in front of Wade. The small one followed her with his eyes. He knew she stood so that a bullet sent to Wade's heart would strike her first. His eyes seemed to look straight into her mind, to search out her thoughts.

She said, her words coming like an echo from a great distance, "Wade, supper is ready. Would you like to ask your friends to stay and eat with us?"

No one spoke. They all stood frozen in the moment, like leaves in an ice-bound brook. It was the little man who finally broke the silence.

"Well, Ma'am," he said, "that is very kind of you. But I don't know that we can. We're—we're rather in a hurry—"

The half-breed laughed, a short, hard laugh.

"So I guess we'd better be getting along," added Poco, "but thank you for asking us."

The half-breed spoke for the first time, his voice slurred and gutteral.

"—the horses?" It was a question he asked.

"On second thought, I don't believe we need the horses."

The half-breed spat out a single word. "Fool—" he said.

The small one sat straight in his saddle. For one moment Bethany had a crazy notion that he was tall, very tall. And, strangely, that the half-breed shrank until he was almost small.

50

"You are not to call me a fool, my friend," the one called Poco said. "Understand—?"

He turned again to Bethany. "Once more, I thank you," he said. "We must be going now. Another time, perhaps, we'll eat with you—"

He lifted his hat and bowed again. Then he turned and rode off, the half-breed at his side.

Bethany watched them go and as she looked, she felt strength draining from her, like water pouring from a glass. She reached out blindly toward Wade.

When she came to herself she was half-lying on the ground, half supported across Wade's knees. She could feel the wetness of her face, of her clothes; she felt, rather than saw, that he was preparing to dash yet more water over her.

"Don't," she sputtered. "I'm all right—"

And promptly fainted again.

This time when she regained consciousness she was in the wagon. Wade was undressing her, pulling off her clothes as if she had been a child. He threw the wet garments across the wagon seat, and seeing that her eyes were open asked, "Where's your gown?"

She motioned toward the box in which she kept it. Not yet was she able to bring herself to speak.

He slipped the gown over her head, straightening it out, touching breast and limbs with impersonal gentleness. He pulled the pins from her hair, letting it fall loose across the pillow.

"Now," he said, "you try to rest—"

She looked at him, her eyes very dark in the whiteness of her face.

"I'm sorry I was such a baby," she whispered. "But I was scared. I thought he was going to shoot you. And if he did, I wanted him to shoot me, too—"

"Well, he didn't," Wade said, trying to speak lightly. And then he gathered her up in his arms, holding her tightly.

"Bethany, honey," he said, his voice ragged and uneven. "You—you shouldn't have done it. A little bit of a thing like you, walking up to Poco and Charlie. You knew who they were, too—"

"Sure," she whispered. "That's why I came—"

She lifted her hand to stroke his face, to feel the solid reality of him, to know he wasn't lying out there on the ground with Poco's bullet in him.

"I was so scared," she repeated with a child's insistence.

He nuzzled his chin against her head. "Don't you feel bad about that, honey," he said. "I reckon I might as well tell you. I was scared myself. I was as scared as the devil—"

They left the main trail now, Wade driving and making Bethany take things easy. They came to Wolf Creek. Here the land was ragged and broken. Everywhere there grew a little reddish-purple flower. Acres and acres of it, stretching on and on.

"Buffalo clover," Wade told her.

There were, too, bushes with sharp sword-like leaves and tall stalks thrusting up from these. Some of these stalks bore waxy white blossoms, cup shaped.

"How beautiful!" Bethany cried.

"That's bear grass. They say the Mexicans call it candle of the Lord."

"Candle of the Lord," Bethany mused. "I like that."

"Little early for it yet," he told her. "Come June, the country will be full of it."

Cattle grazed on hills that faded into blue distances. Now and then she saw horsemen riding. They sat their saddles easy, about them a sense of completeness, as if they, and the horses they rode, and the country itself were one.

"Bethany," Wade said, about his voice a kind of suppressed excitement, "We're in Texas now."

Something prickled in the backs of her hands. She remembered the tales of the grey herds and the men who drove them, and the big talk her childhood had known. She was here at last, in the country that the home-keeping men of Star Hill had dreamed about. She and Wade were in the middle of it, yet they were no part of it. The very bigness of it accentuated their littleness.

She said, her voice sounding strange and faraway, "We're on a ranch, then?"

"Sure—the Lazy Q. Good country for cows, this is. They can find shelter in the breaks. It's good to be close to the breaks. Especially if you get north of them. Then the cattle can drift south when a storm comes and find shelter from the worst of it. There's wood in the breaks. And water."

They drove through these breaks and came at last to the plains.

The first thing Bethany saw was nothing. Nothing at all. She pitched her mind in nothingness, found herself drowning in it as a swimmer drowns in water too deep for him.

Here was more sky than she had ever seen before. That was all there was—sky. No houses, no trees, no roads. Nothing to break the landscape. She shrank back from it, as one draws back from sudden bright light.

"Aren't there—aren't there any *trees?*" she asked Wade.

"Not on the high plains. Too dry for them. They grow down in the breaks, though."

She thought she could not bear a place without trees. They broke up nothingness. They cut a land down to something you stand to contemplate.

"Just look at the grass," Wade told her.

She looked at it. Green and lush, it came to the horses' knees. The wind ruffled its surface as it would the bright face of water. Grass and sky and levelness—they were there. And a great aching loneliness in which there was no sense of direction, no landmarks to tie to. Bethany remembered her Father's words of long ago, "They say the grass out there is all that a cow needs to live on."

"We leave the main trail here," Wade told her. He showed a feeling of great elation, of joy and purpose running full and free through his body. "A couple more days and we'll be there—"

They were blazing their own trail now. Wade would guide himself by things she did not even see—a swell in the land, a clump of grass higher than the rest. By now he rode Rex ahead of the wagon most of the time and Bethany drove the team.

"Oh, Wade," she called, "look in front of you. That butterfly—I never saw one so huge—"

Either the sound of her voice, or of Wade's uproarious laugh, sent the butterfly bounding into the air. Only, it wasn't a butterfly at all. It was a rabbit, and it was the tips of his enormous ears which she had mistaken for a pink butterfly. He ran ahead of them; like the wind he ran, those huge, mule-like ears standing straight up in the air.

"It's a jack rabbit," Wade told her. "Young ones make mighty good eating. Tender as chicken."

A long-legged bird raced ahead of them, waiting until they got almost up with him, looking over his shoulder to see if they were following. Then he would start running again.

"Road runner," Wade said.

There were other sights not so pleasant. Death, as well as life, covered the face of the prairie. Half hidden by the tall grass were countless skeletons of animals, their whitened bones looking as if they might be posted as warnings against the land. Wade saw Bethany's half-fearful glance at them.

"Mostly buffalo bones," he explained. "Hunters killed them by the thousands for their hides. A few cattle, too—got caught in blizzards."

That helped a little, but not much. There was a careless cruelty about a land like this, about his matter-of-fact acceptance of it, that set her shivering, although the day was warm. Life was cheap here—animal life. Maybe human life was just as cheap.

"Now don't you go worrying about the buffalo," Wade told her. "They had to kill him off in order to get rid of the Indians. If it hadn't been for the buffalo hunters, we'd probably be minus our scalps by now."

She didn't worry about the buffalo over much. She felt she couldn't worry about anything, even if she tried. The sun shone in a sky brightly blue. The air felt light and thin. She had a sense of exhilaration, as if somewhere ahead of her in all this nothingness she was going to find something pretty fine. Something that would make up for the sight of skeletons lying bleaching in the sun.

Two days later, about noon, they came to the dugout. Wade, who was riding ahead, stopped Rex, and Bethany brought the wagon to a halt. He got off and came to her, lifted her down from the wagon, set her feet on the ground.

"Well, honey," he said, "this is it. This is home."

CHAPTER THREE

THE DUGOUT sat against a slight rise in the land, was buttressed by it, reinforced and protected. It crouched against this elevation, small though it was, as if it were unconsciously shrinking back from the terrifying vastness surrounding it.

"It's like a cellar," Bethany thought. "Or maybe like a cave."

Even the things Wade had told her had not prepared her for this: unpainted boards rising above the prairie grass, and on the top of these boards again grass—prairie sod making the roof over their heads. Close to the house was a small shed and an enclosure surrounded by posts driven into the ground. It looked like the pictures she had seen of stockades, but she supposed it must be the corral he had talked about. These things— the corrals and the shed and the dugout—seemed to stand out with pitiless clarity in the great expanse of the land. And at the same time they seemed to shrink back into it with an awed and fearsome apology as if they were questioning their right to be here and in their questioning became bumptious and aggressive.

"The poor things," Bethany thought. "They need a few trees and bushes to hide behind. They look like eyes without lashes."

She'd plant trees. She'd have to. Somewhere—in the breaks he talked about, maybe—Wade would have to find her some trees to plant.

"Well," Wade was saying, "it's just like I left it. It looks fine."

She had to say something. He was waiting for her to say something.

"It looks fine," she said.

Later she'd tell him about the trees.

Wade walked ahead of her and opened the door, lifting a rough homemade catch to do so—a catch anyone might have opened from the outside. He saw Bethany's eyes on him, felt the question in them.

"We don't lock doors out here," he said. "Might somebody come along that needed in real bad."

He stood back and let her pass inside.

There was a single room, and it was not large. A homemade bed, strong but with no pretensions toward beauty, was in the corner. It was really a sort of frame across which lengths of rope were woven. Crude though it was, it would hold the feather bed and homemade quilts and make a good enough bed. Not like the ones back in Missouri, but things were different here. There were also a stove, a rough table, and a few chairs. One of these was a rocker, low and shiny. A woman's rocker. Bethany flicked her eyes quickly away from it, brought them squarely back to it. Save for these things, the room was bare.

Wade said, almost timidly, "See— I told you there were glass windows—"

One thing the trip had done for her—she knew what glass window panes meant in this country. They had to be freighted in, and that cost money. You had to think a long time ahead. And when you paid for them, you weren't paying for the windows alone. You were paying for endless miles of space over

57

which they must travel; you were paying for the little bit of space they occupied in the wagon; space that might better be taken by food or by some other vital thing. It was no wonder that the freighters were none too patient with people who wanted any but needful things. Glass windows were a symbol.

She said, "They are lovely, Wade."

"Do you—do you like it?" he asked.

She said, "It's nice—"

No need to tell him she had not thought to find it so small or so primitive. No need to say that, even though he had told her how things were, she still had not quite realized that they would be living like animals in a burrow—dirt for a floor and dirt for a roof and dirt for walls. No need to let him know she was remembering he had built this home, crude though it was, had freighted in the precious glass and the rocking chair, for Rosemary. That the bed was meant to hold Rosemary's dowry bed things. Rosemary was not here. She, Bethany, was here. This house, such as it was, was hers. Hers, and Wade's.

She said, "Why, Wade—it's wonderful—"

"Well," he said, "we'll be getting things moved in."

It was as if someone had handed them a great piece of nothingness and commanded them to make a home from it. There were not the faintest indentations to guide them in their work. Always in Missouri she had taken for granted the equipment of a home. Clotheslines in place, held steady by stout poles. Chicken houses made tight against the weather. Outbuildings and sheds and storerooms. Surely there must have been a time, even at her own home, that these things did not exist. Now they clung about the house like fungus growth on a rock, so much a part of the picture that they would be conspicuous only in their absence.

The dirt floor was hard and smooth beneath her feet. She'd have to get the carpet in and lay it, though how one fastened a carpet to a dirt floor she was not prepared to say. Wade would have to figure out a way. And there wasn't a cupboard to put the new dishes in. They'd have to do something about that. And no shelves. There was, to be sure, a ledge that ran all around the room, up where the boards met the dirt wall of the dugout. She could set a lot of things there. But she needed cupboards and shelves. She did not remember ever having seen a shelf being nailed up at home, and yet they were always magically there, the only problem concerning them being what to set upon them—whether to put the clock, or the blue willow dishes or the coffee mill. Nails too were always where they were needed—close to the stove for pot lifters and behind the door for aprons. There wasn't a nail anywhere in the dugout.

She took off her bonnet, rolled up her sleeves.

"It all looks nice, Wade. But it's going to look a lot nicer when we get the things in."

"Sure," he said. "I'll put the horses in the corral and then we'll start. Anything special you want brought in first?"

She said, "The calendar."

"The calendar—" he thought she was joking.

At home, the kitchen calendar was always covered with cryptic notes, the diaries of domesticity. "Paid Noah fifty cents." "Planted sweet peas." "Set the speckled hen." These were the small, but pertinent, notations of daily life, set down in her mother's neat writing. To Bethany, they were the symbol of the woman who ruled the home.

Here there was no calendar, no nail to hang one on. As yet, there was no home life to record on one.

"Wade," she said, as if the thing she had in mind was tremendous, portentous. And so it was—the first command she would give in her new home. "Wade, I wish you'd get the hammer and drive in a nail for me."

He looked doubtful. "It won't stay," he protested. "These lower walls are dirt."

"It can go above the dirt, into the wood."

"That will be too high for you to reach, to do any good."

"I won't want to reach it often, and if I do, I'll stand on a chair."

He gave in. "Now, before we move things in?"

"Yes—now—"

He found nails in a box in the wagon, and drove one in the spot she indicated. And when that was done, she went to the wagon and got the calendar—the one on which Wade had marked the days of the journey. With a bit of pencil she encircled the day, a Thursday in mid-May.

"Moved in," she wrote beneath it, in her clear round childish hand.

"Now, hang it up," she said.

Wade put in the nail, hung the calendar on it. At the top was the legend, "W. R. Fulton, General Merchandise, Star Hill, Missouri."

He stepped back to contemplate his work. "That the way you wanted it?" he asked.

He spoke with a constrained stiffness. Bethany looked at him quickly.

She knew what was wrong. Even after you had lived with a man only six weeks, you got so you understood what lay behind his words almost better than you understood the words themselves. As well, or maybe better, than you understood your own thoughts. He was scared she didn't like things. He was seeing the dugout as she might see it; for the first time he was realizing it was not as fine as he had thought it was.

"Yes." She went to him swiftly, slipped her arms around his neck, kissed him. No light kiss, this, but something warm and sweet and generous. She could feel surprise running through him—rarely was she the one to kiss first.

"I think it's *all* just beautiful," she told him.

His arms grew tight around her.

"Gosh," he said, "I'm glad you like it. There for a minute, you had me worried—"

They began to move the things into the dugout. Bethany thought it was well that there were so few of them. Even so, some would have to be left in the wagon until Wade had contrived some shelves. They put the carpet on the dirt floor, with a layer of prairie grass beneath it. Wade pegged it down at the edge of the room. She moved the table back against the wall to make more room, and then had Wade bring in the little center table from the wagon. She hung curtains at the windows, and put the straw tick, feather bed and sheets and quilts on the bed in the corner. They worked until it was late, and then she said.

"I'll get supper now. Tomorrow we can move in the rest of the things. And plant the rosebush—"

Quietness settled over the land. Darkness did not seem so much to fall as it did to rise from a hushed earth to the bright face of the sky. And the sky, at first, strained away—resisting, retreating. But at last the night won—slowly, inexorably, until at last all of earth and sky were cradled in its arms.

Bethany lay at Wade's side, awake and listening. It was as if she strained her ears to hear nothing, as if she went out looking for nothing to hear. During the long journey out here she had come to think that perhaps the night sounds of a country were the true essence of it. Then it was that the underlying design of the land came out—the shy, unseen things that hid beneath the bright surface of the day. In Missouri the night sounds were friendly ones—breezes caressing thick-leafed trees, and drowsy night birds chirping sounds of tenderness; horses stamping companionably in barns and chickens making subdued noises when something disturbed their sleep; neighbors' dogs, their barking emphasizing their friendly nearness, calling to other dogs across the moonlit fields. All these were signs of compactness and an established way of life.

61

Now she could hear the wind moving across the prairie—a slithering, vacant sound, as if it were seeking in vain for something substantial to pit itself against, as if it were tired of the cloying acquiescence of grass as a man would tire of a woman whose conquest he found too easy.

The most different sound of all was the sound of the stillness itself. It was not mere absence of noise. It held a positive quality; it had a character of its own, and a substance. She knew it for an adversary—powerful, constant, waiting—but not necessarily unfriendly; rather, it seemed to be taking her measure while it reserved judgment.

And then sound broke the stillness—shivering, tattered fragments of a great and tragic sadness filling the air, like loneliness mourning for all things lost beyond hope of recovery. It shattered into a kind of eerie laughter, and died only to be taken up again and repeated.

She knew it for what it was—the voice of the coyote, that lonely, brooding essence of this lonely, brooding land. She shivered and crept closer to Wade.

The next morning they planted the rosebush. Wade got it out from its box of dirt on the side of the wagon. The leaves had long since dried up and fallen off, so that it looked like nothing more than a few dried sticks. But the soil still clung to its roots—Missouri soil. And when they looked closely at the stems, there was a living cast of green to them.

"It's still alive," Wade told Bethany, answering the urgent question in her mind. "That's not saying it will live when we plant it, but it's alive now. Where do you want it planted?"

She said, "Right here—right by the door—"

The words were thick on her tongue and the taste of salt was in her mouth. She remembered the other doorway it had come from, and the two who had stood there, watching her drive off to Texas. She felt as she had used to feel when she was a little girl away from home to spend the night. Things were all right until dark came, but with it came, also, a sharp, quick rush of homesickness so that it was all she could do to keep from running back to the warm sweet comfort of home—Mama, and Papa, and her own room, and all the dear familiar things.

She stooped and took a bit of dirt from the rosebush, rubbed it gently between her fingers. She and the rose—they were in Texas now, but Missouri had nourished them in the beginning. Only time would tell whether those roots—hers and the rose's—would bear transplanting.

Wade put his spade in the place she indicated, turned up a shovel full of dirt, in the prairie sod. He dug the hole deep, set the rose into it. She poured in some of the precious water and together they packed the soil—Texas soil—back around the roots.

"That's good," Bethany said, rising to brush the dirt off her hands. "Now the next thing we'll have to do is plant some trees."

"I wouldn't get too impatient about that," Wade told her. "They won't grow without water. Better wait until I can manage to dig a well at the house."

They had told Great-grandmother Allen the Virginia rosebush wouldn't grow in Missouri. But it did. Maybe it felt at home there among the log houses and the men in coonskin caps. Maybe it felt even more at home there than it did in Virginia. Bethany's mother had told her that one of the cousins went back to Virginia, after Great-grandmother's death, and tried to find the parent bush. The roses weren't there; they had died out. Maybe some plants and some people were just meant to come to a new place and make a fresh beginning. If they stayed in the old place, they would just die out, like the rose did in Virginia.

She could wait for the trees. The rosebush was planted now.

63

To her, it was like a sign saying that she and Wade were here to stay, that they were together. With the planting of the rosebush, things seemed a little more permanent.

"It's right here by the door," she said. "I can water it with no trouble at all."

Once the rosebush was planted, she set about getting the house in order. She and Wade pegged feed sacks to the walls. That would help to keep the dirt from sifting in. This, with the rag carpet on the dirt floor, made the dugout seem less like a cave.

(Old Aunt Polly Porter always wove a rug on her loom for every bride in Star Hill. But she did not have time to make one for Bethany, things went so fast.

"You can take the one she just finished for me," Mama said. "She can always make me another.")

Now Aunt Polly's bright stripes shone bravely, as if they had never intended to be anywhere except in Texas.

Wade made cupboards from some boxes, and in these she stacked the dishes and other kitchen needs. The curtains she had brought from Missouri went up at the real glass windows. And on the table she put a bit of embroidery she had stitched long ago for her hope chest. On the ledge where the board top met the dirt wall she put the clock and *Pilgrim's Progress* and the poems of Mr. Longfellow. But she placed the Bible on the table, exactly in the middle of the centerpiece.

So it was that, by the time the two cowboys rode up, the place had begun to look like a home.

Wade had prepared her for their coming.

"The Triple T has branch headquarters up toward Coldwater Creek," he told her. "There'll be cowboys riding by every once and awhile, going from one ranch house to the other. Right nice fellows—I got to know some of them when I worked on the ranch."

She listened to him absently, her mind on another matter.

64

"Wade," she said, "I've meant to ask you several times. Where are your cattle—the ones you said you bought?"

There were cattle all around them, grazing in groups—hundreds of them actually, although at first glance she thought that there were scarcely any at all. It was only because they were so widely scattered, because they grazed in so vast a meadow, that she was deceived in their numbers.

"They're out there—" He waved his hand largely.

"You mean—with the rest of them?"

"Sure. My Lord, Bethany, you didn't expect them to be here in the shed, did you, like the milk cow we brought from Missouri?"

She did not quite know what she did expect.

"They're running on the range now. Come round up time next year, I'll cut out the ones with my brand and send them up the trail with the big herd."

"Don't they mind?" she asked. "The ranchers, I mean—?"

"Wouldn't do them any good. As long as we have open range, it won't. What we have now practically amounts to that. But it won't last long. Things are changing. That's because of the new laws down at Austin. Anyway, don't be surprised if the cowboys wander in right often."

So she was not surprised when Butch and Slats came.

Wade was working on the wagon when they rode up, taking off the canvas and the bows that held it so that it could serve for errands and farm work. Bethany almost hated to see him doing this. So long as the canvas was in place, the wagon was a thing shaped for adventure, a ship with sails furled. Now it was only an ordinary home-keeping thing, prosaic and dull. Looking at it, she felt, for the first time, their complete isolation from the home they had known in Missouri. She wondered if the Pilgrim women, seeing the Mayflower sail back to England without them, felt somewhat as she did now.

"You ole son-of-a-gun," she heard a man's voice say. "Here you've gone and got yourself married."

"Sure did," Wade said. "Get off and come in and meet her."

They came into the dugout, the cowboys carrying their hats, walking softly as if they feared to waken some unseen sleeper.

"Bethany," Wade said, "here's two no-good friends of mine. This is Butch, and this is Slats."

"Pleased to meet you Ma'am," they said.

"Do sit down," Bethany invited them, pushing forward the two best chairs in the room.

They sat down, their movements shy and gentle, like adolescent boys trying to behave as their mothers had taught them to. Butch was only a boy—he could not have been much past twenty. His youth showed in his smooth skin, his candid blue eyes, his grave timidity. And his blushes, if anyone so much as looked his way.

Slats was not young. He might have been thirty-five, and he might have been fifty. There was no telling his age. It was as if, at some past stage of his life, he had hardened into a mold in which he would stay forever. At twenty-five he might have looked as he did now; at sixty, there would be little difference. Like the prairie itself, he was ageless—neither old nor young, but timeless and unchanging. The prairie sun had shone on him, its wind had buffeted him, until now he was the color of it—eyes and skin and hair melting into the tones of each other until it was hard to tell where one left off and the other began.

His face was deeply lined, like the maps in the geography books with their little streams running into larger rivers. So, Slats's face was webbed with lines—fine ones running up and down from his eyes to meet the deeper ones in cheek and forehead.

He was the spokesman for the pair, but when his face settled in repose there was about it a great and tragic sadness, a brooding melancholy like that of the land itself. His look was both rebellion and acceptance. It was not just the weather that had put those lines in his face.

Both men wore spurs and, at their hips, guns. These they did not offer to remove, a fact which, at first, Bethany found a chilling note in an informal call. She supposed that those guns were so much a part of them they were not even aware of carrying them. Not until the time came to use them. Now, although they were both regarding her with a hunger that was at once both disconcerting and wholly delightful, they kept their guns in place.

"We don't get near enough women out here," Slats said to Bethany. "We got a saying that this country is good for men and cows, but—well—" he stopped, and then went on carefully, "well—hard on women and horses. I hope you make out to stay."

"Oh, I'll stay," Bethany assured him.

"She'll stay," Wade said. "She made me plant a rosebush this morning, and now she'll have to stay to look after it."

"A rosebush," Slats said doubtfully. "A rosebush—Ain't you told her yet about water?"

"Sure. I told her." He looked at her and grinned, and then looked back at Slats. "But it didn't do any good. You can't bluff her down. You should have seen her standing up to Poco and Charlie."

"Not them two—she didn't do that?"

"She didn't do anything else—"

Wade told the story, pride spilling from him like water from a fountain.

"And they just turned tail and ran—" he finished grandly.

"Well, I'll be—" Slats brought himself to a quick halt. "Well I'll be ever-lastingly-dad-burned."

He turned to regard Bethany with searching, somber eyes, as if he were not seeing her at all.

"It was a right brave thing you did, Miz Cameron," he told

67

her finally. "Them men are as mean as—excuse me, Ma'am, but them men are real mean. Ain't they, Butch?"

Butch said nothing. He had begun to blush, once he sat down, and now he continued blushing but did not cease staring at Bethany with an open and childlike candor.

"Ole Wade said he was going back to get married," Slats went on. "But we didn't in no ways believe him."

Almost the same words Hud Johnson had used. What sort of a girl did they think she was, she wondered—someone who didn't keep her promises? And then she remembered—. She felt, rather than saw, Wade move restlessly.

"Are there—are there other women out here?" she asked quickly, grabbing at the only thing she could think of.

"Well, there's the Boss' wife," Slats leaned back in his chair, evidently quite pleased with his role as neighborhood news sheet. "She's down at Fort Worth to be with her girls while they are in school there. Then there's Miz Newsome, but she's back visiting her folks. She stays there most of the time. They're the women who ain't here."

"Aren't there any *here?*" Bethany asked.

"Of course, there's Miz Dillon, but she's sort of kept at home with a passel of kids."

"And Milly Finch," Butch put in quietly. He spoke softly, and somehow, he did not look young when he said the words.

"Sure, there's Milly Finch. She came out to the ranch to teach the Boss's girls, and it wasn't no time until she got herself married to Tom Finch. Unmarried girls get snapped up right quick, once they come out here," Slats said.

"She has a baby," Wade spoke now. "Some of these days we'll go see her."

Slats's eyes were roving around the room, taking in all the details. "You sure have got things fixed up pretty good," he said. "Living out here, a fellow sort of forgets what a real home looks like. This is—well, this is just real elegant."

"Thank you," Bethany said. "I'm glad you like it. And would you two stay for supper?"

They scarcely waited for her to finish speaking. They leaned forward in their chairs, and their answer was a single thing.

"Would we—oh, Miz Cameron—"

She put on the best table cloth and the best dishes. She hadn't thought her first guests would be two cowboys who kept their guns on, even when they ate. But that did not matter. They were people. They were company. She fried some of the ham, almost the last of what they had brought from Missouri. She opened a jar of preserves. She sent Wade outside for the big tin bucket that held milk and butter and buttermilk—the bucket she kept lowered in one of the barrels of water. She put the butter on the table in a glass hen butter dish, the one Mama had given her before she left. She poured the guests a glass of buttermilk apiece. It all had to go very fast, but she managed with a sort of skill that came to her almost automatically. When the meal was ready, she lined them up around the little table.

"Well, I'll be—" Slats paused. "Well, Miz Cameron, if you ain't got butter, and buttermilk."

He regarded them with awe and wonder. He took a sip of buttermilk, then drained the glass before he set it down.

"Can you beat that, Butch," he said. "Buttermilk—"

Bethany filled his glass again. "With all those cows around, I'd think you could get plenty of milk," she said.

"Milk a range cow, Ma'am?" He considered her ignorance with interest, even with compassion. "My God, Miz Cameron, you don't know what you're saying! It would be a sight easier to break a wild bronc. Besides, it ain't right to take the milk away from the calves."

"Besides," Wade said, "you'd sooner be caught dead than milking."

"Well," Slats admitted reluctantly, "it ain't what I'd really call a man's job. I guess it's all right for women."

Bethany opened her mouth to say, "But Wade does," and then she closed it again. Maybe Wade didn't want her to tell that. This was a funny country, all right. An outlaw like Poco would refuse to harm a woman, and a kindly man like Slats would consider it a disgrace to milk a cow for her.

"I milk that cow," Wade told him. "And don't you go saying I'm not a real man."

"I ain't telling you *anything*," Slats said. "You learned me better, first time I ever saw you."

He drained his glass again.

"Main trouble with milk is," he said, "you got to farm to get it."

"Now come on, Slats," Wade protested. "There's nothing wrong with farming. A fellow could do a lot worse."

"Well, maybe," Slats agreed. "I reckon he could start raising sheep."

CHAPTER FOUR

W<small>ADE</small>," Bethany said one morning at breakfast, "do you suppose we could have a garden? We have those seeds Mama gave us."

Missouri was fresh and green now with uncounted hundreds of gardens. Roses were beginning to bloom, and peonies were great fluffs of whiteness against their own emerald leaves. Now, in Missouri, one could almost hear the sound of roots reaching down, of green shoots sprouting up.

He hesitated.

"I know it's late," she said. "Here it is, almost the last of May. But it would be a start, and next year we could plan for a real one."

"It isn't that," he told her. "Nights are too cool out here for early things to do much good, anyway. But you have to remember it's different from Missouri; we don't get much rain, and gardens need rain."

"We can try, can't we?" she persisted.

"You won't fret if it dries up from lack of rain?" he asked.

"No," she promised stoutly. "No—I won't fret."

"Well," he said, "I had sort of planned something else for

71

today, now that we are moved in and all. But—yes, I'll start your garden. Where do you want it?"

She did not know. She walked around the dugout, considering the matter. There seemed no place to pick from all the sameness that surrounded them. She supposed that at one time Mama and Papa had been confronted with the same problem back in Star Hill, but as far as she could remember the garden had always been in the same place, like a thing created by God at the beginning of the world.

No matter what direction she looked now, there was no difference. She was like a child turned loose in a candy store, unable to make up her mind among such great richness of choice. She could not say where she wanted her garden. To add to her confusion, she felt Wade's growing impatience, as if the thing she was asking for was an incongruity and an insult to the vastness of the country. He would humor her, he seemed to say, but she must be quick in her decision, for it was a trivial thing she asked for.

She chose without reason, as one would indicate a number in a lottery.

"Here—to the south—"

And then, as if to justify her choice, she explained, "It will be close to the house—so I can tend it—"

"How big?" he asked.

"Oh, I don't know. Just as big as you want to make it—"

"Bethany," he said, "from where we are standing I could plow a straight furrow for forty miles before I hit a fence."

She was feeling utterly foolish by now—sorry she had brought up the matter in the first place and therefore all the more sure she was going to see it through.

"Go as far as you like," she said stiffly. "So long as you get home in time for supper."

He laughed, and went for the plow and the team.

It was prairie grass, virgin soil, that he plowed up, and the

72

work was not easy. For hundreds of years, and longer, those grass roots had been there—inviolate, undisturbed, twining themselves within the safe darkness of the earth, giving to it and taking from it so that, by now, the roots and the earth were one. And now, even when the roots were turned up to the sun they lay there, stubborn and strong, still blocking the planting that Bethany would do.

The rows fell behind the plow, straight and precise, like the lines around the mouth of a good woman showing disapproval of her light-minded neighbors. Wade plowed the little plot a second time, and the clods were broken up now. After that he and Bethany raked it, and then they put in the seeds she had brought, smoothing the earth back over them— earth yet warm with the sun, having a vital, fresh feel to it.

She stepped back to look at their work. How little it looked —how ridiculously little that bit of plowed ground looked among the vast greenness of the ocean of grass! No bigger than a postage stamp, it seemed. Yet a letter had to have a stamp before it could go anywhere. This garden was a start.

"Now that we've got that done," Wade said, "I reckon we'd better hook up and go for water."

By this time Bethany knew that the need for water, and the supplying of that need was the thing which all the other details of their lives must work around. They hauled it from Newsome's spring almost three miles away, and in this country that was like having water at the back door. Wade told her he had considered another section. It was a good one, too, but it was fifteen miles from water, so he gave up the idea pretty quickly. Besides, this section of Newsome's was fairly close to the breaks. When he went for water he could sometimes drive on and pick up some wood. Wood and water—they were the things you looked for, searching with painstaking care, treating your find with great respect once you came upon it. Because Wade's land was so close to water it was a great deal more valuable.

Already Bethany had learned to guard water with automatic caution. Back in Missouri, except in drought years, one took water for granted, like air and sunshine. Women washing clothes sloshed great tubs of it carelessly, as if it were a thing meant to be wasted, had come into the world for no other purpose. People filled tubs with it and cooled themselves on hot afternoons. They went to the river and fished in it; they led stock to drink from brimming tanks of it. At the foot of every little green hill small streams flowed free and beautiful.

Here it was as if every year was a drought year, so much more grievous, so much more prolonged, than ever any could be in the cruelest of Missouri dry spells. Here one had to realize the value of every teacupful, of every drop. More than that—one had to learn to re-use it, so that a bucketful could serve several times.

The rosebush came first. It got its drink from the last rinse water left from washing, which was not soapy enough to hurt it. After this, if there was any left, she was going to carry it out to the garden. The soapy water was used for scrubbing stove and table. Oh, she managed all right. But she didn't intend to tell anybody back home how little water she used—for clothes, or dishwashing, or bathing. They'd never believe you could get yourself or your house clean with just that little bit.

In order to go for water, Wade hitched up the team and loaded the barrels on the wagon. Two were the barrels they had brought from Missouri. One had held coal oil and in order to make it usable Wade first burned out the inside. The charred wood gave the water a better flavor; Bethany used the contents of this barrel for cooking. The other had been a whiskey barrel and still smelled faintly of its former usage. The third was at the dugout when they came. In case the claim was ever sold, some of the barrels would go with it, so precious were they out here. This third barrel held water for the stock.

Bethany liked to go with Wade for water, although the first trip had taught her it was no easy task. Three endless jolting miles there, following no road at all save the faint markings their own wagon had made on its last trip; three miles back, over the same trail. The endless, endless dipping until the barrels were full. Wade dipped the water from the spring and handed his bucketful to her as she stood on the wagon, by the barrels, and she poured it in, handed the empty bucket back to him. Afterwards her back ached for hours from the lifting, but this she did not tell him. She felt very useful, out there helping with the water. Besides, she wanted to be with him.

Why hadn't somebody told her, she wondered, that one of the nice things about marriage was having someone to talk to. Your talk could flow on endlessly, without effort. You didn't need to say smart things; you didn't even need to answer what was said, or maybe even listen to it always. Just the sound of a voice was a comforting thing, filling up the void of loneliness. Wasn't it funny—a little thing like the sound of another's voice could squeeze the land down until it was a thing to be encompassed easily, something almost your size.

"Want to go with me?" Wade asked.

"Sure—" she said. "It will take less time with me there to pour it in."

"Good Lord, Bethany," he protested, "you don't have to go just to help. You're—well, you're sort of company—"

"I'll go," she said. "Wait until I get ready—"

She put on a fresh print dress. And, after a moment's hesitation, her second-best shoes. She was a little defiant about this—looking first at the ones she wore, seeing them for what they were. Sturdy, but a little on the clumsy side. When she

75

found out how far it was to Mobeetie, which was the closest place one could buy things, she had packed her second-best shoes away with her Sunday ones. But she got them out now. Going for water was fun, sort of like a picnic, and she felt like dressing up for it. Besides, when you rode in a big wagon you put your feet up on the dash board to brace yourself and your shoes were out in plain sight all the time. Wade might not say anything, but he'd notice if her feet looked neat and pretty.

After she was ready, she stopped a moment to gather up some food left over from breakfast and put it into a basket.

"I'm ready," she said, coming out of the dugout with the basket on her arm, pulling the door shut after her. She did not lock it, although she had not yet learned to like the idea of leaving the house unlocked in her absence. Wade had told her she mustn't feel put out if she came home some time and found somebody she had never heard of cooking dinner on her stove, or maybe even sleeping in her bed.

"It will probably be some cowboy. He'll leave things neat, and not hurt anything."

Wade took the basket from her when she came out, helped her in the wagon. "Picnic?" he asked.

"Yes—sort of—"

"I brought the rifle. Thought we might see an antelope. Short on meat, aren't we?"

"Yes—"

"Don't want to shoot quail or prairie chicken right now. You pick off a mama bird before she's had time to teach the young ones to watch out for coyotes and you might as well to kill them, too."

She had not expected to find so many birds out here. It didn't seem possible that birds would thrive without trees, any more than you'd think to find fish without water. But here there were many birds. There was the road runner who had dared them to run races with him as they came out. There were the quail and the plover too, and a bird which Wade said the cowboys called the fe'lark. The name must be a corruption of field lark, for it was like the meadow lark back in Missouri. This one perched on the tall center stalk of the bear grass, that waxy white candle of the Lord, and poured out his haunting, liquid melody as if he was aware of the loveliness on which he rested. At dusk the bull bats came out—birds half as big as a crow with huge mouths that folded back to scoop up grasshoppers and insects. They would swoop down upon their prey, gorging themselves until their bodies were full and distended, continuing to feed until their mottled grey-brown feathers faded into the darkness of evening. Then they would disappear, only to come back at dusk the next day. Oh, there were plenty of birds here!

And there were flowers too. The prairie was aglow with them. Where the breaks had been overlaid with the delicate blueness of buffalo clover, the plains flowers ran to warmer tones, with yellow and orange and brownish-reds predominating. There were yellow ones with tones of red and orange, as if a paint bucket had been upset on them. There was a little yellow flower covering the land with a rift of gold.

And everywhere were the whitened bones of the buffalo, as if they too were a strange plant native to the land.

There was a shimmering brightness in the air. Surely it was not possible to see so far, it must be some sort of trick, like the one worked with mirrors where a scene is thrown from one to another, like a ball tossed in play, so that the same one is extended on and on, far beyond its actual dimensions.

"How far do you suppose we can see?" Bethany asked curiously.

"I couldn't say. Twenty miles, maybe—"

She saw a lone horseman, riding toward some cattle in the distance.

"Maybe it's Butch or Slats," she said.

"Not likely," Wade told her. "Usually you see them to-gether. Unless—unless, well, sometimes Butch does ride alone. But I don't think he is now."

"They are a strange pair, aren't they?" she remarked. "I mean, one so much older, and Butch hardly ever saying a word, and all that—"

She had sensed a strangeness she could scarcely express.

"Yes," he agreed. "They sure are. Sort of funny, too, the way they got together—"

He told her then the story of Slats and Butch—the story men told around campfires from Montana to the Rio Grande, in one version or another. Because no man knew all of it for sure, each one pieced in details to suit himself. The Boss probably knew as much as anyone, but even his was only part knowl-edge. There were, however, some parts on which everyone agreed.

Slats—he had another name then, a name which had been lost in the years. Perhaps by now he did not remember it him-self; some there were who swore he didn't. Slats had started across the plains with a small wagon train, just a few families going West. He had a wife and some children—a couple any-way, maybe more. But there was certainly a boy, so the story went; blue-eyed, he was, and trying to act grown-up. Carrying a little wooden gun every day and wanting to walk alongside the men instead of riding in the wagon with the women. And, still according to the story, there was also a little girl—"Just a baby; looked like her eyes were going to be black, but it was too soon to tell yet."

People warned the party against the Indians, but they said they were not afraid. There was a string of forts across the country—the Indians would not bother them. Besides, the days of Indian scares were past.

The days were not past. The Indians came, at night, while

78

the people were sleeping. They surprised the man doing the night watch and killed him. They fell upon the sleepers before anyone knew they were there. What they did to the members of the party were things best left untold. Best left unremembered, if a man could manage to work it that way. Everyone except Slats was killed—the wife and the little boy who had begged to walk with the men and the little girl whose eyes had not yet had time to turn dark. None of the people were spared. No one except Slats, and the Indians surely thought he was dead or they never would have left him.

That much of the story was pretty sure. How long it was between the massacre and the time he came wandering up to the Triple T Headquarters was a point in dispute. Perhaps Slats himself did not know. The Boss gave him a job and asked no questions, which was not remarkable for no one asked questions of a man in those days.

Slats had stayed at the ranch for six months and then disappeared. Just rode off into space one night, saying nothing about his destination. He was gone three months and then he rode back, still without explanation.

"Hello," he said to the cook, as if he had been gone only over night. "How about breakfast?"

That went on for several years. He would stay awhile and then ride off. From another man the Boss would probably have taken no such conduct, but he never seemed to notice Slats's behavior. It got so they could all tell when he was getting ready to leave—his eyes would begin to take on a strange baffled look, as if something was happening the nature of which he could not quite understand; didn't want to understand, as far as that went—as if he had to get away from it and yet at the same time was afraid to go. Usually he was a great talker, but when those fits came upon him he scarcely said a word. Men began to say he talked because he was afraid to remain silent, because when he was quiet he thought. Speech, for Slats, was a thing to fill up silence, to keep thought from flowing into his mind as air pours into a vacuum.

And then he came back from one of those trips bringing a boy with him. A slight, timid boy, with blue eyes and a manly way about him.

"This here is Butch," Slats said to the Boss. "Found him up in Kansas City. No place for a kid, the city ain't. He's a good kid, willing to work. Reckon you could sort of let him hang around, Boss."

The Boss reckoned he could.

The story of the finding of Butch got around. The boy was sick and alone in Kansas City. Starving, really. Slats nursed him until he was well and then brought him to Texas. Butch had more than justified Slats' faith in him. He had become as good a cowpoke as a man could wish for. You couldn't judge him by that boyish face of his, that quiet way. He could handle cattle with the best of them, Butch could.

Strangely enough, with Butch here the character of Slats' journeys into forgetfulness altered, too. Where once he took off for long periods of time to places whose names he did not divulge, now he was content to go no farther than Mobeetie. Often as not, these trips would come immediately after pay day. Slats would look his roll over, consider it, and then peel out some bills and hand them to Butch.

"You keep these for me, huh? Reckon I'll just light out for Mobeetie for a spell."

"Want me to go with you?"

At first the refusal had been quick and positive. Now it was automatic. Butch understood both.

"No—I'll just jog along by myself. You behave while I'm gone, mind you—"

"Sure—"

"Be back before too long," Slats would tell him and then

ride off toward Mobeetie—a lone man riding into the lonely broken hills around the Canadian River.

What he did in Mobeetie was legend. The saloons were there and the girls on Feather Hill and the freighters and the soldiers from Fort Elliot. They all knew him, knew the story of the thing that drove him there. Perhaps in their own way they felt a need to help him crowd into a few days the essence of all he had used to find in his long wanderings. Indeed, when he came back to the ranch he had the look of a man who had been gone long, had wandered far from his own kind. There was also a look of having been purged, if only for a while, of the horror that had plagued him.

"And the way he watches over Butch," Wade said, finishing the story. "Good Lord—you'd think he was a mother hen looking after a brood of chicks."

Now Bethany thought she understood better that strange look in Slats' eyes; maybe that was why Butch scarcely talked at all himself. He knew Slats needed to be talking. Butch would understand—Butch, with his blue eyes and that manly way about him.

Loneliness bit into people here. You clung to someone for companionship, a thing as needful as food. Maybe that companionship was only a makeshift thing, but anyway a person had to have it. It was no wonder Slats and Butch rode always together. There were plenty of problems here besides that of earning a living. And goodness knows that would be hard enough.

"Wade," she said, asking the question that had been on her mind ever since they arrived, "how are we going to manage until we get started?"

The supplies they had brought out would not last forever. Neither would the money in the bottom of the sack of seed.

"I have my cattle," he said. "Of course, they won't be ready for a year. Anyway, I'd like to use the money I get from them to buy Newsome's section, if he'll sell. And I think he will—the way his wife acts, it's just a question of time before he'll have to pick up and take her back to East Texas. Close to the breaks the way he is, and with the spring—well, that makes it a fine place to run some cattle."

"But until then?" she persisted.

"Now don't you worry, Bethany," he said. "There isn't any call to worry. I can pick up work at the ranches. Or sell them lake hay. Or sell them some of my crop. Tomorrow I'm going to start breaking up a piece of land and sow it to maize. After that, I'll fence it in, to keep the cattle out—"

"Fence it in—" She was saying words news to the country and the very grass, swaying beneath their wheels, seemed to stop to listen. "How—"

"That new barbed wire. When we saw Hud, I asked him if he'd bring me down some from Dodge City. Told him I'd meet him and pick it up, so it wouldn't be any trouble for him."

"Did he say he would?"

"Yes. He thinks I'm crazy, but he says he will. You see, Bethany, there's been considerable—well, there's been some trouble up in these parts over fences. Serious trouble."

"You mean—shooting—?"

"Well," he admitted reluctantly, "yes—some. But not much. More just sort of hard feelings, and so on. And cutting it, so it was ruined almost as fast as it got made. But there's a law now, saying you can't cut another man's fence. Anyway, I'm going on and build mine around my maize field."

"But will they let you?" she asked. She did not know whom she meant by "they." The spirit of the country, maybe. Somehow law seemed a feeble and puny thing out here—far away and ineffective, something "They" might not listen to unless it suited them.

He said, so quietly that it was a sort of charter of rights, "If

82

it's my land, Bethany—if I filed on it and keep my payments up—I've got a right to do anything I want with it. Anything within the law, of course."

He was silent a moment.

"I came out here to work on a ranch," he went on, almost as if he were talking to himself, "I thought before I'd been here too long I'd start a herd of my own. That's the way a lot of ranchers got their start—helping out at first with somebody else's cattle. That's what Tom Finch did. Newsome would, too, except he's not got too much push about him. If he had his say, he'd go out and live on his claim. But his wife makes him stay close to the ranch house because it isn't so lonesome there. Besides, he's sort of secretary or something to the Boss and she thinks that sounds big."

He stopped a moment and went on.

"I hadn't been here very long before I saw a field of maize the Boss had grown. Maybe I told you about it. He cautioned his men not to mention it. By that time they had passed the law down at Austin about homesteading, and he knew if people found out how maize would grow here, he'd be surrounded by nesters. But I saw. And when I did, I went straight out and filed on my claim."

"So that's the seed in the sack with the money. Maize seed. I had meant to ask you."

"Yes. I got it up there because I figured it would be hard to buy down here. Next year I'll have my own seed."

"Sure—" Bethany agreed.

"And another year I'll be ready to try—well, something else—"

"And you'll be having more and more cattle—" she said, caught up by his planning.

"Bethany," he said, as if he were thinking something through, something he had pondered many times and had always come up with an answer which was not the one most people got. "I'm not too sure about cattle. For me, I mean. They've had a long try at cattle out here, and the business is a big thing. It will go on being big. But I think there's another day opening up."

"You mean—?"

"Farming."

"But Wade, everyone says there's such a little rain. You said so yourself."

She was remembering rain falling on Missouri fields. Remembering, too, the pitiful barrenness of those fields when the rains did not come.

"Oh, it won't be like we farmed back in Missouri. We'll have to feel our way along in this farming job. We get some rain. I keep remembering the way that maize crop looked— green and thick and heavy. A ton to the acre, and heads so big they bent the stalks over. This is good land. And when you have good land, and use it right, you get returns."

If he made a go of farming, she was thinking, that meant others would come. That was good. People who came seeking homes put down roots. They held the soil as they were held by it. People had a feeling for land. They had it back in Missouri; Wade had it here. She supposed it was the same everywhere. And they were good for a land. They filled up its emptiness. After them came good things—schools and churches and towns.

"But, Wade," she said, remembering the way Slats had looked when he mentioned farming, "they aren't going to— well, maybe the ranchers aren't going to want you to start farming."

"Maybe not," he said cheerfully. "But I never yet heard of a person who got any place by waiting for the country to invite him to come. Well, here we are at the spring."

Sure enough they were. It scarcely seemed they had started, and now they were there. After the water was in the barrels,

Bethany unpacked her basket. Wade made a fire of chips and she heated the coffee. They ate at the water's edge and it was all good fun.

"Sure is a good spring," Wade said. He eyed it with a combination of a small boy's wistfulness and a man's purpose. "Well, I guess it's time we were getting along."

He put out the fire with single-minded and meticulous care. He did not have to say the words "grass fire" to make Bethany know the reason back of his care. Even though it was not the season for fires, one still watched out.

They were nearly home when Wade saw the antelope he had hoped for. He gave the lines to Bethany.

"Hold 'em steady," he told her, and took aim.

It was all her fault. She should have been prepared for the fact that the noise of the gun might startle the horses. She should have held the lines taut, instead of letting them go loose in her hands. Wade, intent on his shot, trusted her to keep the team steady. And she failed him.

She did not know quite how it happened, but, quicker than eye or hand could follow the motion, the lunging team flung Wade off the wagon, went careening across the prairie toward home.

She tried to guide them, standing up in the wagon, sawing on the lines. It was no use. She tried to keep them away from the dugout, but she was only partly successful. They dragged the wagon across the very edge of the rise; the wagon rose on two wheels, hung precariously for a moment, and then turned over. With it went the three barrels of water. And Bethany, like a stone out of a child's slingshot, went over the side of the wagon to land in the garden.

She struggled to rise out of what she thought was a gigantic pool of blood. And then she knew it for something almost as precious.

The water from the barrels, the work of a day, was spreading over the prairie grass. Only a little bit of it, enough to get her thoroughly soaked, was going where it might have done the most good—on the newly made garden.

She was just picking herself up, when Wade came running around the corner of the dugout.

His face was white, whether from anger or fright she did not know. She was more concerned about the way she must look. Her dress was sticky with mud; the ooze was filling her shoes, dripping off her fingers. She thought she knew how people dying of thirst in the desert might feel—tantalized with the memory of the bright beauty of water, but unable to get to it. Water, the great fundamental need of life itself. Not for drinking alone, but for the food it grew.

All these things flashed through her mind, as his past runs through the mind of a drowning man. She tried to speak to Wade, found no words would come. The loss of three barrels of water in a land like this was the very drying up of the spirit.

"I'm—I'm sorry—" she tried to say.

"My God—" he said. "You might have been killed—"

He helped her to her feet, and she started to walk around the corner of the dugout to the door, trying to go with dignity and no tears. One step, and she sank ankle-deep in the ooze just at the garden's edge. At that, Wade began to laugh.

"Go look at yourself," he said. "You are—you are about the funniest thing I ever saw—"

He doubled up with renewed laughter.

The reaction from the fright had set in. This, added to her physical discomfort, set her trembling. And, because she was frightened and miserable, she was also angry.

"I'll thank you not to laugh at me," she stormed, and went toward the dugout.

She was trying to get the mud off when he came to the door. He was not laughing now.

86

"I'm sorry I laughed," he said. "But I couldn't help it. A muddy person, out here—"

She averted her dirty face. By now, it also had the grey-white tracks her tears had made.

"I'm going for more water," he told her. "I'll be back as soon as I can."

She could feel his renewed laughter as he turned to leave.

She set about cleaning herself as best she could with the little bit of water left in the dugout. It would be almost night before he could get back, filling the barrels alone, as he would have to do. At best, she could do little with herself. Her face was drawn and caked with the mud. Her neck smarted from the alkali. She did not want to put fresh things on over her soiled body, so she did not try to change.

And her second-best shoes were ruined. She had paid for her vanity, all right.

She wondered soberly, as she supposed maybe Great-grandmother had wondered in her time, if the story of a new country was written so much in a man's heroic struggles against dangers as it was in a woman's against nature's ravages. The trail of the Forty-niners had been marked by the men who died on the way, but something surely died in the women, too. The Indians may have got scalps, but the weather got the roseleaf skins and toil took slim figures. Maybe Aunt Clara was right in wanting a look at Mrs. Daniel Boone's diary.

Already she had been here long enough to know what wind and sun and alkali water could do to the skin. Her face felt dry and drawn. The wind seemed to lift the moisture out of it; the sun shone with a brightness that made her blink when she passed out of the shade of the dugout into its full force. If only the wind didn't blow all the time; if only there were a few cloudy days to give you respite. She rubbed glycerine into her skin each night, but, like the money in the sack, that wouldn't hold out forever. What would she do when it was gone? What did the other women do?

And with the thought of other women came a great and shaking desire to see one. She had not been homesick until now; the force of it reached out to enfold her. A bright dream of home took possession of her—women in light dresses, walking up and down the streets of Star Hill. It was almost too beautiful and too real to be borne. She must see another woman —any woman.

Wade got home just before dusk. He unloaded the barrels, and came inside for buckets.

"Still mad at me?" he asked, looking at her sidewise.

"No," she said briefly, still occupied with the wish she had. "No—but, Wade, you said there were other women out here. I want to see one."

He faced her with wide and startled eyes.

"You aren't sick or—or anything—?" he asked uncertainly.

For a moment she looked at him questioningly, not understanding the nature of his concern. And when she did, she laughed.

"Good heavens, no," she said. "I'm perfectly all right. I just got homesick to see another woman, that's all."

"I thought—" he began. Then he stopped and grinned at her shyly, looking almost as young as Butch. "I thought maybe—well, I just thought. Oh, thunder—you know what I thought!"

"No, you goose. Not yet, anyway." Then she went on curiously. "Would you mind?"

He considered the matter. "I don't reckon I would," he said. "We sure need some more people out here—"

CHAPTER FIVE

I've been thinking," Wade said the next day. "I've decided we're going visiting."

"Oh, Wade—" she exulted.

"The way you act," he grumbled. "It's enough to make a man think you're tired of him. Going all to pieces over a visit to the neighbors—"

She couldn't tell him how she really felt. It was not just neighbors she wanted, welcome as their presence would be. It was rather that she craved, without being able to name her want, the feeling of being a part of a group. For Wade, the bright promise of land might be enough. But she wanted more. She wanted not only a home, but the sum of homes—those things that add up to a church spire, a school, a store and a doctor with a neat sign over his office. No woman knows how to express this want; she lumps it all together by saying contentedly, "Yes—we have good neighbors."

"The boys said Mrs. Newsome isn't here, which is not surprising," Wade went on. "It's ten-twelve miles to the Dillons, but I don't think you'd enjoy her much. The Finches are on another ten miles or so. Tell you what we'll do—we go to the Finches, stopping off at the Dillons on our way over. I'll fix the stock up so we can leave them, and we'll stay all night."

"But, Wade," she protested, "we can't. Without letting them know, or anything. People I've never met—"

"Now you just go and get ready," he told her, "and stop worrying. It will be all right."

She dressed quickly, but carefully. Aunt Clara had said all pioneer women wore calico dresses and sunbonnets. Maybe they did, but that wasn't the way she was going to look when she went calling on Mrs. Dillon and Milly Finch. As she dressed, she wondered how much Milly knew about—well, about Rosemary.

She was just ready when Wade came up with the horses. Rex was almost human in his restless eagerness, like a child who well knew he was going off on some sort of an adventure. Bethany's side saddle was on the other horse, a gentle, docile little animal. Bethany had named him Star.

"Because he has a star in his forehead. And," she added wistfully, "for Star Hill."

Wade helped her on her mount. "M-m-m—" he said, "we look right nice—"

"I didn't want Mrs. Dillon and Milly Finch to think you'd brought out a tacky wife," she said.

He grinned at her. "Mrs. Dillon isn't going to think much about how you look." And then he went on seriously. "Now, Bethany, don't you expect too much of Lizzie Dillon. She's—well, she's not like folks you've known back in Missouri. With Milly it's different. She came out to the ranch to teach the Boss' girls. Nobody could figure out why she married Tom Finch, but she did."

"She has a baby, hasn't she?" Bethany asked.

"Yes— Now let me see—the Dillons are over in that direction—"

They rode off across the prairie grass in "that direction."

Even though she had not expected much of the Dillons, Bethany was not prepared for what she saw.

"This is it," Wade said, and stopped his horse.

They were before a dugout, scarcely more than a hollowed out place in the ground, with a wagon sheet at the door.

"Hello," Wade called, raising his voice to greet some unseen person within.

At his words, five children, of varying sizes, scuttled behind the slight protection the dugout gave. Where they had come from, Bethany did not know, for she had not seen them until they ran. Once in a position they considered safe, they stood peeping around the dugout with the small, wise eyes of young animals. There was an age-old fear and an endless caution behind their actions. By and by when instinct told them all was safe they would emerge—slowly, by degrees, testing each step they took.

A man lifted the wagon-sheet door and came out. He was tall, with a dark thick beard, curiously well cared for in comparison with the rest of his appearance. His clothes were so ragged and dirty that it was impossible to tell what their original cut and color might have been.

"Howdy," he said. "Light, and set a spell. God-a-mighty, where'd them kids run off to? Act like you was horse thieves, or something. Zeke, you come here and take Mr. Cameron's horse. And—and—" he paused, the gallant question on his lips.

"This is my wife," Wade said. "Bethany, this is Tobe Dillon."

"Pleased to meet you, Ma'am, and I must say Wade done well by himself. Now you git right off and come in—the ole woman will want you to stay for dinner. 'Tain't often she gits to see another woman."

Bethany's quick look was not lost on Wade.

"Oh, no," he said. "We can't stay this time. Maybe another day, but now we are headed for the Finches. We just stopped to say hello."

"Good thing you did. I hate to answer for what Lizzie

would a-said if you had rode by without stopping. Lizz-ee—"

And then Lizzie Dillon lifted the canvas and came out.

Bethany saw a tall woman in a soiled mother hubbard. She had a long face, strong and patient, with deep-set eyes and high cheek bones. Somewhere back, and not too distantly, there was sure to have been a strain of Indian blood. It showed in the dark straight hair, in her black expressionless eyes. There was no age about her; she was like the hills in her look of strength and endurance. Her face was the sort that was meant to be forever framed by the bow of a covered wagon; her body was one that carried children easily and bore them, if not without pain, at least without great fuss. Birth and death—and what was most mysterious of all, life itself—gave her no great concern. She took everything as it came, bearing within herself an animal's power for self-healing. She was the true pioneer type—the one who is destined never to eat the fruits of the vineyards she has planted.

"You come right in," she said, a kind of dignity folded around her like a cloak. "You come in, and I'll fix a bite—"

The children were beginning to come back now, slipping across the grass with animal-like quietness, looking as if they belonged nowhere so much as in a cave.

"Oh, no," Bethany protested. "We just stopped to say hello—"

"I'd be proud to fix a bite," she repeated, a great hunger in her eyes, and in her voice. Bethany knew it for what it was—hunger for the sight of womankind. She herself had been out here long enough to know it, feel it.

"I'll come in awhile," Bethany said impulsively. "But don't you go and cook anything. We'll just visit."

The woman led the way to the dugout, lifted the sheet and threw it back so that the doorway remained open. The door furnished all the light that came into the room; it furnished, too, the means by which the smoke from the crude stove escaped. A makeshift bed stood in one corner, and about the small room were other straw ticks on which the small Dillons slept. A baby, perhaps nine months old, lay on the bed. A rough table and a few boxes, serving as chairs, made up the remainder of the room's furnishings. On the rusty stove were a coffee pot and a skillet—apparently all of the family cooking things.

"Set—" Mrs. Dillon said simply, waving her hand toward a box.

Bethany sat down.

"It was real kind of you to come," the woman said. "I git a turrible cravin' to see another woman now and then—"

"Have you been here long?" Bethany asked.

"Well—not in this-here spot—"

And then her story began to fall from her lips, softly, with a monotonous inflection of voice. Almost it was as if she talked in order to be sure she was still capable of speech. And Bethany listened, knowing that, however much she wanted to be out of this burrow and on her way, she must give ear to the woman.

When she first came to Texas, so Lizzie Dillon told Bethany, there was not a white woman within a hundred miles. She and Tobe had come from Tennessee—not directly, but by stages, along a trail which was marked by the realities of birth and death. Part of her story she told Bethany now—part came later, bit by bit, as a puzzle is put together.

"We moved to Missoury," she said. "Jennie was a baby. She died there."

They went to Arkansas, and a baby was born there. And to East Texas, and two more were born.

"—and one wasn't right. He was a blue baby. We buried him in a little graveyard, out in the country somewheres. I've always said some day I'd git back and put a headstone to his grave. But I ain't never done it. I could find the place, jest as easy. I know I could. We was camped in a grove right by the little graveyard. We stayed there quite awhile—two weeks, maybe—because I was turrible sick, too. I've tried to remember the name of the town we was close to, but I can't. But I could find the place, if ever we git back that way—"

There was another baby born "on the way out here." And two after they got to the first place they settled on the plains. Those children both died.

"—measles—we was in a wagon, and a norther hit, and they taken cold—"

And now here was the baby, thriving pretty good. Seemed like this place was right good for the children. No chills and fever. Arkansas was a bad place for that. But East Texas was about the worst there was for chills and fever.

Bethany stirred, and Lizzie Dillon knew the visit was ended. She made no protest.

"You'll come back?" she asked.

"Yes," Bethany told her. "Yes—and you must come over and bring the children to see me."

Bethany did not know what made her give such an inclusive invitation. Certainly she couldn't look forward with any pleasure to having those little animals scuttling around her neat dugout.

The woman did not promise to come. She followed Bethany out the door.

"You must bring your wife over to see me," Bethany told Tobe, once they were outside.

"I sure will," he promised gallantly. "That is, if we stay here. I'm thinking of moving. There's some powerful good land, just for the asking, over in New Mexico. The way school lands are a-cluttering up things here in Texas, a body just about has to leave to git any land all in a piece."

Lizzie Dillon stood there, immobile and patient, waiting, like the land, for the will of the man beside her. Bethany wanted to ask her how she felt about moving, but hesitated. About the woman, for all her unkempt looks, there was a sort of inviolate dignity.

"Come back," Lizzie's voice followed them as they rode off. "I'd be proud to have ye—"

They had scarcely halted in front of the Finch dugout when Milly came running out, a little child-like woman, frail and delicate looking, with an apple-blossom coloring about her.

"You're Wade's new wife," she cried, her voice a child's voice, soft and light and unformed. "Butch and Slats told me you were here. But even before you came out, I felt I knew you—"

Wade, lifting Bethany off her horse, went red and then white, and then got the scared look he had had the day they got married, as though he wished this business was over, and fast. He stood Bethany down on the ground, put his arm around her shoulder.

"Milly," he said, "this is Bethany. This is my wife."

Milly regarded her uncertainly for just a moment. And then a look of great and adult wisdom spread over her child-like face. She came forward impulsively and took Bethany in her arms.

"You are Bethany," she said. "How nice. Wade used to talk about you a great deal."

She could have said no better words. Wade brushed back his hair quickly, as if to say now everything was fixed up just fine and he'd leave the two of them for their visit.

"Where's Tom?" he asked.

"Out around the corrals somewhere. Go find him. Of course you've come to spend the night."

Wade looked at Bethany. "What did I tell you?" he asked.

"You've not eaten, I know," Milly said. "I'll go fix something."

She put her hand on Bethany's arm, holding fast to her as if

95

she were afraid of losing her. She looked over her shoulder at Wade.

"Now don't you men get to talking and forget to come in to eat," she said. "I'll have something ready before long."

She turned toward Bethany, linking her other hand around the one with which she held her, as if she could not believe this was a real woman she held to, or, if Bethany were real, that she might not take it into her head to escape.

"The men are as glad to see each other out here as the women are," she said. "Now you come in with me—oh, do come in—"

The dugout was no larger than that of the Dillons, and it had scarcely anything more in it. But there was a neatness and order about it that was somehow more pathetic than the squalor of the other one. There were books on the ledge where the frame top met the dirt foundation. Calico curtains hung at the windows and the walls were papered with newspapers. The floor was dirt—packed as hard as rock, but dirt, nevertheless.

"I want a rag carpet the worst kind," she told Bethany. "Slats told me you had one. But we just haven't been able to manage that yet. Next year, maybe, if things go right. This year we had the baby. You must see her—"

She led the way to a small wooden box, lined with soft pink material. In the midst of this pinkness the baby lay. She wore a little lace trimmed dress, clean and dainty—as if Milly had been expecting company to come, although of course she had not.

"Why—she, she is a darling," Bethany said. She found herself speaking very low, as if the baby were asleep. But she was not—her eyes were wide open, very blue against the whiteness of her small face.

"Isn't she, now!" Milly cried. "My folks have never seen her. I keep writing them, trying to tell them how she looks.

But I can't seem to find the words, exactly. If we could just have her picture made. She doesn't look like other babies, does she?"

She did not. She looked more like a doll, Bethany thought, or a picture of a baby. She was little, but that word did not describe her either. It was more that she didn't look quite real.

"She's beautiful," Bethany said. "You must bring her and come over to see me."

"We don't take her out much," Milly told her. "Tom thinks I should, but I know the sun's not good for her. It's so hot out here, with no trees or anything to break the heat—"

She said "out here" as an exile breathes the words, as a shipwrecked sailor who has lost all hopes of rescue and so has reconciled himself to that hopelessness. She said it with a bright courage that was at once both moving and pathetic.

"Now you just sit down while I fix a bite to eat," Milly said. "We've already had our dinner and I have things left—it won't be a bit of trouble."

Bethany sat down by the table. On it she saw a mail order catalogue, its pages open to the carpets—Brussels, with pink roses of unbelievable brightness. Milly caught her glance, colored,

"I—Tom laughs at me because when I'm sort of blue I play a game. I get out the catalogue and make an order for something I want awfully bad. I measure and plan colors and sizes and everything. And after I've written the letter, I go burn it!"

She looked at Bethany, smiling faintly. "I guess you think I'm crazy, too, don't you?" And then, before Bethany could answer, she went on.

"You'll understand after you've been out here for awhile. You'll know for yourself what the mail order catalogues can do for us."

"I've found out already," Bethany said. "I've written for one. Sixty miles to Mobeetie—my goodness, I don't see how I could get along if I couldn't order things."

Wade had thought he needed a rifle and a shotgun and a plow to tame the country with. She'd take the catalogue, if she had to make a choice. She wondered if maybe most women on the fringes of things didn't feel the same way—if maybe the catalogue didn't go marching clear across the continent right along after the covered wagons. Rifles and plows might take a country, but if a woman was going to stay in it she'd have to have a few pretties to help hold her there.

"And how," Milly asked brightly, "do you like it out here? No—I won't expect you to answer that. It isn't fair to ask you so soon. Everything's so different—so big and sort of fearsome. Like a dream of being lost, when you're a child."

Bethany agreed that it was different, especially from Missouri.

"It's just as different from Austin, where I came from," Milly said. "When I first got to the Triple T I thought I must be mistaken—there couldn't be that much land in the world!"

"Oh, we're not bothered too much with land," Bethany laughed. She thought she had better explain to Milly. "You know Wade isn't trying to—" she hesitated for lack of words to express what she meant to say and then hit upon the vernacular of the country. "He isn't trying to run much of a herd. He is more interested in farming."

"I know—Butch and Slats told me."

"They didn't seem to think so much of it," Bethany remembered. She repeated their remark about raising sheep.

"You mustn't mind them. They don't mean all they say. Cattlemen don't like sheep because they eat the grass too close. You can't run cattle where sheep have been—the grass is ruined."

"And they think we'll ruin it, too," Bethany said. "Fencing it in, and so on—"

"Now, don't you pay any attention to that; if I had my say there'd be farms so close together they'd be sitting in each

98

other's laps! I guess that's the way most women feel. We don't like the loneliness—"

She was preparing the meal, her movements awkward and unsure. It was easy to imagine her reading a book or playing the piano. But handling black pans in a dugout—well, that was another thing.

"—and the coyotes," Milly went on. "They give me the shivers. I always have the feeling that they are trying to tempt me to come out, so they can get at me."

Bethany said that she too hated coyotes.

"They sound so lonely," Milly said. "Seems that I get twice as lonesome, just listening to them."

She was also, she confessed with a sort of defiant shame, afraid of lizards and prairie dogs.

"My goodness," Bethany told her, feeling very wise and motherly, "the prairie dogs won't hurt you."

Wade had said the prairie dogs were nuisances, making holes for stock to step in and injure themselves. They dug up what was planted. And they sat and sassed you while you went for a gun, disappearing the minute you got back. They were smart, those dogs, but nothing to fear.

"I can't help it," Milly said. "Tom says I'm silly. I've heard that they let rattlesnakes stay in the holes with them. Tom says that isn't so. But all the same, I can't think of one without thinking of the other. If they do give the snakes house room, maybe some day when I'm not looking one of those very snakes will get in and bite the baby—"

"A snake is not going to bite the baby," Bethany reassured her.

"I know." Milly laughed once more. "I'm silly, just like Tom said. But anyway, the people who come out here have a lot to learn—"

She had her own wisdom about the country which she passed on to Bethany now, the words incongruous and unreal on her lips. There was a difference in cow chips. The white ones were best for kindling, the brown ones made the hottest fires. A person should eat plenty of tomatoes. There was something about canned tomatoes that helped you withstand the dryness; if you ever got caught out without water, canned tomatoes would see you through. One could make several rooms in a dugout by using curtains.

"See," she said, pulling some bright calico curtains so that they formed a screen around a bed in the corner. "See—I had Tom put up a wire arrangement and now I can just pull them around and make a bedroom for you and Wade."

"But that's your bed," Bethany protested. "Where will you sleep?"

"Oh, don't you worry. I have that managed. I have a mattress stuffed with prairie hay and we'll make a pallet. And don't you think it's a hardship for me. When you've been out here as long as I have, you'd welcome a woman if you had to sleep right on the hard floor for a week. Now you call the men —it's ready—"

Milly held her wrist close to her skirt, trying to conceal the burn she had got, partly through her haste, partly through ineptness.

The men came in and Bethany had her first look at Tom Finch. Certainly the baby looked nothing like him. He was a stocky man, slow moving and stolid, with big clumsy feet and square strong shoulders. Bethany remembered what Wade had said, "None of us could figure why she took Tom Finch."

Seeing him, Bethany could not understand it herself. He was not unkind—he was really quite cordial, telling her how glad he was to see them and how good it was they could spend the night. About him there was nothing furtive or at all amiss. It was just—well, one could not imagine Milly married to him, and that was all there was to it.

They sat down at the table and Tom made a show of eating

again. But Milly did not even try and scarcely talked at all. Her joy was too great for food or speech or any other thing.

"We stopped and saw the Dillons," Wade said. "He's talking about leaving."

"He's been talking that ever since he got here," Tom said. "I wouldn't be a bit surprised if Newsome didn't have to pull out, too."

"That's where we get water," Bethany told Milly. "At the Newsome spring."

"Yes," Milly found her voice and there was a kind of desperate wistfulness in it. "I know. They live over close to Triple T headquarters. Mrs. Newsome says it's too lonesome to live out on their claim."

"He'll keep on fooling around until he loses it," Tom said impatiently, as if he were justifying himself, as if he were explaining, for the hundredth time, his actions to a child who could not, or would not, understand him.

"I'd like to meet her, too," Bethany said, smoothing over a moment that had become a little awkward.

The meal was finished and the men went outside once more. Bethany and Milly washed the dishes.

"When I first came out here," Milly said, "I didn't see how a person could get dishes clean enough to eat in, with no more water than I use. And now all I think is whether maybe I'm being a little wasteful with it—"

"I know—" Bethany agreed.

Milly cared for the baby, touching her with loving gentle hands. Then she rocked her to sleep, singing a plaintive little melody that was all subdued sounds, almost like sighing. The sadness of it touched Bethany, made her want to cry. Milly laid the baby down, turned to Bethany once more.

"I've been talking too much," she apologized. "I'm not giving you a chance at all—and you must be as anxious to talk as I am—haven't you been awfully lonesome?"

Bethany said yes, she had.

"It's really harder for you than it was for me. I came to the ranch first and was around other people. But I still get lonesome. Tom gets out of patience with me because I'm always wishing we could move closer to the ranch."

"I don't blame you a bit," Bethany said. "I wish it myself."

The women were silent for a moment, looking out across the prairie.

"Well, we can't, either one of us," Milly finally said. "Tom's bound to stay right here and build up his herd, and Wade's going to have his try at farming. We can wish all we want to, but we know we'll stay with them—"

"Sure—" Bethany said. "I guess I don't mind—really—"

They stayed until the next day, and even then Milly did not seem to be able to bear having Bethany leave. "You'll come back," she urged. "Oh, do come back—"

Bethany and Wade rode away and left Milly standing there, a small, frail woman at the door of the dugout, until both of them—the woman and the house that sheltered her—were lost in the immensity of a brooding land which was as unmindful of them as a mountain is unmindful of an insect upon its crest.

Ahead of them the land stretched out, flat and table-like. The sun, already low against the horizon, shed an amber glow upon the greenness of the grass. In the distance cattle were feeding, looking like little cardboard toys silhouetted against the low-hung sun.

"I was—I was glad you were so nice to Mrs. Dillon," Wade said, breaking the silence.

"I felt sorry for her," Bethany told him.

"And Milly—it was better than a letter from home, for you to go see her."

"I'll go again. And she must come see me."

"I doubt if she will. Tom says she won't leave the baby five minutes. And she thinks it isn't good to take her places. But Tom says she might come, now that she's met you and liked you so much."

The sun was just about gone now. Bethany wondered whether, even if she lived out here the rest of her life, she would ever become accustomed to the beauty of the sunrises and the sunsets. Twice a day this stupendous miracle came to the plains. At night the sun went down in a blaze of beauty—reds and purples and golds. These faded out slowly, to be replaced by greens and roses and lavenders—the soft colors of flowers one tucked away for remembrance's sake. You looked, and looked, and there was nothing to break the sight of all this beauty. And then in the morning, the whole thing was repeated, as if the sunrise were only an extension of the sunset.

And now the moon came up, as if it and the sun were playing on one giant see-saw. The land took on a luminous glow, a milk-white translucence. At home the moon never looked like this. In all her life she had never seen so many moon-washed miles, spread out before her like a giant cloth of silver.

Wade rode close to her. He put his arm around her, almost shyly. She could feel him hunting for words, knew he was trying to say something that would make up for the awkward moment when Milly first saw her.

"I was right proud of you," he said. "The way you looked, and all—"

He held Rex close to Star. He rubbed his face across her cheek, coaxingly, until she turned so that he could kiss her lips.

"I sure was, honey—" he whispered.

For just a moment, before the two horses pulled apart, Bethany leaned against him. It might have been Rosemary that Milly was expecting, she thought, but it was Bethany who came. And it was Bethany leaning against Wade now, tilting up her face to be kissed.

CHAPTER SIX

THE next day Wade began plowing. After he hitched the team to the plow, he came to the dugout.

"Bethany," he said, "do you have a bucket around handy?"

"There's the gallon one I keep milk in."

"Mind if I use it?"

"Not if you'll bring it back so I can put the milk in it to-night."

"Well," he told her slowly, "after I get through with it you can't use it for anything again."

He stood there before her, his hat pushed back on his head, a queer mixture of little boy and grown man. A bucket was a hard thing to come by out here; it represented weeks of waiting, miles of travel, and money besides. But he asked for it, as a small boy might ask for a crock to lick.

"I—I have an idea," he said. "I need a bucket to carry it out—"

She turned back into the kitchen, emptied the milk from a bucket into a pan, took it back to him.

"Here it is," she said.

"You wait and see," he told her. "Wait and see what I'm going to do."

He took the bucket from her.

"I'm going to make a planter out of it," he explained, his face intent upon the thing he held.

He punched holes in the bucket and mounted it on a sort of spindle arrangement. He filled it with seed, and then set it down.

"Now," he said, "I'm ready to start. Want to come watch me?"

She said "Yes—" her throat tense with excitement. This was a big moment. This was what they had come to Texas for. She followed him outside.

He set the plow into the soil, the plow they had got from the homesteader up the trail.

"Look, Bethany," Wade said, his own voice deep with emotion. "Look—it's never had a plow in it before. It's been lying here like this since the world began."

The plow was turning the sod over, exactly upside down. Where it went it left the plain brown dirt and, by the side of it, the green waving grass. Bethany watched him, feeling not only excitement, but a sense of responsibility. They were plowing up that grass now, the grass that had grown by itself, and they were putting in another kind of seed. They would have to stay here and watch this new seed and harvest it when the time came. This thing Wade was doing would tie them to the land; it was almost as if they were planting a part of themselves. Milly was right when she said they'd stay.

At the end of the third round, Wade came back and attached the improvised planter—Bethany's riddled milk bucket filled with seed—behind the plow. And then he drove off again. He had a sizable portion planted when Tobe Dillon rode up.

"What in tarnation you doing?" the man asked.

"Planting maize—"

"That's the dad-burndest thing I ever saw," he marveled.

"That bucket tied on behind your plow. Don't see why the team ain't run off. You look jest like a kid playing horse."

He laughed uproariously.

It did look a little funny, Bethany thought, even while she resented Tobe Dillon's laughter. Who was Tobe Dillon, who never seemed to do anything himself, to laugh at the efforts of another? And yet that piece of plowed land did seem ridiculous when you stopped to think about it—like a grain of sand in an ocean of space. The ranches were to blame. They made anything you did seem small by comparison. A section was a lot of land, until you set it down in the midst of ranches. A dozen cattle made a number not to be despised, until you saw them grazing among thousands. The twenty-five acres Wade planned to plant had seemed important until Tobe's laughter showed it up for what it was—only an insignificant scratch on the face of the prairie.

Wade did not seem disturbed by Tobe's laughter. "I'm getting the job done, though," he pointed out.

"You ain't got no right to treat the land this-a-way," Tobe went on, his tone changing. "This is cattle country, not farmland."

"Oh, I wouldn't be too sure of that," Wade retorted. "Look at the color of that soil, at the lay of the land. It won't wash—"

"You're gol-darned right, it won't wash," Tobe agreed. "It won't because there ain't nothing coming down to make it wash. You been out here before. You know this country. All a farmer out here will ever do is stand in the way of the ones that know what the land's good for. This is cattle country. 'Twon't never be nothing else. It's agin nature to try to make it anything else."

"Oh, I don't know about that," Wade said. "You can't make a real country out of cows alone. You have to have some bread along with your meat. And people to eat them both."

Tobe spat mightily.

"Too many people cluttering up this place already," he said. "I'm a-fixin' to leave because of that. I came out here a-plannin' to run a few head of cattle and send 'em up the trail with a big herd. Figured maybe somebody would take 'em, and maybe give me a job helping besides. But first one thing, then another happened. Lost all my herd last winter. Now the gol-darned nesters are a-coming in and a-taking up all the land. A fellow can't run his cattle free and open like he used to."

"There's just me," Wade told him. "I've got just one section. And I'm planting only twenty-five acres of it. That can't hurt anyone very much."

"But you're a start. Others will be coming along, if you make a go of it."

Wade filled the bucket with seed and hooked it back to the plow.

"Oh, come now, Tobe," he said. "Don't take it so hard. You're no cattleman. Neither am I. We are going to have to start a game of our own."

"You mean farming?"

"Well—yes. Farming adapted to this country."

"It won't work. Won't rain enough to wet a pocket handkerchief."

"We get some rain here. You know the way this soil is—it holds water better. Besides, it doesn't rain other places sometimes, either. Remember how it was back where you came from? I certainly haven't forgotten the dry years in Missouri."

"Seasons ain't right for regular crops. And it's too high. Man, I remember how the team had to pull gitting us up on the caprock when we come from East Texas. Straight uphill. Thought we wasn't a-goin' to make it. And the nights are cool—mostly the ole woman has to git her quilts out every night, even in summer. You can't raise cotton or corn with nights like that."

"We'll raise what we can."

"And that ought to be cattle. The Lord made the grass out here for 'em and 'em for the grass. If you don't do things that a-way you are workin' agin His plan."

"You might as well say he made Missouri for the trees and us to be monkeys and stay in them," Wade said shortly.

"Oh, hell," Tobe retorted lazily, "I ain't no man to argue. Go on and pull that crazy bucket after you and scatter seed as much as you want. The Triple T cattle will take care of it, soon as ever it comes up. You may be planting on your own land, but a cow ain't a-goin' to know, or care, about the difference between what's yours and what's God's and meant for her to graze on."

"As soon as I get this planted," Wade told him, "I'm going to start building a fence. Hud Johnson is bringing the wire down from Dodge City—"

"A fence—" Tobe did not believe the word he heard. It hung on the still summer air, a weight rejected of earth and sky and man. "My God, man, that ain't a safe word to say in these parts. I seen men git killed for stringing up wire. Served 'em right, too. Got no call to fence off cattle pasture."

"That's over now," Wade said. "You forget the law they passed down at Austin."

"Cattle men ain't a-goin' to like that fence of yours. Maybe they ain't even a-goin' to stand for it, regardless of how many laws got wrote on the books at Austin. That's a long ways from here, Austin is."

Wade straightened the crude implement attached to his plow. "I have to get busy, Tobe," he said. "Come by again sometime."

"Get up," he said to the horses and started off, the bucket making a clanging sound as he went.

"My God," Tobe said, watching him, "if there don't go the funniest crazy man I ever saw!" He turned to Bethany. "Can't you talk some sense into him, Miz Cameron?"

"I don't want to," Bethany said firmly. "I think he's doing exactly right."

She did. She did indeed! Suddenly Wade didn't look funny at all. Maybe people had thought the first ranchers to venture up here were crazy. Somebody had to be first; somebody had to endure the hardships, not the least of which would be laughter.

The man rode off, sitting loose and easy in the saddle. Until he was out of sight he continued to shake his head at the foolishness of the thing he had just seen.

Finally the seed was all in.

"Now," Wade said, "I'll start fencing. By the time it begins growing good I ought to have that fence pretty well finished. Hud will be along in a few days, and he's promised to have my fence for me. I'll drive over to meet him. And I'll go to the breaks for the posts."

He was full of plans. He was full of hope as he set about fencing his land. He went to the breaks for posts, and began to dig holes for them. It was backbreaking work, and slow. But he did not give up. He set the posts deep and firm, so that the cattle would not knock them down. He took the wagon and team and went out to meet Hud Johnson and brought the barbed wire back with him. And then he set about nailing it to the posts.

The fence he built was at once a barrier and an inclosure. It looked, at the same time, childishly inadequate and menacingly businesslike. Bethany touched the frail thread of wire, and wondered how it could keep out anything. She slid her fingers along it until she came to a barb, and then she felt the chilling import in its prick.

"What if—" she hesitated. "What if the cattle run into it and get hurt?"

"Cattle have too much sense to get hurt on it. Horses, now, are different. They get excited and don't know where they are going. But not cows."

The fence was going well when Slats and Butch rode over. They sat sideways on their saddles, and rolled a cigarette apiece. Not until then did they speak.

"Well," Slats said, "Tobe told us, but we didn't believe him. A fence. Old Wade, fencing cattle off the grass. And planting stuff. Garden stuff."

They came into the dugout, carrying their hats in their hands, their faces wearing the same frank admiration they had displayed on their first visit. Seeing them, the story Wade had told her about Slats came back to Bethany—Slats, and the wagon train with the children in it, and Butch, who had perhaps in a measure taken their place. Now she understood the look in Slats' eyes, the reason Butch let him do most of the talking.

"Come in and sit down," she said. "I have some fresh bread, and maybe even some buttermilk."

"She thinks we come to eat," Slats said, addressing no one in particular. "Everytime we come, first thing she says is don't we want to eat."

"Well, don't we?" Butch asked, grinning shyly. Coming from him, it made them all laugh.

"Sure—but she ain't supposed to let on like she knows. It would be nicer if she pretended maybe we had just come calling."

"I've been calling since you left," Bethany told him. "I've been to see Mrs. Dillon, and Milly Finch."

A sort of stillness fell over the dugout. Its core was in Butch's face, but it reached out to embrace them all. The boy's eyes were alive and questioning, but his lips made no sound. It was Slats who asked how Milly was.

"All right," Bethany told him. "The baby doesn't seem well, and I think she worries about her."

"She never has been well," Butch said softly. "From the first she looked sort of—well, sort of frail-like."

"Butch ought to know," Slats said. "He was the one that rode for Doc the night the baby came. Tom was off on the ranch, and the young'un sort of decided to slip in on 'em. Good thing Butch came by just when he did."

"I just happened to be riding by at the time," Butch explained simply.

Bethany felt it was not so simple as it sounded.

"What do you think of Wade's fence?" she asked, changing the subject.

"You're a lady, Ma'am," Slats said, "and I can't say before you. It isn't his fence we mind—it's just fences in general. It's like this—"

He crossed his knees, relaxed in his chair, warmed up to his subject.

"One fence is like a sprig of loco weed. By itself it ain't so bad—maybe you can pull it up, if you see it in time. But leave it there, and it spreads. And pretty soon you got loco weed everywhere. When that happens—well, you just about as well to move your herds to another range."

"It can't be as bad as that," Bethany protested.

"Miz Cameron, Ma'am," Slats went on, "did you ever try to handle cattle around fences? I hate to say it, but sometimes they act like their brains were way down below nothing. A cow and her calf are as sure as shooting to get on opposite sides of the fence."

"And then both a-bawling at the top of their lungs," Butch put in, the nature of the subject loosening his tongue.

"Oh, to be sure," Slats said. "And if you cut the fence so they can get back together and quit bawling, you'll get your seat full of buckshot, because there's a new law down at Austin that says you can't cut fence. And the man who built that fence will sure know about it. And if you try letting the fence down, the calves stand still and the maws all rush into the field the fence is around and tramp down whatever is planted there."

"You just don't have a chance," Butch said.

"Nary a ghost of a chance. Only thing you can do is to get off your horse and lift that fool calf over the fence. And while you're doing it, you get your pants tore on the wire and the calf kicks your shins. By the time you get the baby back to his nit-wit maw, the rest of the herd has wandered off maybe ten-fifteen miles. No, Ma'am, no angle I can see looks good to me."

"Oh, my goodness," Bethany was half laughing, half convinced. "I don't wonder that you hate for us to come out here. You make me think maybe we ought to pack up and leave."

"No, *Ma'am*," Butch broke in so quickly that she could not believe it was really he speaking. "No, Ma'am. You stay right here. Slats didn't mean you were to leave—"

"No," Slats said. "I didn't mean you weren't to stay, now that you are here. Or that we aren't glad to have you—personally. If it hadn't been you, it would have been someone else. It was bound to come."

"Well," Bethany said, "pull up to the table. Maybe after you've eaten you'll feel better about things."

They sat eating and talking until it was almost sunset. When they got up to leave, they stopped at the door of the dugout to look at the rosebush. A few green shoots were showing. Each day it seemed a little greener than it had been the day before. Each day it had its drink.

"Looks like it's going to live," Slats said. "A rosebush, out here. A rosebush, and a patch of maize. Looks like you mean to stay, all right."

"You never thought anything different, did you?" Wade asked.

"No—I guess we didn't. And if you are bound to stay, we have to admit the things you are planting aren't so bad. Rosebushes and maize. Got any other ideas?"

"That's all—for the present," Wade said. "Later on, maybe—"

He was silent, contemplating his idea, whatever it was. Bethany, watching him, felt at once his remoteness and his nearness. She could understand how Mrs. Cameron must have felt when he used to play the harmonica. But this was different, because he was planning for this place, and those plans included her.

Slats, too, was silent. Bethany saw Butch's eyes on him, questioning, anxious. Finally, the boy's look seemed to get through to wherever it was Slats had retreated. The older man shook himself a little and said, almost as lightly as usual, "Guess we'd better be getting along. See you later."

"Come back," Bethany urged, "any time—"

They rode off together, their shadows long and grotesque. As they rode, the evening swallowed them up so that they were absorbed by the twilight long before they should have been out of sight.

Bethany and Wade walked together toward the fence he was building. Wade gave the wire a sharp rap. It picked up the sound, hummed with it, seemed alive with meaning and power. The sound, low though it was, reached out toward the two figures, lone and lonely, riding away into the dusk. Something about the sight of them made Bethany shiver a little. Suddenly she wanted the shelter of the dugout—the sight of the center table with its Bible; the rocking chair with the bright cushion; the striped carpet. She felt she could not hurry toward them fast enough.

"I'll get supper while you milk," she told Wade.

By the time she got to the dugout door, she was almost running.

It was several days later that Wade called to Bethany excitedly, so that she knew something important had happened.

"Bethany," he said, "can you come here a moment—?"

She went quickly, drying her hands on her apron as she walked toward him.

"Look—" he said. "The seed—it's coming up—"

She followed him to the plowed field. The seed indeed was coming up. In the cracks that marked the edges of the strips of turned-over sod, frail shoots of green were showing. About them, even now, there was an individuality, a certain something that set them apart from the other green around them. They set upon the monotone surface of the plains a passementerie of curious design—frivolous, even incongruous. They did not change the real nature of the original fabric which seemed to endure rather than to embrace them.

"It looks good," Wade said, his voice tense with excitement, with triumph. "It looks pretty good—"

"It's—" Bethany wanted to cry, although for the life of her she could not have told why. "It's—it's the most beautiful thing I ever saw—"

She reached for Wade's hand and, together, they stood looking across the field. Suddenly that little piece of maize looked big—big as the prairie itself.

CHAPTER SEVEN

O<small>N ONE</small> of his trips to the breaks for posts, Wade brought back some wild plums.

"Millions of them growing down there," he said. "Want some?"

They were small, but even so the first fruit she had seen since coming to Texas. Back home her mother would not have thought them worth the picking, or wasting sugar on, once they were picked. But here they seemed precious.

"Of course," she said. "I'll go with you next time and we'll bring back all we can get."

They made a picnic of the plum gathering. They took lunch and spent the day, returning at night with the washtub full of fruit. She set about putting it up, adapting her mother's recipes, always using as little sugar as possible.

Sugar was cruelly expensive. Not the article itself so much as the freighting charges. That was what cost out here—getting the stuff in. Whether it was people or supplies to keep the people alive, there was the long pull from the source of the supply. Water. Lumber. Food. Fuel. So they hauled water and made out with dugouts and cow chips and wild plums, so small and sour that back in the land of plenty one would have fed them to the hogs.

"Sugar is so hard to get," she said.

"Sure—everything is. We're going to have to have a railroad."

"A railroad—my goodness, Wade—" He might as well have told her that they needed the moon, or the stars, or a sizable portion of the planets. "A railroad—"

"There's nothing impossible about that," he told her. "They are spreading out. Getting ready to go beyond Dodge City. There's talk down in Austin about one coming in this direction. Of course, we don't know how close it will come to us. But we can hope—they're in the air, all right."

He spoke so convincingly that Bethany almost expected to hear the long, mournful whistle of a train, as she had used to hear it in Star Hill. Back of her the rosebush was sending out green shoots, not despising the portion that the new land gave it—rinse water from the washing. Why should she, at the memory of a train's eerie whistle, feel a wave of nostalgia that threatened to overcome her?

"I'd like a railroad," she said simply.

"First time I came out here," Wade said, as if he were thinking aloud, "I knew the railroad had to come. I even had a silly idea that maybe I'd go back and play big and try to get one through myself. You see, the first look I had at the soil, I knew it was farming country. But until you get railroads close you can't farm enough to do any good. Cattle can take themselves to market, but grain and stuff have to go a different way."

She sat quietly listening, as she had learned to do years ago in Star Hill.

"I gave that idea up," he went on. "And now, it's sort of funny, but I know I'm right. I'm going to help build that railroad after all. If enough people come out here, they'll build that road fast enough."

"And somebody has to start," Bethany said. "Maybe that's

why the ranchers don't want us. It isn't just because of the land we plow up or the fences we build. Maybe it's because the railroads will follow us."

"I shouldn't wonder," Wade agreed. "They know they can't have ranches, the way they've been having them, on land that's all cluttered up with people. When railroads come, that will mean towns all up and down the track. You'll see—when the first engine comes chugging in, there'll be a big change around here. Bound to be—"

Bethany had a strange feeling as if she and Wade had found a page that had been used before and had erased the record so that a new one might be written. When Great-grandmother had come from Virginia, Kansas City was nothing more than a trading post—a wild, ripsnorting dot of restlessness on the banks of the Missouri. And then it had grown to be a city, with a city's ways. From the things she heard she guessed maybe Dodge City was pretty much as Kansas City had been in the old days. Perhaps Dodge City too in time would be replaced by another town like it—maybe one that would grow up where she and Wade were now. There was really nothing so strange about the idea. Papa, who had a feel for such things, said that in America anything could happen where you had good land. Well, this land was good enough.

The summer wore on. There was rain. Not much, but still some. Enough to make the maize grow lush and green.

"Look at it," Wade said. "It's even better than the piece the Boss grew. Did you ever see anything like it?"

"No," Bethany said honestly, "I never did."

The garden did well enough too. Next year Bethany would know what to plant. Lettuce and things like that were not so good. Peas, beans, melons, squash—those seemed to do best. She saved back seeds against next year's planting.

The rosebush, too, was doing well. It had, as Bethany called it, a "belonging look."

As July slipped into August the days got hotter.

"They say that ordinarily June is the hottest month," Wade told Bethany. "But it sure missed it this year. I'm glad the crop is made before this set in."

Although the wind blew, hot and searing, he would not let her complain about it.

"The wind is what makes the heat bearable," he told her. "I'll bet it's ninety today, but we don't feel it. Think what this would be like back in Missouri."

She did not tell him that it seemed very hot to her here too. The sun was vital, strong, pitiless. It rose in an immensity of space and wheeled across a limitless sky all day long, to sink into a nothingness which gave no promise of clouds to hide its rising in the morning. To her, the wind seemed almost to make the sun's flames hotter, as bellows fan a fire.

She wanted to say, "Goodness, Wade, the heat seems pretty bad to me. I feel like it's curling me up around the edges."

But she kept quiet.

"And think how cool the nights are," he went on. "Remember how we used to suffer on hot, still nights in Missouri?"

There was no denying the wind made the heat more endurable, both by night and by day. But even so she could not bring herself to like it. About it there was an all-pervasiveness from which there was no escape. There were no hills to break its force, no trees to temper it. There were no streams to cool it. It came sweeping down across the miles of nothing, with nothing to challenge it save nothingness itself. It bore the essence of the land over which it passed—the sound of its loneliness, the heat of its sun, the smell of its growing things. The odors of grass and sage and cattle were in it, so faint that their blending served only to make the air seem more pure and clear.

Bethany did not know whether it was the heat or the wind that was responsible for the mirages that came to plague her when she went outside the dugout. There were shapes of trees in them, and blue water, and white houses with flower gardens. When she told Wade about this he said a person saw what he wanted to see in mirages. As for himself, he saw forty acres of maize one day—thick and green and tall as a man. It even had a good stout fence around it. She knew this wasn't true about mirages, but still it was the legend.

Bethany said maybe he was right. Lots of times she saw a group of women, in bright summer dresses and carrying pretty parasols, coming toward her. They were so real, she started to go change her dress in order to be ready for them.

"Why, Bethany," Wade said, as if her words had set him to thinking about something that hadn't occurred to him before. "You get lonesome out here. No woman to run across to see. It *is* hard—"

"Oh, nonsense," she said. "Don't worry about me—"

"Tell you what I'll do. First money we make, I'll send you home for a visit. That be all right?"

"That's fine."

He seemed quite pleased with himself for thinking of it. "Guess I'll go for water," he said.

"Want me to go?"

"Better not; it's pretty hot. Besides, I want to go for some extra posts. You won't get lonesome?"

"Goodness, no." And when he seemed disappointed, she relented. "I'll write to Mama."

When he was gone, she got out her writing things.

"*Dear Mama,*" she wrote. "*Things look fine for us. The crop is good. I have put up a lot of plums. We had a good garden, too. The weather has been warm, but the dugout has been comfortable. Wade was right—it is cool in summer.*"

She nibbled her pen, sat looking across the miles of prairie grass. She could see the corral, the shed for the stock. She could see the patch of maize, and, in the distance, cattle grazing.

"In fact, everything that Wade said about this country is true—"

The pile of pages grew, all of them filled with information about the country. She was surprised at her knowledge—she had not realized how much of Wade's talk was in her mind until she began to set it down.

And after she had finished with that, she came to what she knew would be, for her mother, the heart's core of the letter.

"Wade is very good to me," she wrote, *"as he promised he would be. I am very happy."*

She signed it, *"Your loving daughter, Bethany Cameron."*

She had addressed the letter and was ready to seal it when she decided to add something else. After her name, she wrote, *"Tell Rosemary hello."*

It was the first time she had put that into a letter.

She could see her mother when the letter reached Star Hill. She would walk down the shady street, holding it in her hand, not realizing through what devious paths it had come to her —from the hands of Wade to those of a cowboy who happened to be passing by, to a stage driver to Dodge City—and thence by rail until it came at last to Mama in Star Hill.

"And how is Bethany?" neighbors and friends would ask, stopping on the shady street as they talked.

"She's fine," Mama would say. "I have a letter from her, just today. She likes Texas."

Rosemary, too, would hear about the letter, would get the message. Rosemary in her big house on the hill—the house that was filled with things which had belonged to another woman. Rosemary, who was now Mrs. Brad Bishop, wife of the banker. Brad Bishop—an old man!

It was late when Wade got back, but she had a good supper

ready and had changed into a different dress and made herself fresh and nice.

"My goodness," Wade said, "somebody looks might fancy. Had company, or something special while I was gone?"

"No," she said. "I just wrote Mama."

It was a few days later that Mrs. Newsome came calling. Mr. Newsome brought her over. Bethany saw them when they drove up to the corral, and even as the man helped the woman out she knew who it was. She had only time to smooth her hair a little, to cast a hasty glance around the dugout, before Wade appeared at the door with the visitor.

"Bethany," he said. "This is Mrs. Newsome."

"Oh, do come in," Bethany urged.

Wade turned with what Bethany felt was almost indecent haste and went back to join Mr. Newsome. Evidently he had no intention of accompanying the guest inside.

"How do you do?" Mrs. Newsome said. She took the chair Bethany indicated. "No," she said, when Bethany offered to take her hat. "No—I'll just keep it on."

And Bethany found herself flushing, like a child caught in fault. Of course women didn't take off their hats when they came calling! Even in little Star Hill, you kept your hat on when you called formally on a new neighbor.

Mrs. Newsome was a woman no longer young. Fine lines were etched in her face as if a delicate instrument had carved them there. Her nose was pinched in the merest trifle. The heaviness of her jaw was a surprise, set off as it was by the delicacy of her other features.

She wore a grey dress, smartly made. And on the hat with which she had refused to part was an ostrich plume. About her there was an air of calculated effusiveness, as if everything she did or said she practiced first before a mirror. Beside her, Bethany felt young and awkward, conscious of her print house dress, her clumsy shoes, her work-roughened hands.

She saw the woman's eyes darting around, missing nothing, taking in the curtains, the table cover, the quilt on the bed, and all the other furnishings of the room in a swift and single glance.

"You have things very nice here," she said, her very approval a condescension.

Bethany thanked her.

"I should have called on you sooner," she went on, her words not so much an apology as a way of airing her knowledge of what was right and proper. "But I've been back home visiting. You must forgive me."

Bethany said that was all right, she quite understood.

"Goodness knows, one needs to keep right customs alive out here. There are all too few at best who try to do things as they should be done. With Mrs. Marcy gone—she's the wife of the owner of Triple T, you know—there's really no one I enjoy. Except you, of course," she added hastily.

Bethany noticed she did not say "the Boss" as the others did.

"You mustn't feel bad if the other women out here haven't called on you," Mrs. Newsome told her.

Bethany pushed back in her mind, lest she laugh aloud at the thought, the picture of Mrs. Dillon coming to see her with white gloves and her calling card!

"I haven't," Bethany said. "Milly can't come because she won't leave the baby, and Mrs. Dillon doesn't go anywhere much."

"Mrs. Finch is quite a sweet little thing. All the cowboys were crazy about her—especially the one they call Butch. I understand he was quite broken up when she married Tom Finch."

Bethany understood now, if she had not before, the hushed look on Butch's face at the mention of Milly's name, his eagerness to know how things went with her.

"It is a great shock for gently reared women to come out

here," Mrs. Newsome went on. "Had you realized that there isn't a church within miles? Not even at Mobeetie. I did not always go to church back home, but still—it makes me feel downright uncivilized to know I can't go if I *want* to."

"I do miss church a great deal," Bethany admitted, feeling suddenly a great aching desire for the little church back in Star Hill, the white building with its steeple pointing like an admonishing finger toward God.

"Of course, you know we live thirty miles from Mobeetie," the woman went on. "That's our nearest town. Though why they should call it a town, my dear, I cannot say. Clyde took me over one time when court was in session. I was never so shocked in all my life."

She leaned forward, as if she must relate in whispers the scandals of this visit.

"The town is right in the shadow of Fort Elliot," she confided. "So, they have a place called Feather Hill, with all those —*those women*—in it, living shameless and open. But I couldn't see that the rest of the town was much better. We stayed in what was supposed to be the best hotel, and my dear—we had buffalo robes for covers!"

She paused, to give her remarks time to soak in.

"When the rooms at the hotel filled up, the manager just let the cowboys sleep on the dining room floor. They yelled and swore all night long. And towards morning, a man got killed. Right under our window. And nobody seemed to think anything about it."

She sounds like Aunt Clara, Bethany thought, wondering how much of the woman's story really happened, how much she imagined.

"Of course," Mrs. Newsome added primly, "I'm sure there must be some good people in Mobeetie. In fact, I've been told they have many social events there. But after that night, I wouldn't care to share them."

She paused a moment, her look distant and far away.

"I go back to East Texas very often," she went on. "I stand it as long as I can and then either give a party or go back home for a visit."

That was why they lived closer to the ranch house, she explained. Clyde had a silly notion of building a dugout on the section where the spring was, but she put her foot down on that.

"Of course, that was before you came, my dear!" she simpered.

By living closer to the ranch house, she was able to see people oftener. And if they got sick or something, they didn't feel so stranded, as it were. The cowboys were a real help. Of course, they didn't know much about the way to act at a real party, but you'd be surprised at the way they fitted in. She always asked them and they always came. In fact, everyone came to parties, whether they were asked or not. It was like a picnic back home—when the word gets out that someone is giving a party everyone assumes he is invited.

"The Dillons—pardon me, Mrs. Cameron, for saying so, but they are—they are impossible. I've never been able to give a really nice party because they always come, with that wagon full of dirty youngsters, and ruin things—"

Bethany agreed they were pretty awful, but she did feel sorry for Mrs. Dillon.

"Yes—I'm sure it's hard on her. I suppose she goes for months without seeing anyone but her own family. It's enough to make her go—go crazy—"

There was a strange, fearful look in the woman's eyes as she said it.

"The loneliness, my dear," she went on, almost in a whisper. There was no acting in her now. "The loneliness—it gets you. Sooner or later, it does—"

And then she caught herself, and spoke with dignified correctness.

"I must be going," she said. "You must come see me. And now that I've called on you, will you come to the next party I give?"

Bethany said she'd love to.

After Mrs. Newsome was gone, Wade came to the door.

"Got any carbolic acid?" he asked. "I've cut my finger."

She went for the bottle, brought it to him. The cut he had was only a scratch, but she dressed it for him. He stood quiet under her ministrations.

"How'd you and Mrs. Newsome get along?" he asked. This was, she knew, his real reason for coming to the house.

"Oh—all right—"

"You mustn't mind what she says. She's sort of silly. Harmless, but silly. I should have warned you."

"She didn't bother me any. It's good to see another woman, silly or not."

"Even if she does all the talking."

"Even if she does all the talking. By the way, she says she's going to be giving a party some of these days. Wants to know if we will come."

"Sure. She didn't even need to invite us. Everybody goes to parties out here. Reckon she'll stay home long enough to give one?"

He turned to go back to his work. And then he stopped. He grinned at her, running his hand through his hair, brushing it back into place.

"Oh, Bethany," he said, "don't you let her put any ideas in your head. If you start trying to run around the way she does, I'll chain you to the fence."

CHAPTER EIGHT

O NE thing Mrs. Newsome's visit had done for Bethany—it had made her realize how much she missed going to church. As yet, all the Sunday observance she and Wade had known, outside of a day of rest, was the continuation of the plan they had used on the way down. Wade read from the Bible and together they sang.

"I will lift up mine eyes unto the hills," Wade read, even as the minister back in Missouri had read.

Bethany, looking out the window, saw no hills—only sky, and, under that, promise of distances that seemed to have no end to them.

And yet, there was something about the very vastness of the land that was, in itself, strength and assurance. She felt this especially in the evening when a mauve veil fell softly over the landscape. Twilight was magically generous with this country, giving it a sense of mystery, and, at the same time, a feeling of fulfillment and brooding tenderness. Anything could come from a land like this—or so one was lulled into thinking at evening. Perhaps that was why Wade felt about it as he did. He got his dreams at evening, and was so busy pursuing them that daylight could not dim them. At evening, anyone could look at the land and feel God must be near it.

But, if there were no hills to which one could lift one's eyes, there was always the sky. It was bluer than she had ever seen in Missouri, and clearer. The clouds in it formed an ever-changing pattern, assuming shapes of grandeur no less impressive than the look hills took on. The clouds seemed to hold the majestic dignity of the land over which they passed. If this country must be covered by any sky at all, she thought, the one it had was right—bright, and big, and free, with shapes of clouds that caught at your heart and lifted it up to them.

She said, "Wade—I wish we could go to church somewhere. I suppose there isn't any way—"

"Not unless we went to Mobeetie some time. There's no church, but they have services there."

Mobeetie. Sixty miles away, with the treacherous Canadian between. And when you got there, you would not find a real church. As Mrs. Newsome had said, it sounded downright uncivilized.

"I tell you what," he said, "there's a traveling preacher somewhere in this country. I'll try to get word to him to come and hold services. He's quite a character."

Wade got word to the preacher and he sent back a message saying he would come, naming the Sunday.

He came late one Saturday afternoon. By this time Wade had told her about him, so she was not surprised at the sight of him—a tall thin man on a rangy, loose-jointed horse that no cowhand would have ridden. He carried a camping outfit, a few extra clothes, some song books wrapped up in oiled cloth. In his pocket was a Bible, and across his saddle a Winchester. And always he wore the breastplate of Righteousness, the sword of the Spirit. No meanly accoutered soldier, this.

He carried his head a little forward, as if he was always listening for something others could not hear. He might have

been a wandering farmhand or a barker at a circus, or any one
of a dozen other things fascinating to men who will not follow paths set by ordinary men, or obey the rules they must
set for themselves. One would scarcely have taken him for
a minister of the Lord, unless you looked at his eyes. They
were not quite the eyes of a prophet, but they held something
of a prophet's vision. They saw visions, but they were not
visionary.

The horse he rode was named Devil, and they said he was
rightly named. He was as black as sin, and as wicked. As a colt,
so the story went, he promised to be as good a horse as anyone would want—tireless and enduring and easy enough for a
knowing man to handle; not one to be picked for riding, but
one that might be good at working—hauling the chuckwagon,
and such things. It was a great mischance that the man who
set out to break him was drunk, and maybe a little crazy besides. He had his own methods, sinister ones which men dis-
cussed darkly and some refused to believe. It was these
methods which he used on Devil who, at the time, bore no
name except "The Black One." He did the breaking in secret,
so that nobody knew quite what happened. The breaker
claimed the horse tried to paw him, and maybe he did. At any
rate, the man gave up the job.

"That's an outlaw," he said. "Better leave him alone, the—"

He gave his opinion of the horse in language the cowboys
understood.

The horse himself came out with one eye gone. Forever
afterwards the socket was a blank and staring thing, like that
of a lesser cyclops brought to everlasting blindness by a lesser
tree. From that blankness shone a vast promethean rebellion
against life and fate. No puny thing, this anger, but rather a
god-like wrath directed not so much at man himself as at the
forces which made him less than he was meant to be.

The breaker said the horse was a potential killer, but he was no killer. He had no reason to trust man, that was all. Had he been whole, and a good riding horse, the cowboys would have felt themselves honor-bound to try to ride him. As things stood, they left him alone.

One day the traveling preacher came walking to the ranch— walking, in a country where no man walked. He said, "Brother, have you a horse for sale?"

"How much you want to pay, Parson?" they asked him.

"I have ten dollars," he told them. "I have asked the Lord to provide me with a horse that will cost no more. And He will —if not here, somewhere else."

They laughed at that, but not with unkindness. He was like a child offering a nickel for the moon.

"Tell you what, Parson," one of the cowboys said, "we got a horse out there you can have—and us boys will throw in a saddle and a bridle—if you can ride him."

"I can try," the man of God said quietly. And they respected his quietness, for it had something of strength in it.

"Maybe you better not," one of them said. They liked this man, and thought perhaps things were getting a little ahead of what they had planned. "He's a devil, that one is—"

"I am accustomed to wrestling with the devil," the preacher told them. "Let me see him—"

They tried then to talk him out of his plan, but he was firm.

"My friends," he said, "I have need of a horse to do the Lord's work. With His help, I'll break this one."

They roped the Black One and got the saddle and bridle on him. And then they ranged themselves along the corral fence, laying bets on the outcome. When the minister found this out, he turned upon them and banished them.

"I'll have no betting," he told them. "And no watchers, either."

He rode the Black One. There were as many stories of the way he did it as there were men who tried to get a glimpse of the performance. Some said he prayed over the horse, and the Black One came and knelt at his feet. Afterwards, when they marveled, the Minister said,

"It was not so hard as you might think. Daily I conquer the Devil."

He named the horse Devil, and the two of them—the tall rangy horse and the tall rangy man astride him—became a familiar sight through all the plains country.

Bethany saw him riding up that Saturday evening, and went to the door to welcome him, feeling that she was re-living the days of her childhood. There was a feel to Saturday then— cakes and pies and hams and chickens ready in the kitchen, and canned things in the cellar to draw upon. Fresh-baked loaves under a white cloth. The very feel of Saturday was one of opulence coupled with sanctity. She used to think it was like the Israelites, who, after all the wanderings in the wilderness, had come at last to Canaan, to the land of milk and honey. They themselves had come through the problems of the week, and were at last looking upon the full abundance of things that Sunday promised, both for the body and for the spirit. It was all a part of this glad feeling when a visiting minister, or the Presiding Elder himself, came to spend Saturday night in the home.

"I am Brother Fenton, the Traveling Preacher," he told her.

"I am Mrs. Cameron," she said. "I'm so glad you came."

"It was good of you to send for me."

He spoke with a curious formality, at variance with the land in which he had cast his lot. Although he was not a learned man, his speech was more than a little tinged with the intonations of the scholar. At first Bethany was puzzled that this man, product of a frontier culture, should speak so. Later she came to know that it was the majestic cadence of the Bible language that colored his speech. He had read so much from it that the rhythm of the style, as well as the words themselves, had crept into his speech.

"I have taken the liberty of spreading the word that there will be services at your house tomorrow. This is a fine location."

He requisitioned her house, appropriating it for the Lord's work as he had requisitioned the horse. She bowed to his will, even as the horse had done. More than that—she felt a pride that she should be the chosen one.

"I'm glad you will have the services here," she told him.

He said, now that the matter was settled, he would go out and visit with Brother Cameron.

She poured chips into the little stove and began preparations for supper. There were beans and canned tomatoes and roast prairie chicken. She put the coffee on to boil and set the table with a white cloth and the best dishes. This was the way she had been taught to do things for a minister of the Lord. And all the time she worked she worried about sleeping arrangements. Why hadn't she asked Wade to make her some curtains, like Milly's? Why hadn't she asked him to build another bunk over in the far corner? The best she could do now was a pallet on the floor. A minister sleeping on the floor! Perhaps it would be better if she and Wade took the pallet and let the minister have their bed.

Presently he and Wade came in together talking earnestly. The preacher knew men as well as horses. He talked honest man-talk, colored with no unctuous piety. He knew cattle and grass and all the good wisdom of the land. He knew them because they stemmed from the source of all good, the One who was Master of all.

"This is a nice place you have here, Sister Cameron," he said, looking around him.

His look took in the curtains, the white cloth, the best dishes. With that look, he also took her measure. Here was a good woman. She had made the house ready, not for him alone, but for the One he represented.

He asked the blessing, a deeply personal note in his voice. It was not just the food on which he invoked the Lord's blessing, but the house, and the people in it, and the land they lived on. It was almost as if his prayer was answered on the spot so that one could see the blessing descending visibly upon them, spreading its benign presence over the little house.

When the meal was finished, Wade, prodded by Bethany's meaningful look, asked the preacher if he would "read a chapter." The preacher reached for the Bible which his discerning eye had already discovered on the little table.

"I always use the Bible of the household," he said.

He began to read aloud, his voice low and deep, filled with a great and aching sadness like the wind passing over the prairie.

"For the Lord thy God bringeth thee into a good land—" he read.

He believed what he read. His voice invested the land with magic—not with promise alone, but with the actuality of homes and people and all good things.

"—a land of wheat and of barley, and vines and fig trees—a land wherein thou shalt eat without scarceness, thou shalt not lack anything in it—" he went on.

His voice was beautiful, filling the little dugout with its music.

"When thou hast eaten and art full then thou shalt bless the Lord thy God for the good land which he hath given thee—" he went on, and then closed the book and said, so that his own words might have been ones he read from the book, "—let us pray."

"Oh, Lord," he said, "I pray thee, bless this home and all the other homes of this country."

His voice gave the homes substance. Bethany half expected to rise from her knees and see them ranged neatly outside her window, with green clipped lawns about them and rustling trees and, at the end of the street that held them, a white church with a steeple pointing upward.

And when he had risen from his knees, he said, "If you will excuse me now, I will retire. I need time to refresh my body and my spirit if I am to have anything to give those who come tomorrow."

It was then that Bethany, pink with embarrassment, said, "I'm sorry, Brother Fenton. I have no extra bed. I am going to make you a pallet on the floor."

"Sister Cameron," he told her, "I would not sleep inside had you a dozen beds. I always sleep out—under God's stars—as do most of my flock. I work much with cowboys, you know," he explained.

He bade them goodnight and went out, as he had said, to sleep beneath the stars.

"They will be coming early in the morning, I'm thinking," he told Bethany. "But perhaps you know that already."

Bethany did not know, and she was glad she had been warned, for, sure enough, they began to arrive by mid-morning. From a radius of eighty miles they came, the people in that sparsely settled land. Many of them she had never seen before. But they brought with them baskets of food, for, even in this open-handed country, no one would expect a hostess to feed a group of this size without assistance.

The Dillons were among the first to come.

"I brought a kettle of beans," Lizzie said. "The kids'll relish them when they won't eat nothing else. I'll jest set 'em on the stove to het."

Bethany privately resolved that beans were one thing she would leave off her own plate today.

"If you'd set me to something," Lizzie Dillon said, "I'd be proud to help. A meetin' is awful nice, but it comes hard for the woman where they have it."

"I don't mind," Bethany said. "I'm glad it could be here."

Lizzie Dillon looked at her thoughtfully, her eyes deep and inscrutable.

"I sez to Tobe," she went on, "first time you come to see us, I sez—now that Wade Cameron has gone and married hisself a good woman. You ain't a thing like he made out you was, before he fetched you here."

There was no answer Bethany could make. It was well that Milly came just then. She and Tom drove up in a light spring wagon, Milly carrying the baby carefully.

"It was such a nice day, I didn't think it would hurt her," she said anxiously, as if she were not convinced she was right. "Tom was determined to come, so I finally said I would. It's the first time I've taken her anywhere."

"I'm sure it won't hurt her," Bethany reassured her. "My, that's a pretty dress she's wearing."

"Isn't it! I made it myself. I'd hate to tell you how many hours I spent on it."

She put the baby on Bethany's bed and it lay there smiling gently, like a woman resigned to the fact that life has passed her by. No baby smile, that.

"There, there, sugar," Milly crooned. "That's a good baby to smile so sweet when mama puts you down—"

She straightened up, and turned to Bethany.

"I brought you a plum cobbler and some roast prairie chicken. There's no telling how many will be here before it's over. A church service is a great event out here—you wouldn't believe how much the cowboys enjoy it."

The crowd was growing now. The men and the Dillon children remained outside. Bethany saw a half dozen cowboys who were strangers to her before Butch and Slats rode up. Between them, they carried a big piece of beef which they brought inside the dugout.

"We brought you some meat," Slats said. "Don't ask us how we wangled it out of the cook. You just take it, and be glad to get it. Hi there, Milly. Good to see you. How's the little tyke?"

134

"She's over there on the bed," Milly told him. "Go say hello to her."

Butch and Slats tiptoed over, as if they feared to waken her. But the baby was not asleep. She looked up at them, smiling her wise unchildlike smile.

"Well, the little booger," Slats exulted. "She smiled at us—"

Butch reached out his finger, slowly, and the baby's own small hand closed around it. His face turned red, but he stood there quietly, smiling down uncertainly at the child.

"My gosh, let's get out of here," Slats said. "Here comes Miz Newsome. Better get your mouth set just so, Miz Cameron."

The two cowboys hurried out, just before Mrs. Newsome came in. She was wearing a hat with a veil, and white kid gloves. In her hands she bore a plate—carefully, lest the contents soil the gloves.

"Why, how do you do, Mrs. Cameron," she said. "It's good of you to have us here today. I'm glad you felt you could come, Mrs. Finch. Good morning, Mrs. Dillon."

She set her plate on the table, unwrapped it to show the contents.

"I brought a cake," she announced. "It ought to be good—I used eight eggs and a cup of butter."

"I'm sure it is," Bethany told her.

The cake sat there, among the beans and prairie chicken and plum cobbler, looking as much out of place as the kid gloves and the veil looked by the side of Lizzie Dillon's mother hubbard.

"Won't you—won't you take off your hat and things—" Bethany asked her uncertainly.

"I suppose I will, although one really should wear them at a church service—"

"We're going to eat first," Bethany told her.

Brother Fenton, a practical man, had arranged this.

"You have ridden far," he told the people. "It is best that we all refresh ourselves. After that, we will hold services."

The men had already improvised tables in the yard, and it was to these that the women carried the food. Brother Fenton looked at it appreciatively.

"Ah, this is good," he said. "Now let us ask God's blessing upon it, and then we will eat."

He lifted his hand, and a reverent hush fell upon all the people. Even the small Dillons, made restless and eager by the sight of food, stood quietly while the preacher spoke to a God of whom they had scarcely even heard.

They filed around the tables, helping themselves to food, laughing and joking each other. Here was food, not only for the body, but for the spirit. It was good to hear a preaching, but it was good, too, to eat with their own kind—to hear talk and laughter, to know themselves a part of a social unit. The preacher knew this—he let them savor the last bit of food, the last bit of companionship before he again raised his hand and said:

"And now it is time for services. Let us help the good women clear away first, for they have done much and are tired."

Finally, the work was finished, and it was time to begin. The men lounged around the yard, the cowboys, with the exception of Butch and Slats, looking uneasy and doubtful whether to sit erect or to relax easily on their haunches, the way they would do if they were out among themselves with no women or minister to set them thinking about proprieties.

The preacher passed around the song books.

"Let us sing 'On Jordan's Stormy Banks I stand,'" he said.

"On Jordan's stormy banks I stand
And cast a wistful eye—"

They sang together, their voices lifted to the Lord in a strange land.

My goodness, Bethany thought, that's the song I sang the first Sunday Wade and I had services on the road down.

"I'm bound for the promised land," they sang together, their voices lost in the vastness of the landscape.

And then they went into the next stanza, and Bethany knew why the preacher had chosen this song.

> "O'er all those wide extended plains
> Shines one eternal day—"

He led them until the last syllable had died away.

They sang others, "Beulah Land," and "Come Thou Fount of Every Blessing,"—the words warm and lovely on their lips. In a land far removed from fountains they sang of them, but no one thought of the lack.

After that he took out his Bible and read to them—words so familiar to him that he did not really have to look at the page at all. But the feel of the book was good in his hands. He held it, even as he talked to them. He talked easily, almost as if it were a conversation he was carrying on. Perhaps he knew that what he said did not matter—they were not listening to him so much as they were remembering other sermons, in other churches. His business was to keep alive in them the thing that other ministers had nurtured. Never for him the church with walls, stained glass windows and an altar rail. Some day there would be such a one in this country, but by that time he would be somewhere else, off to another place that would be as this one now was. For he was a traveling preacher, and his work was clear and sure in his heart. He knew this, and he did not mind.

"We will pray," he said. And he prayed earnestly but not too long—these people had far to go, and besides, they needed contact with their fellow men as much as they needed communion with their God.

"And now may the grace of God go with you," he said. "Amen."

It was late afternoon before the people finally rode off—the Newsomes in their buckboard, Milly and Tom in the spring wagon, and the Dillons in the larger one with its wood end bows still standing up, like the bare skeleton of some grotesque monster. The cowboys rode off together, too, but there was a difference in their togetherness. It seemed to accentuate their loneliness, instead of assuaging it. Milly and Tom were a unit, as they went away; the Dillon children, most of their shyness now gone, gave that wagon a comfortable family look; even the Newsomes had an air of destiny shared.

Brother Fenton left, too. "You were good to have us, Sister Cameron," he said. "The Lord will bless you."

Bethany watched them go, and then she turned to Wade. When she spoke, it was not of the services, but from some inner knowledge, some great hope within her.

"Lone men have it hard out here, don't they?" she asked.

Here was his chance to tell her—she did not quite know what she hoped for. The essence perhaps she knew, but not the words.

"Now aren't you ashamed," he said. "Fishing around for compliments like that. I'm a good mind not to tell you."

He put his arm around her, drew her to him.

"If you mean, am I glad you came out here with me, honey— I sure am!"

(*It's just to spite me, he's taking you to Texas*, Rosemary had told her.)

Bethany leaned against Wade, thinking she was silly even to let herself remember the things Rosemary had said.

CHAPTER NINE

Summer slipped into fall.

It was a strange thing, this fall in Texas. About it there was little of the rich opulence of Missouri autumns—no shocks of corn like Indian teepees keeping watch over the land, no orchards bending with loads of ripened sweetness, no leaves of red and gold. But, in spite of this, there was something in the air—a sense of hushed expectancy, a feeling of fulfillment.

Wade headed the maize by hand with a knife. Part of it he hoped to sell to the Boss. He would keep some for next year's seeding, and to feed his own stock. It was slow work, alone, and by hand.

"Almost wish it hadn't done so well," he grinned.

But Bethany knew he did not mean it.

Often when he went to the spring for water he drove on to the breaks and gathered wood. This he piled against the side of the dugout.

"Come in mighty handy this winter when the chips are wet," he said. "Could be we'd need it, before the winter is finished."

Strange, she hadn't thought of that, hadn't stretched her mind to a time when chips would not be available. She remembered how she had felt about them at first—the loathing with which she touched them, the inner shamed disgust that kept her from writing home that she used them for fuel. And, even after she grew accustomed to using them, she was oddly embarrassed when she and Wade drove out on the prairie to gather a supply of them. They went in the wagon, just as if they were going for water, taking wash tubs in which to carry back their loot.

"It's—I feel just like a scavenger," she told Wade. "Or a buzzard looking for carrion."

"You'd feel a darned sight worse if we didn't find any," he told her.

He grinned at her, pushing back his hair with his wrist. He might tell her how clean the chips were and all that, but she noticed he was mighty careful not to touch his hands to his face while he was out gathering them!

"They tell a story about a man up the line who pays the trail bosses to let their cattle bed down on his place—so as he can get the chips."

He was thin, she noticed. Or was it that the wind did that to men out here—chiseling off every ounce of excess flesh, molding them into lean taut things fit to stand the buffets of the land? Slats and Butch had much the same look—as if they had been carved by destiny to fit the niche they occupied.

"You're thin, Wade," she said. "I'm going to have to feed you better—"

"You aren't so fat yourself," he said, looking at her closely. "But then, you've had a lot of things to get used to—like using chips, and so on—"

"I don't mind," she told him staunchly. "All I worry about now is maybe the cattle will go off too far to graze."

The grass was the real richness of the country. One way or another, it sustained them. The wind blew over it, cool at night, hot and searing in the daytime. The heat of the wind was enough to dry out the very marrow of the land, but the grass bent to it easily and gracefully, like waves of the sea. Under the wind and the heat the green summer grass changed, turning brown, becoming one with the earth.

This autumn grass did not have a dead look, such as Missouri grass held in time of drought. That was pitiful, like a woman who had given up trying because it was no use anyway. About the dried grass here was a resourcefulness, a feeling of adaptation, different from the green of spring, but no less good. Into it were sealed all the real values, as a woman seals into her heart and mind all the real good that has happened to her, preserving it for future use, drawing upon the actuality of it when the need comes. Looking at the grass, one knew that the earth, bursting with plenty, waited serenely as a woman who has fulfilled her destiny waits for old age.

"It's rich as hay," Wade told her. "Take a cow off it and send her down to Galveston to that stuff that's all water, and she'll starve to death in a week."

Maybe Tobe was right when he protested the plowing up of grass.

With the coming of autumn, too, they began to worry about fires. For fire menaced this source of life, the grass. The fear of fire, and precautions against it, were inherent in every action of the plainsman. Bethany had grown accustomed to the meticulous care with which Wade put out matches. It was not enough that the flame was out; the match itself must be broken and then, often as not, put into his pocket instead of thrown down on the ground. It was as if only in his own safe-keeping would he trust the firemaker.

"I saw one burn a hundred miles once," Tobe said. "Looked like there was jest no stopping it, once it got started. You'd think it was stopped, and sure enough the wind would change and it would all start over again. Caused considerable ruckus— some said the freighters got kind of careless like with their camp fires. I wouldn't know. Sometimes I think fire jest breaks out by itself here—"

Did it? Bethany wondered. Was the country wanting to be rid of them and took this means, thinking to wipe them out as a wave washes away the sand castles children build on the beach?

It was while the preparations for fall were being made that Mrs. Newsome sent word she was going to have a party, and hoped she could have the pleasure of Mr. and Mrs. Wade Cameron's company. A cowboy brought the written invitation, grinning as he handed it to Bethany.

"She'd like an answer," he said.

Sure enough, the letters R.S.V.P. were in the corner. Bethany, trying hard to remember the correct form for answering such an invitation, went to look for ink and paper.

"There," she said, "I've told her I would come."

"Thank you, ma'am," he said. "She made quite a point of it."

Already, when Bethany and Wade rode up to the Newsome place on the night of the party there were a number of horses around the corral. You could tell the cowboys' horses from the others—they stood quietly, with the reins dropped over their heads. Rex and Star had to be tied to the corral fence. The Dillons' wagon was there, looking worn and dejected as if it had just completed a long trek across unexplored lands. Bethany found herself wondering if they, too, had received a written invitation, and, if so, what Lizzie Dillon had done about the "R.S.V.P." in the corner. At any rate, they had come, with or without benefit of invitation.

And that was as things should be. A party here was a public thing—it was a law of the land, a law enforced by grim necessity. Just as people left their doors unlocked in order to succor their fellow man in a land where nature offered such grudging shelter, so they must offer as well an anchor against loneliness, that greatest enemy of all. Here, the only invitation needed was the fact that a party was being given.

The Newsome half-dugout had two rooms, which awed Bethany before she alighted from her horse. On the inside, it was different, too. Although most of the furniture had been removed from the "front room" in order that the dancing might take place there, enough was left to set this house apart from the others Bethany had seen. A coal oil lamp with red roses painted on the shade stood on a shiny oak table. Two mahogany rockers with crocheted tidies on arms and back were pushed into the corners. Mrs. Newsome had rolled up the rug and placed it against the wall, taking precautions that the design side, with its roses, was rolled out. Perhaps the greatest difference of all was the floor, which was wood instead of dirt.

"Oh, how do you do, Mrs. Cameron," Eva Newsome said, extending her hand elegantly. "And Mr. Cameron. I'm *so* glad to see you! You know Mr. Newsome, don't you?"

She and Clyde Newsome stood at the door to receive the guests, she in a yellow party dress, delicate shoes, and an elaborate hair-do. In every word and gesture of his, cordial though he strove to be, there was an air of embarrassed reluctance. He would do this because it meant so much to her, his attitude said very plainly, but he would have liked to do things in another way—the casual, backslapping friendly way that was native to the land. But that was not his wife's intention. She would insist on an air of elegance, such as was the fashion back home. Her guests might take this for a public affair, but she herself would never give in to such impropriety. She would handle the situation as any lady would when uninvited guests came, with dignity, even though she knew it was not right for them to act so.

"Take your things into the other room," she told Bethany, her words consciously important.

Bethany went into the "other room," really a combination kitchen, dining room, and general utility room. A table had been extended by some ingenious method so that it looked like a table, and not planks laid over saw horses, as it surely must have been. On it was a linen tablecloth and over that a humped-up whiteness, a thin material which covered the food and decorations, already on the table. Milly was in the room, bending over two chairs which had been made into a sort of bed for the baby.

"Oh, it's good to see you," she cried when Bethany came in.

"I'm glad you came," Bethany told her.

"I didn't want to come, really," Milly admitted. "But Tom was so anxious, I didn't have the heart to disappoint him. I didn't think it would be good for baby. But it doesn't seem to bother her—she just lies there."

The baby was, indeed, lying quietly—too quietly, Bethany thought. She must be more than nine months old now. By that time, most babies were beginning to wave arms and legs and make a great fuss to be taken up. But this baby made no fuss at all—just lay there smiling that sweetly-sad little smile of hers.

Milly, wearing a white dress which Bethany suspected must be a part of her wedding clothes if not the wedding dress itself, looked little more than a child herself. Her hair hung soft and loose about her face. Bending over the baby, she might have been a child admiring a beloved doll, except that the look in her eyes was not that of a child.

Butch and Slats came in just then. At the sight of Milly, Butch's young face was illuminated, as if some inner light burst into flame in a radiance of which he himself was either unaware or did not mind exhibiting.

"Why, hello, Butch," she said. "Come see baby—she's grown so much since you last saw her." On her lips the words had a sort of bright pathos.

Butch went over to stand beside her and looked down at the baby. His eyes were kind, and a little sad.

"Isn't she growing?" Milly said. "Just think—you haven't seen her since the day of the preaching at Bethany's."

She begged him to agree, to say yes and allay the doubt in her own heart.

"Tom says she's the littlest thing he ever saw, but she's bigger than she was that first night you saw her, isn't she?" Milly went on eagerly.

"She was mighty little that night," Butch agreed. "I thought at first it was a doll Doc was holding when he called me to come in. Yes—she's grown, all right—"

It was the longest speech Bethany had ever heard him make.

"Oh, thank you," Milly cried, as if he had conferred some great gift upon her. "Oh, thank you, Butch. You were so good that night," she went on, a little diffidently—being, at the same time, both self-conscious and more mature than Bethany had yet seen her. "I—I don't think Tom or I have ever thanked you for it."

Butch's face glowed crimson; he moved his hands restlessly, as if he were in sudden, and secret, pain.

"It wasn't nothing," he muttered. "I just happened by. I didn't do any more than anyone else would have done—"

"Oh, yes, you did, Butch," Milly assured him earnestly. "I was awfully sick, but I knew all about it. And I thank you. If it hadn't been for you, maybe baby and I both would have died."

They were silent, standing there together. For them, neither the party, nor Bethany, nor anyone else existed. Finally Milly spoke, quietly, as she might have spoken to a child, "We must go back with the others, Butch. Thank you for looking at her."

They all went into the front room together.

The Dillon children were there, looking like young wild things cooped up in the smallness of the house. They sat in corners, peering around fearfully at the unaccustomed grandeur that surrounded them. Bethany was half afraid they would bolt if she spoke to them, but risked it anyway.

"Hello," she said.

They regarded her with unblinking shyness, unsure whether her move was a friendly one. Bethany wondered if the party itself was so much an ordeal as was the fact that their mother had evidently insisted upon clean hands and combed hair. It was a great relief to everyone when Tobe Dillon said,

"Git out in the yard and play, kids. Night's too pretty for you to stay inside."

They scuttled out with frightened suddenness as if they suspected someone of setting a trap across their path.

More guests were coming in now. Several ranchers and their families from as far as sixty miles away; three or four of the cowboys brought girls from Mobeetie. One of these women was drawing a great deal of attention. She was not very young, and she was not very pretty. Her reddish-gold hair was piled too high on her head, her dress was a bit too tight, her laugh a little too loud—in fact, everything about her was just a little *too* much. But she was a woman, and women were rare out there, so she was not without a circle of male admirers. The women were more reserved toward her. They knew there was nothing bad about her—she was only a little silly. But even so, they liked neither her actions nor those of the men who gathered about her, joining in with her too-loud and too-frequent laugh.

"She does have pretty red hair," gentle Milly said, just as Mrs. Newsome, thinking that all the guests had probably arrived, came by.

"It's no more red than mine," Eva Newsome snapped. "*She puts soda on it.* She got here at noon today—and me with all I had to do—and said she was dusty from riding and did I mind if she washed her hair before the party. And what did she do but empty most of my box of soda in the water!"

For the first time, the women were all lined up solidly behind Mrs. Newsome, impressed with the magnitude of the crime committed by the red-haired visitor from Mobeetie. Not so much that she had stooped to the trick, for did not they all—perhaps even Lizzie Dillon—have their own ways of overcoming the ravages of this raw country? But that she should employ a means so thoughtless was beyond forgiveness. Soda was a two days' trip away!

"Miz Newsome," Slats said. He refused to be awed by anything, even the attempted correctness of this party. "Miz Newsome, ain't it about time you let us start dancing?"

"Indeed it is," Mrs. Newsome told him. "I was going to—"

The fiddler, who might have been very old or quite young, for all one could tell by looking at his weathered face, took his place in a chair which had been set on a box in order to lift him above the level of the dancers.

"Gents, git yore pardners," he called.

Wade came to Bethany, led her out on the floor. The rows of men and women faced each other.

"Salute yore pardner," the fiddler commanded.

Wade bowed to her as she stood there in her best dress and Sunday shoes, her eyes bright with excitement and expectation, and with that gesture of his started an experience she was never to forget—her first dance on the plains.

Things moved too fast for her to be sure what did happen. For her, as well as for the other women, the party was a sort of endurance test. Even Lizzie Dillon did not sit down during the evening.

The cowboys were frankly, naively woman-hungry. A fellow could ride for days, seeing nothing but men and cowcritters. Then he came to something like this where there were women—good women, like you'd known back home. It was almost as if he were seeing them for the first time. They were little. You forgot how small their hands and feet were, how soft and delicate the stuff in their dresses. A man could get drunk, just looking at them.

A woman sensed this feeling of theirs, gauged it for the strength and gentleness and great yearning that was in it, so that their own enjoyment of the party was tinged with woman-compassion as well as woman-pleasure. They danced with everyone, and knew no fatigue.

"Excuse me, Ma'am, will you dance this one with me?"

A cowboy Bethany did not know took her from one whose name she had heard but had forgotten. As they stepped back on the floor, she saw Lizzie Dillon go by, stepping light and free, led by a boy scarcely older than her own oldest son. Upon the woman's face was something which, if not beauty itself, was so near akin to it that the difference was not worth considering. She was not conscious of her grey mother hubbard nor of the tight knot into which her dark hair was screwed. She was not aware of herself at all as she really was— a heavy, middle-aged woman who had known little but pain and trouble. She was as young as the spirit of the girl this boy might have loved; she was as old as the mother he had left somewhere back in the piney woods of Texas.

Bethany saw Milly across from her, daintily lifting the skirt of the white dress; she saw the red-headed woman from Mobeetie, her hair loose and disarranged now, as her cowboy partner lifted her hand in a gesture as courtly as he would have used for a young princess; she was aware of Eva Newsome, forgetting her stiff party manners in an abandon almost as complete as that of her guests. She heard the hoarse voice of the fiddler, calling out the steps; she felt, as much as heard, the quiver of the floor as the dancers stamped their feet, clapped their hands. It was almost like a dream—as if she stood still and let all this flow past her.

At intervals the men who "couldn't snatch a pardner" left

the room to smoke, to look after the horses, to rest. But none of the women took rest, nor felt the need of it.

It was not until after midnight that the dancing stopped, even temporarily, and then only because Mrs. Newsome signaled the fiddler. He laid down his bow; the dancers stood still.

For Bethany, the room settled back in place. She saw the Dillon children asleep in the corner on the "suggan" their mother had brought for a pallet; she saw Milly slip into the kitchen to take a look at the baby—knew she must have gone several times before this; she saw Wade glowering at her across the room, realized she had scarcely danced with him all evening. The etiquette of the land demanded that he let the other men dance with her—all those lonely cowboys who had ridden through miles of loneliness for the privilege of dancing with a woman. That he was resigned to. But that she should be enjoying it so much—well, he didn't mind showing her he didn't like it! She moved over to him now, slipped her hand through his arm just as Mrs. Newsome said with correct primness, "Refreshments are served."

She led the way into the "other room." She lifted the table cover to reveal food rarely seen in this country. Not content with the delicacies of the land, she had sent out for things hard to come by. Oranges in a bowl in the center of the table, so beautiful and rare they might have been real gold. The freighters had brought them in, and not a soul there did not know full well the cost of such a venture. There were chicken salad and delicate sandwiches which the men eyed with instinctive distaste. There were nuts and bon-bons in silver dishes. On one end of the table was a huge white cake, decorated with a most intricate icing, the whole thing representing an outlay of eggs which must have been a piece of extravagance scarcely less than that represented by the oranges. The sight of so much unfamiliar food, resting on a lacy white

149

cloth, awed them all a little. Which was exactly what Mrs. Newsome had meant it to do.

The table seemed out of place in this dugout kitchen. Like the party itself, it lacked both the real gentility of the land from which the woman came and the ease of this new one. The people who were her guests would have been the first to accept genuine refinement; likewise, they were quick to see through her pretensions. Theirs was the real refinement in that they took, with simple graciousness, the last full measure of enjoyment from the party she was giving.

They had finished eating, were ready to dance again, when Tobe Dillon and some of the partnerless men opened the door of the dugout and started outside. Tobe stopped short of the threshold, pointed his hand.

"Look—" he said. "Yonder—"

Against the horizon they saw a light. No moon it was, or sun, or any natural light. They said, together, "It's a grass fire—"

They said it, knowing the nature of the menace that was bearing down upon them.

CHAPTER TEN

They said, "It's a big one—look at the smoke—"

As a single unit the men moved to their horses, the party forgotten. Where there had been only a light a few moments ago, now there were little red tongues of flame, licking scallops against the sky. Like imps dancing in hell they formed a solid line against the horizon.

"It's headed north," someone said. "And with the wind the way it is—"

North. Away from the breaks, away from the River. And, Bethany thought—knew Wade was thinking, too—toward their place. North. For Wade and her, that was the direction in which fear lay.

They set about fighting the fire, ranchers, cowboys and nesters alike, moving together in an undivided attack, held by a common purpose. In their approach there was no talk of me and mine. They saw the fire against the horizon and they moved toward it, determined to use every cunning as if they were fighting an enemy half-human, half-demon. For the fire, indeed, had about it a human-like cunning, a diabolical cruelty.

"You stay here," Wade said to Bethany. "Later you can help the women bring us something to eat, and some water."

He didn't say, "You couldn't get home now if you wanted to. Not without riding miles out of your way, you couldn't—"

They stayed at the Newsome place, the women and children, waiting as women always wait while their men do battle against the enemy. For it was a battle the men fought, and they used whatever weapons they could lay their hands upon.

They took the despised plow, and put it to a new use. They plowed strips of prairie sod, not for seeding, but to prevent the growth of the seeds of fire. Fire guards, they called these plowed strips. But the red monster hurdled them as if they were not there. Sometimes the wind picked up cow chips, tossing them lightly across the barrier, starting a new fire in fresh fuel. Even the cow chips, which had served them well, seemed to turn against them—friends until now, they had joined the enemy.

The men made backfires between the main blaze and the territory they wished to protect, placing them with cunning, watching them with a care a doctor shows a patient to whom he has given a problematical medicine in a last desperate effort to save him. There was no water here, the natural enemy of fire, so man must make of himself a semblance of that enemy.

It was Lizzie Dillon who took command of the women. She, who had weathered everything, felt no great fear of a grass fire.

"They'll stop it," she said calmly. "They always do. Sometimes it takes longer'n others, but they do it—"

She could be calm, Bethany thought rebelliously. About her place there were no row crops drying, no curtains at dugout windows. No maiden blush rose was taking root beside her door. For Lizzie Dillon, there was nothing to lose. If her burrow was destroyed, she and her mate and her young would move to another.

It was as simple as that.

"Come morning," Lizzie went on. "I reckon we'd best take them a bite to eat—we can load it in my wagon—"

"I'll go with you," Bethany said. "I'll ride Star—"

Morning came, eerie and unreal. The sun rose red in the east; in the west was that other grim redness.

"It ain't quite so big," Lizzie said. "They're a-whippin' it; I knowed they would. We'll take the stuff to eat now, and the water."

They packed the food left from the party into pans and boxes. Among them, they got a small barrel on the wagon, filled it with water. Mrs. Newsome's face showed gray and old in the light of dawn. Bethany knew that she herself should be tired, but she was beyond fatigue, beyond feeling of any kind.

Mrs. Dillon awakened the children, still sleeping on the "suggan," and got them into the wagon.

"Shouldn't some of us go with you?" Milly asked uncertainly.

"You best stay here and take care of the baby," Lizzie Dillon said kindly. "And you ought to lay down and rest, Mrs. Newsome. You're plum wore out from the party."

Strange that from her would come the thoughtful kindness— and from her lips, too, the words that threatened to send Bethany off into hysterical mirth.

"It was shore a nice party, Miz Newsome," said Lizzie, as she took the lines in her hands. "Git up, Bess. Git up, Kate—"

Lizzie Dillon and Bethany drove on. The woman did not look back; she drove with sureness and confidence. Bethany followed her, never questioning her decisions. The children sat quiet in the wagon as if they too were sure of her rightness. Afterwards Bethany remembered that not once during all that trip did the children make any trouble, grow restless, ask for some of the food or water which was in the wagon with them. They had been trained in a sort of quiet acceptance of what

153

came. They had been schooled to follow without question the ways of their elders in times of emergency.

They came upon the fire fighters by mid-morning. The men had just killed an old bull and split him wide open, so that his carcass formed a large flat surface. They had tied ropes to his legs, and two men rode to a side, with the other ends of the ropes tied to their saddle horns.

Four cowboys whom Bethany remembered only vaguely were making ready to drag this strange piece of fire-fighting equipment across the grass, where it was burning farther up the line.

"Wouldn't you like some water?" Bethany asked. "And— and something to eat?"

She felt a little embarrassed to be offering them the dainty remnants of the Newsome party supper. Working men needed real food, not party stuff.

They swung down off their horses, which stood with eyes turned questioningly toward their masters, as if they would know the reason for this strange burden they carried. Live cows they knew—plunging and kicking. They could brace their weights with them, even almost anticipate their movements. But this dead thing—

"Yes, ma'am," they said. "We could use some water and some grub, all right—"

Bethany looked at the dead bull, tied fast between the horses.

"Seems sort of a shame," she said. "Killing cattle, I mean—"

"Well, Ma'am," one of them said softly, "maybe so. But I reckon this one would be right proud to know he helped stop a fire—"

It was the ancient ritual of sacrifice—giving one in order to propitiate the wrath of the gods against many. They would drag this carcass across the burning grass, putting out the flames with it. Maybe it was like that everywhere, Bethany was thinking. A few have to suffer so that things will be easier for others.

"How are they a-comin'?" Lizzie asked. "They are a-stoppin' it, ain't they?"

"I can't say, Ma'am," he told her. "Sometimes we think so, and then the wind changes and blows it back into new places —like as not where none of us are working."

He bent over to beat out a small spark with his slicker. The gesture was automatic. The spark had landed on the trail, was out almost before it struck. But all the same, you put out a fire, however small, when and where you saw it. The monster they were fighting now had probably been a spark no larger than this one at one time.

"Seems like the wind blows from all directions at once when we get to fighting a fire," he said. He got back on his horse. "Guess we'd better be getting along. Thanks for the grub and water."

"We'll drive on up the trail," Lizzie told him. "No fire up that-a-way, is there?"

"Haven't heard of one."

"Tell the others where we're headed, and that we got stuff to eat."

"That's right kind of you, Ma'am," he said. "Most of them are back a ways where the fire is worst, but I'll tell them. Maybe they can sort of spell each other off and come for some."

"Tell them I'm workin' on toward home," she said. "I'll git them kids out of the wagon and then bring back some fresh grub and water—"

"That's fine," the boy said. "Looks like we may be at this for quite a spell yet. So long—"

He rode off.

"If you see my husband," Bethany called after him, "will you tell him I've gone home?"

155

Home! It seemed like weeks, like years, since she had seen the little dugout. She felt she could not wait to be back there again. And if she went, as she knew now she must do, Wade should have word so that he would not go back to Newsomes' looking for her, once the fire was over.

"I'm Mrs. Cameron," she added.

"Yes, Ma'am, I know," the boy called back to her. "I danced with you last night."

Last night! That was an aeon ago. She rode off, trying to remember what had happened in that long gone time.

The trail over which they passed, Lizzie driving the rickety wagon and Bethany riding Star, ran through grass already blackened by fire. It looked like soft dark cloth, thick and heavy. When the horses' feet touched it, a black dust arose. The smell was acrid, choking, like the smell of fire itself. Off to their right they could see flames against the sky; the fire, then, was on two sides of them—to the right and behind them. Where it would go next, or whether it would spread at all, was a matter that rested not only with the zeal of the fighters, but on that arch villain, the wind. At any time a new fire could break out, seemingly without cause, sometimes in places widely separated. What was it Tobe Dillon had said one time? "Sometimes I think fire jest breaks out by itself, here—"

Ahead of them now an expanse of unburned grass fanned out. Seeing it, Lizzie said, "Looks like we ain't a-goin' to have a chance to git rid of this grub."

She had turned to speak to Bethany, and what she saw when she looked around brought a strange expression to her face. She stopped the wagon, stood up. She put her forefinger in her mouth, then removed it and held it up to the air. Her face was quiet and intent as she waited for her judgment to tell her what she wanted to know. Finally she turned to Bethany.

"Miz Cameron," she said, "the wind is a-changin'. We'd

best git down the trail as fast as we can. It don't look so good
—back of us—"

Bethany looked around. The thing she saw made panic well
up in her.

On three sides of them was fire—behind, to the left, and to
the right. More than that—the wind was behind them, pushing the fire forward as a child would roll a hoop. Only the
way ahead was clear. And, even as they faced front again, it
seemed that the bright edge of fire was spreading closer to the
trail.

"I think you'd best tie yore horse to the endgate and git in
the wagon with the kids," Lizzie said quietly.

There was something about her voice that made Bethany
obey instantly, and without question. She tied Star's reins to
the back of the wagon; she got in the wagon and sat down on
the suggan with the Dillon children. They received her with
unblinking regard, as they would have received any other
fresh discomfort. One of the older girls reached over with a
womanly gesture to pick up the baby. She held it close to her,
dropped her face against its head.

Lizzie slapped the lines over the horses' backs. They started
off at a smart trot, tossing their heads in nervous excitement.
Star, following behind, also seemed uneasy. Bethany hoped
she had tied him securely. It would be too bad if he broke
loose in his nervousness and fright. Turning to check the knot,
she saw what was probably the strangest sight she had ever
beheld.

The wild things were coming—running swiftly, with terror
distended nostrils. Side by side they ran, the coyote, the antelope, the lobo, the deer. Cattle came too, and the birds, and the
jack rabbits, their great ears erect. Hunted and hunter were as
one, joined in a great exodus of fear and horror, fleeing the
thing that was more fearful than fear itself. Desire to kill was
lost in desire to live. The strange horde passed the wagon as if

they did not see it at all, as if they knew that man, their enemy, was fleeing as they fled.

And now the fright of the horses almost matched that of their wild brothers. Only Lizzie's expert handling of the lines kept them steady at all. The wagon rattled perilously. *What if it falls to pieces entirely*, Bethany thought. *We'll be left in the path of the fire!* Why hadn't she stayed on Star? She heard Lizzie's voice calling to her. The woman did not turn, but kept her eyes on the fear-maddened horses.

"Now listen, Miz Cameron, and you kids—you do what I tell you to—"

Lizzie had long since lost the last of her hair pins. Her black hair was hanging loose, whipping back from her face like some strange banner which they must all follow. And, as if she knew they felt this, she gave her directions, quick and tense, like a general who sees one chance to win a battle, and that only if his men obey him without question.

The boys were to peel off their shirts, she said, and Bethany was to take them and wetten them with what was left of the water they had fetched for the men. One of them Bethany must put on her head, protecting her face with it as much as possible. The other she was to hand Lizzie, who would do the same. The kids were to get under the suggan.

"—and Eli, you shuck out of them britches of yores—"

Eli, already divested of his shirt, hung back.

"Eli—" his mother's voice was terrible. Eli, hearing it, forgot false modesty. He pulled off his pants, stood for one moment as naked as the day he was born, and then plunged under the suggan.

"—now you git them britches real wet, too," she told Bethany. "—and when a spark blows in on the wagon, you beat it out with them. See—?"

"Yes—" Bethany said, dipping Eli's pants into the keg of water.

"—and if the wind lands a burning chip in the wagon, you jest shovel it out with one of them plates Miz Newsome put the grub on—"

"Yes—" Bethany said again, locating a plate from the box of food. Part of the cake was still on it, that fancy party cake which looked all the more foolish now in the face of the red terror that menaced them.

Bethany looked around. The red wall was closing in. By now it was a sound and a smell and a red light. She realized what had happened—a new fire had broken out so swiftly and unexpectedly that there were no fighters near it. If they came out of this, it would be because Lizzie Dillon brought them out.

"And now," Lizzie said, knowing that her commands were understood and heeded, "now—we'll jest make a run fur it—"

She stood up in the wagon and struck the horses. "Git up," she said, although it did not seem possible that they were capable of any greater speed.

The road was a narrowing wedge whose outlines were sketched in fire. The fire did not seem so much to come toward them as they seemed themselves to drive into the face of it. Even through the wet shirt, Bethany could feel the heat. The smoke stung her nostrils; water streamed from her eyes. A flying disc of fire shot into the wagon—a burning cow chip which hit the suggan under which the children were cowering. Bethany scooped it up on Mrs. Newsome's plate, threw it over the side of the wagon. She beat out the smoking place on the comfort with Eli's wet pants.

By now, the team was frantic. They sped across the prairie, down the trail. Lizzie Dillon still stood up in the wagon, leaning forward slightly, as if she would push them along with her own stout heart. The air was full of chips, flaming like meteors. The wagon swayed from side to side. Once Star stumbled. Maybe he had stepped in a prairie dog hole, broken his leg. If he had, Bethany knew what she must do—at once, and with no holding back. She must untie him, leave him there to perish in the fire.

He righted himself, came on after the wagon, as if he knew that in that action lay safety, lay life itself.

"Good old Star," she whispered, feeling her cheeks wet, knowing it was not moisture from the Dillon boy's shirt.

Could they make it?

Lizzie had said they would. She was matching her instinct, her wisdom, against the cunning of the fire. More than that—she was matching the courage of a mother who was taking her children to safety. They had a chance.

The path was very narrow now. The path was not there at all. There was only a line—a thin line—a line through which no human being could pass, and live.

Bethany shut her eyes. Her lips moved stiffly; she knew she was praying, but did not know what words she said. The texture of them was there, though, the need, the appeal.

To perish by fire! To die in a blazing funeral pyre, there in the wagon with Lizzie and the children. With the little naked Eli and the girl who held the baby against her breast. A wave of love for the doomed children passed over her; she wished that she, too, might reach under the suggan, hold one of them close to comfort it in this last hour.

To die by fire. Never to see Wade again. Never—Oh, God—

She felt the slowing pace of the horses. All was over. Lizzie, too, had given up. Lizzie knew it was no use. Lizzie had consigned them to the flames. Bethany reached out blindly for one of the children.

"Well, Miz Cameron," she heard Lizzie say shakily, "we're through—"

Bethany opened her eyes. The prairie stretched out ahead of them, free of fire. Behind them, a red wall had closed in.

"Looks like it's already burned off here," Lizzie said, surveying the burnt grass ahead of them. "Must have happened last night."

They were on burned grass. They were safe.

"You kids can come out now if you are a mind to," Lizzie said. "Eli, we'll turn our backs whilst you put on yore britches. And don't you fret about 'em being wet—"

They came to the Dillon dugout, a small humped up place in a great ocean of blackness. Fire had passed over the place, burning corral and rickety shed. But the dugout itself was there, and Bethany thought she had never seen anything so wonderful, so safe, as it looked when Lizzie stopped the creaking wagon in front of it.

"Well," Lizzie said, "we're safe. And I reckon I better be gittin' in. I don't feel so good—"

"Oh, Lizzie—" Bethany cried, "you're ill—you look terrible. Here—let me help you—"

She put her arm around the woman, started with her toward the dugout. Sweat poured off Lizzie's face; her hair was dank with it.

"Now, Bethany," she said, "—you ain't to worry about me. I'll be all right—jest let me git to a bed—"

Bethany helped her inside, helped her to the bed in the corner. The woman closed her eyes, lay perfectly still. She was so motionless, it was almost as if she did not breathe at all.

"Lizzie—" Bethany cried, "isn't there something I can do for you—"

The woman roused herself.

"No," she said. "There ain't. If I lay right still, like this, until morning, I'll be all right. I ain't never lost one yet with a mishap, and I ain't a-goin' to lose this one."

She closed her eyes again.

Bethany built a fire in the stove, cooked whatever she could find in the way of food. She fed the children, who by this time accepted her almost as calmly as if she were one of them. She took the baby in her arms, lulled it and when it was asleep, laid it beside its mother. Lizzie lay with closed eyes, taking no notice of what went on around her. Like an animal she rested, seeming to draw strength from some deep reservoir within herself. She had said she would be better by morning. Bethany found herself believing the woman was right. Bethany lay down on a suggan on the floor, beside the Dillon children. She knew she wouldn't sleep a wink.

She had scarcely straightened out on the hard bed, when she was asleep.

Bethany rode toward her own dugout.

Lizzie was better, even as she had promised. "I knowed I'd be," she said. "You didn't have no call to worry about me—"

"Oh, Lizzie—Lizzie," Bethany cried, clinging to the woman, "you saved our lives—"

"I didn't do nothin'," Lizzie said, stroking Bethany's hair, "nothin' at all—Now you better be gittin' on to yore own place. You're a dyin' to see about it, I know—"

The fire had stopped short of her own dugout. There it stood, beautiful and unharmed, in grass unmarked by fire. The corral was there, and the shed, and the maize patch. The rosebush would be there, too. Shame on her to be so exultingly glad they had been passed by the fire when her own neighbors had suffered! But even as she thought this, gladness swept over her afresh.

Everything was safe. And Rex was standing by the corral.

That meant Wade was home, that she would soon be in his arms. She urged Star on, her heart racing ahead of her, on to the haven of Wade's arms.

She did not bother to tie Star at all. He'd stand, here at the home corral. She ran toward the dugout, not caring how she looked—her party finery bedraggled and stained by smoke, crumpled from two days' wear. She flung open the door, and as she did so Wade wheeled to face her.

"Wade, darling—" she cried, and rushed toward him.

It was Wade, and it wasn't Wade. His face was black with smoke; his eyes were red-rimmed. But the worst thing was the look on his face. She had never seen him like this before.

"You—" he said, in a strange choking voice she did not know for his.

He began to hurl words at her—horrible words, words she had never heard him use before. But she got their meaning, fast enough, as he spilled them over her. Horror and unbelief engulfed her. Wade, talking to her like that!

She remembered once, long ago when she and Rosemary were little, they had quarreled and thrown at each other some of these words, not in the least knowing what they said, repeating something they had heard heavens alone knew where. She could still recall the look of horror on Mama's face when she heard them; knew she herself must look much the same now as Mama did then. And, even when she knew how silly she sounded, Mama's old threat rose to her lips.

"Wade Cameron," she said facing him, drawing herself up very tall. "Wade Cameron—you stop saying words like that. If you don't I'll—I'll wash your mouth out with soap—"

Suddenly he was laughing. He sat down weakly in the little rocking chair, bending forward from the waist to laugh. He reached out and pulled her down on his knees. At first she resisted, but he held her fast, bent her backwards so that she was cradled in his arms, like a child. He tilted her head, brought his lips down on hers.

163

His body smelled of smoke, of sweat, of the acrid bite of fire. But it was heaven to be here in his lap. She put her arms across his shoulders, found it was partly the back of the chair she was embracing. She moved her arms so that she brought them up around him.

"You crazy little idiot," he said. "Starting out in the face of a prairie fire. You don't know what I've been through—"

"I was with Lizzie Dillon," she said. "She got us through—"

"In that rattletrap wagon—" he shuddered.

"Well, anyway we're home," she said.

They were the most beautiful words she had ever heard.

"Yes," he said. He rubbed his chin against her hair, against her face. He had not shaved for three days, and his beard rasped against her skin. It felt wonderful. She tried to crowd closer to him.

"I'm sorry I talked like that to you," he whispered.

"Oh—that's all right. You were upset."

"Going to wash my mouth out with soap, eh?" He stood up, still holding her in his arms.

"You're a spunky little devil," he said.

He lifted her, held her on a level with his shoulders. "I went through hell," he told her simply, looking straight into her eyes. "When I got here and found you weren't here—"

He set her down.

"I don't even want to talk about it," he said unevenly. "The boy told me you were headed for home, and I knew what you'd have to come through. And when I got here, you weren't here—"

"I know—" she said.

She could not tell him about her experience with Lizzie. Not yet, she couldn't—.

He walked over to the little stand with the wash pan on it. He looked at himself in the mirror.

"You go get your soap," he said. "I can use it on my face!"

And then, they both were laughing. Much of the grass on which they hoped to run their stock this winter was burned. Now their own precious maize crop must go for feed instead of for money with which to pay on the land. But still they laughed.

They were young, and they had the most important things —the dugout, each other, the rosebush. And laughter.

They would manage.

CHAPTER ELEVEN

I F THEY felt that they could manage, it was not a sentiment shared by Tobe Dillon.

Bethany was washing dishes one morning when she heard a great commotion outside. A man's voice called "Hello," and she went to the door to answer.

It was the Dillons. Lizzie sat in the seat of the wagon, her face patient and immobile, a blankness on her that might have passed for resignation. The young Dillons peeped from the back and the sides of the wagon, their eyes bright and alert, like young foxes viewing a new barrow. In spite of the coolness of the October morning, they were all barefooted. About them there was no hint of their mother's resignation, if such it was. Nor did they show any touch of their father's nervous eagerness.

"Wade here?" Tobe asked.

Just then Wade came around the corner of the corral. Tobe swung off the wagon, and walked toward him.

"Want to talk a little business with you," said Tobe. The two of them went back to the corral.

"Oh, it's good to see you, Lizzie," Bethany said. "I haven't seen you since the fire. Is—is everything all right?"

"Yes," Lizzie told her simply.

"I'm so glad," Bethany said, wondering as she spoke why she should be happy at the prospect of the coming of another Dillon child. It would be only an added weight for the creaking wagon, another life to be forever uprooted by Tobe's restlessness, perhaps just one more grave for Lizzie to remember in her heart.

"I knowed I'd be all right if I took care," Lizzie explained. "And I did."

Ah, that was it! To Lizzie, this child was important. Lizzie, who gave life, would recognize the value of the gift. That was why she had been able to bring them all through the fire—the children cowering under the suggan, the one as yet unborn, and Bethany. Lizzie was too wise to question the reason for life; she was content to cherish it.

"Come in," Bethany urged. "I'll make coffee. And I'll fry flapjacks for the children. Now don't tell me you have to rush right off—"

"I don't know as it's worth while," Lizzie said. "Comin' in, I mean. We'll have to be gittin' along in a minute. We're a-movin'."

"Oh, no!" Bethany cried. Tobe mustn't drag Lizzie and the children away, she was thinking desperately.

"Why—why you can't—" she finished lamely, knowing as she spoke that they could, that they would, that they were—

"It's the prairie fire," Lizzie explained. "Looks like it was jest too much fur him. Says he can't winter no stock on burnt grass—"

"Where are you going?"

"New Mex. He says there's good land out there, and free besides. Says it's a-gittin' too crowded here."

"Why don't you put your foot down?" Bethany asked. "You won't find any better land than this, and it's not so expensive. If you stay here, pretty soon we might have a school.

Why I'd even be willing to try to teach one myself, if you'd stay. And maybe we could get Brother Fenton to come for regular services—I've been wanting to ask Wade about that for several weeks now."

"Yes, I know," the woman said.

She knew all that Bethany was saying—had already said it many times to herself and to her man. Bethany's was the quick hopeful wisdom of inexperience, but Lizzie Dillon knew the answers the hard way.

"I know," she said, and in her voice was a sort of compassion now for the ignorance of young Bethany Cameron, so newly married that she did not know the ways of men. "Yes, I know. But it's jest no use to try to talk to a man, once he gits his mind made up."

The children watched the two women, not speaking, the urgency of their wish sitting hard upon them. Little foxes they were, or some other quick young animals, tired of this burrow in which they had been suckled, straining to be off to other, larger horizons. Talk of schools and of churches was a subject alien to them; the words held no meaning, either of sweetness or of woe, for they had never known these things. They were children of a man who moved on when the trappings of civilization were about to overtake him. And they would always be thus—always they would live on the fringes of other men's lives.

"The kids air as bad as he is," Lizzie said patiently. "When they git it into their heads to move—men, and young'uns—you might as well give up to 'em—"

And she had given up to them. Other stronger (or maybe weaker) women would plant a vine and refuse to leave it. Because of them, the men would stay, too. But not Lizzie Dillon. She would go on with Tobe Dillon, her very endurance a kind of weakness, a submission. She would endure all the hardships of a new country save that hardest one of all—staying there.

Never the vine for her, or the hearthstone. Never a maiden blush rose beside her door.

Tobe and Wade were coming back from the corral now, Tobe bearing the look of a crusader who had known from the first that his cause would receive no hearing from those who needed to hear it most. But, his air seemed to say, he had tried and his conscience was clear. So Noah might have looked, when his message concerning the Ark went unheeded. He got into the wagon, took the lines.

"I've been trying to talk some sense into that man of yours," he told Bethany, as if he hoped to gain an advocate in her. "But he won't listen to me. Don't blame me if you starve to death this winter, or if you git yourself all wore out trying to pay for this little piece of land you saddled yourself with."

"We'll manage," Bethany said.

Tobe turned once more to Wade.

"Sure you ain't a-goin' to change your mind?" he asked. "You and me together could stake out a mighty fine parcel of land out in New Mexico."

"No," Wade said, "I'll stay here."

He looked across the land to where the burned grass showed, stretching away to what might well be the nethermost edge of the world.

"I'm staying," he said again.

"They ought to give you this claim," Tobe growled. "The state ought to pay you for living on it. Out here in this God-forsaken hole. They got their nerve, asking a man to pay for land like this—"

In leaving, his hate welled up against the thing he left. He had failed here, and he hated the land, blaming it for his failure.

"Charging money for land like this—" he spat over the side of the wagon. "They ought to be glad to give it away, them smart alecks down to Austin. I'll show 'em. They're giving away better land than this out in New Mexico."

"I don't want anybody to give me my land," Wade said. "I'd rather pay for it myself."

"You'll pay for it," Tobe told him. "Or you'll lose it, and all you've put into it. You'll pay heavy for it."

"That's all right," Wade said. "That way, I'll feel more like it's mine. I'm not meaning to lose it, either."

Tobe slapped the lines across the backs of the bony horses. His anger had spent itself, and he was himself again. He was leaving this spot of failure, disclaiming any part in that failure, feeling that now, at long last, he was going to have his chance. The prospect was pleasing to him. He would forget this place, as he had forgotten Tennessee, and Arkansas, and Missouri, and East Texas. None of these places had done right by him. But in New Mexico things were going to be different.

"Well, so long," he said. "If you ever change your mind, jest get in touch with me. Could be I could git you in on some good free land."

The wagon came to a creaking start, pulled off. The children looked out the back. The pots and pans clanged beneath the wagon. That was all. He wasn't taking a plow. He didn't believe in plows. As far as that went, he wasn't taking cattle. And he professed to believe in cattle.

The wagon moved on, across the prairie, along an unmarked trail. Bethany waved to the little Dillons, looking out the back, but they did not return the gesture, whether from shyness or indifference, she did not know. When they were out of hearing, she turned to Wade in a burst of resentment.

"Of all the crazy things. If they had just stayed on that claim of theirs, they could have made something out of it. It's like throwing away a part of their life."

"He didn't have a claim, Bethany," Wade said. "He was only a squatter."

170

A squatter. That explained everything. A squatter was a different person from a homesteader. A homesteader came with honest intentions and law and order behind him. The ranchers might resent him, might call him a nester, but that did not matter. The squatter simply settled like a parasite, taking all he could get, giving nothing in return. Having nothing invested, he stayed only as long as things were good. But the nester stayed on. This was his home, his future. His fortunes rose and fell with those of the country. Desperate he might be, and at his wits' end. But he would stay.

"It isn't just the land he's interested in," Wade went on. "It's the idea of moving. He won't stay there long, even if he gets a good place. He'll never stay long anywhere. He won't put anything into the land, so he'll never get anything out of it. He'll never feel close to it."

Bethany took another look at the wagon, threading its way into nothingness. And then she turned to look at their own place. Anchored in nothingness it might be, but at least it was anchored. It was not theirs yet, but some day it would be. Maybe Tobe was on his way to something far better, something that would be easier to come by. But she doubted it. Mostly people didn't get something for nothing. Maybe Tobe was right when he said she and Wade were fools to stay here and work the way they would have to in order to pay off the indebtedness on the claim. Maybe he was right when he said the state ought to give them the land. It wasn't going to be any good to anybody until people came out here and made it good. Perhaps the people who did that should have the land coming to them free.

No—Wade was right. Mostly people paid for what they got. She was still young, but already she knew that. Anyway, a body liked a thing better when he had paid for it. Then it represented something.

It was like her plum preserves. Back in Missouri, where fruit grew lusciously beautiful, a housewife wouldn't have given them shelf room. Out here, because they were so hard to come by, they were treasures of worth untold.

"Well," she said, looking after the departing wagon, "they are gone. I hope things turn out all right for them. I hope they soon have neighbors, so there'll be a school for the children."

"Maybe they will, in time," Wade said. "Once somebody starts to a new place, others follow."

"I guess there have to be men like Tobe Dillon," Bethany mused, "to go places first, so the rest of us can follow."

"Sure—" Wade told her, absently.

"Know what I'm going to do?" Bethany asked him. "I'm going in and count my jars of preserves."

She felt very settled, at one with the country.

The Dillons were gone, and with their going, Bethany was conscious of a gap in her life—loneliness seemed to move in a little closer.

Wade was busy making preparations for winter. On three sides of him the blackened earth spread, bearing the marks of the fire. In only one direction was there grass, and that was open range, a thing to be shared. In the middle of this, the field of maize seemed to be only a child's toy, pretty to look at, but wholly inadequate to the demands that would be put upon it. Wade stored part of it away in the shed.

"Some of these days we'll have a snow," he said. "I don't want to have to go out and dig food for the stock when that happens."

The biggest, finest heads he placed in another pile.

"Seeds for next year's planting," he explained to Bethany.

He hauled up more wood. He checked the dugout to be sure that all was snug and tight. Bethany could well believe that those preparations might be necessary, for even in this country, where there were no trees and shrubs to tell about the death of summer, there was still the feel of nature closing in for the winter. The filmy haze of Indian summer, lacking telegraph poles and trees to thread itself upon, filled the very air itself.

There were days of this, so lovely and quiet that it seemed as if each one touched the earth with loving, gentle fingers, reluctant to be gone. And then one night the rains began.

At first they were a fine mist, their coldness seeping through the land. The burned grass was mercifully cleansed. Nature, bearing the power to destroy, bore also the power to heal. Her destruction might come as a raging fury, but her healing was gentle, holding in it the sadness of regret.

There had been times in the summer when Bethany, looking at the bright metallic blueness of the sky, felt she would have given anything for the boon of only one small cloud to break the searing force of the sun. Now, after a week of intermittent rain, she wanted nothing so much as the return of the sun.

"This rain," she complained. "I'm getting sick of it. And besides it's ruined all the cow chips."

"I never thought I'd live to see the day you'd be mourning because there weren't any chips," Wade said. "Remember how you were ready to run back to Missouri the first time I brought them to camp? You acted like a locoed bronc."

"It wasn't quite that bad," Bethany protested. "But, anyway, I've got used to them now."

"You can expect some rain in the fall, out here," Wade said. "Usually the wet spell doesn't last long."

This one lasted.

She was very saving with wood. How helpless a person was out here, how dependent on the whims of nature, on the meager resources the country offered. You complained about the endless blaze of the sun, forgetting that because of it the cow chips were good for fuel. The wind got on your nerves, but it did cool things off. The endless flatness was enough to set you crazy, but level fields were easier to cultivate. She supposed it was always like that. When Great-grandmother came to Missouri, she found trees that could be used for fuel and the making of homes. Here they used chips and prairie sod. Every country offered you something, if you were smart enough to take it.

"If it clears tomorrow," Wade said, "I'll go for water."

"All you need to do is to stick your head out the door," Bethany said.

"Why, you sassy little thing," he laughed. "You're as bad as Rex. Need exercise to keep you from getting mean. I thought you got tired of the sun shining all the time."

"I take it all back," she said. "Besides, we need wood more than we do water. The rain fills up the barrels, but it certainly does ruin the chips."

By morning the rain had stopped, so Wade went for water and wood. He was scarcely back when it started again, falling lonesome and eerie-like. The wind came up, and the sound of it was a sorrowful thing—bleak and lonely. Bethany shivered.

"It sounds as if it wanted to come in here with us," she said.

"Want me to open the door for it?"

"Oh no," she cried, knowing he did not mean it, yet as quick in her denial as if he had.

The wind! She had promised Wade she wouldn't complain about it, but that didn't mean she'd ever learn to like it. The wind and the loneliness and the vast expanses of nothingness—those were the things she found hard to bear. They were her enemies, almost intangible, but ever-present. They were at the same time both impossible to reach, impossible to remove. The courage with which one met them was a thing that must be renewed each day from nothingness itself, for they were things you had never needed to meet before you came out here.

"Don't feel so bad about the wind," Wade told her. "I have a feeling he'll be the fellow that will help to make it possible for our kind to stay out here."

She looked at him inquiringly. He was mending a bridle, peering at it through half-closed eyes, seeming to find it hard to concentrate on this little piece of work when his eyes were better trained for looking into far distances. Two curved lines inclosed his mouth, like parenthesis marks setting off some deeply significant phrase. Maybe the wind had curved those lines, the way it seemed to whittle off every ounce of excess flesh of all the men out here. Perhaps the wind itself was bent on shaping the sort of people who would fit in this strange lonely land.

"Know how far it is to water here?" Wade asked.

"I should. I've gone with you often enough."

"I'll have to beat you yet," he said. "I mean—down. Some of the ranchers dug wells. Went two-three hundred feet, they say. But it was good water, and plentiful. That means machinery. Can't do it by hand, the way we did back in Missouri."

Always there was this distinction in the way they said the words. He said, "Back in Missouri." She said, "Back home."

"And once you strike water at that depth," he went on, "you know good and well there'll be no pumping it up by hand. That's where the wind comes in. Windmills. Once we get them, we'll be fixed."

Of course. Once they got a sure source of water, like deep wells and windmills, they would be independent. Farms were founded on the basic fact of the presence of water. Cattle country needed it, too, but it could exist without wells. If a rancher had four or five hundred sections, or even less, he would be sure to have water running naturally somewhere on it—a stream, or a spring, or even a river. But when you had only one section, it was a matter of chance. Maybe you would have water on it, and maybe not. Newsome had water, but Wade had none. Having none of your own, you had to go to your neighbor for it. Yes—Wade was right.

175

"Windmills and fences," Wade said. "That's us. And you can't have the windmills without wind."

"I guess I'll get used to it," Bethany said, knowing she never really would, knowing that the better thing to say was that she would learn to endure it. "I guess I'll learn to take it, like I have cooking with chips. Wouldn't it be nice, though, to have water close? Sometimes I get to thinking about how it is at home—a sink in the kitchen and a hand pump in the sink. And here, we have to drive three miles for a drink of water."

Wade looked up, a startled expression on his face.

"Three miles for a drink of water," he said. "Why Bethany —I hadn't thought about it like that."

"Oh, I don't mind," Bethany assured him hastily. "It's sort of fun, going for water is."

"Yes—you had a good time all right the day the team ran off—"

"Oh, that—" she could laugh about it now.

He stood up, threw the bridle to the door, where it hung neatly on the wooden peg that served as a handle.

"See what a smart man you married?" he bragged. "Now, how about a little music?"

He got out the harmonica which he had been almost too busy to play since they got to Texas. He cradled it in his hands, feeling for the melodies he wanted. When they came, they were all jolly ones, like "Yankee Doodle," "Dixie" and "Turkey in the Straw." They filled the little room with happiness.

Bethany made coffee. She poured it into the best cups and recklessly cut the cake she had meant to have for dinner tomorrow.

It was not until after they had gone to bed that she remembered about the wind. She hadn't been conscious of it since Wade started playing the harmonica. Maybe it had stopped. No—there it was, moaning around the corner of the dugout. It sounded so lonesome, she felt sorry for it instead of herself.

The next day was bright and clear, so Wade said he would ride over toward the ranch. Maybe he'd find someone who had some mail for them. He left early, Rex stepping high and proud. It was difficult to tell whether man or horse was the happier at the reunion. Wade stroked Rex's neck as if to explain why he hadn't been riding of late and Rex shook his head as if he were saying, "That's all right—I understand. But let's get busy now and have a good gallop."

Once Wade was gone, Bethany set about cleaning house. She opened the windows, and the door. A dugout might have all the advantages that Wade claimed for it, but in wet weather it got damp and musty. The walls felt clammy to the touch. The bed clothes seemed soggy. She hauled them out into the sunshine, put them on the clothesline to air. In spite of sunshine, she didn't quite like the looks of the sky. It had a sort of petulant uncertainty about it, as if any minute it would start pouting and pull a curtain of dampness over the brief brightness that was on the land.

Wade came back late in the afternoon. He was lucky—he had met the mail hack. He brought no letters, but something almost as good—a package of newspapers. There were Kansas City *Stars* and *Times*, as well as their own home town paper. Bethany touched them lovingly, planning to make them last until a new supply came through.

She had been right about the weather. That night the rains started again.

"Tobe Dillon ought to be here," Wade said. "Someone told him once that this country would be fine, if we could get enough rain. He said so would hell."

"Wonder where they are now?" she mused.

"No telling. Say, how about reading those papers to me while I work on this saddle—there's a place that rubbed Rex's back today."

Bethany sat down and, by the light of the coal oil lamp, began to read the *Star Hill Gazette*. It was as if she brought friends and neighbors and kin into the very room with them. Only, when she came to an item about Mrs. Brad Bishop, she skipped it. Later she went back and read these privately, thinking that for a new wife Rosemary was certainly spending a lot of time in Kansas City. Almost every week the items noted that "Mrs. Brad Bishop has been spending a few days in Kansas City." Of course, Kansas City wasn't too far off, and Rosemary would be the one to go there for all her clothes and things. But still—

They were eating breakfast the morning that it happened.

First there was a low rumbling in the side of the dugout nearest the table. There was a slight shivering in the air. And then, a layer of muddy ooze came pouring in.

They got to their feet, Bethany looking at Wade stupidly, a cup of coffee still in her hand.

"The dugout," Wade said. "The side of it is caving in—"

And so it was. The rain, pushing searching, secret fingers down into the earth, had at last found an opening—a prairie dog hole, or even the burrow of some smaller animal—and so had made its way into the larger burrow of the man who forced himself upon the land. The mushy earth had finally pushed back the last frail restraining barrier—the burlap on the dugout walls.

By now, the ooze was half-way across the dugout floor, soaking into the rag carpet, down to the packed earth on which it was spread. Parts of the slimy stuff had even fallen onto the table at which they had been eating.

Bethany found her voice. "Oh, Wade—my carpet—"

They stood ankle deep in the mushy debris.

"My carpet," Bethany moaned again. She was very close to tears.

This was her badge of pride, the thing that had helped to set her apart from the crudeness of the land. It made her different from the Dillons, who did not care, and from poor Milly, who had not the strength to demand the thing her soul so greatly craved. It was the one thing that made her feel equal to Mrs. Newsome. More than that—it was a tie with home, for into it had gone all the old clothes which had been discarded, woven on Aunt Polly's loom into a carpet whose destiny was never meant to be a thing covered with black and slimy mud.

"Stop crying," Wade said roughly. She wasn't really crying, and he knew it, but he must say something. As for himself, he knew a sterner grief, for he saw their very shelter itself menaced. A carpet was a transient thing, something cherished by women—the trappings of vanity. But a home—well, that was a different matter. He waded to the broken wall, put his hand on it in order to ascertain the extent of the damage.

"I wasn't crying—" she sniffled.

"I'll fix it for you," he promised. "I'll fix the wall. And you'll never know anything happened to your carpet, once we get it cleaned off."

He bent over, started getting the carpet up, the brisk purposefulness of his actions as bracing as a tonic for Bethany. She set about getting the mud-covered dishes off the table. As she did so, she tried not to look at the caved-in wall, at the earthen floor under her feet.

And just then, as if nature knew she had gone too far in her harassment of them, the sun came out. Bethany thought she had never seen anything more beautiful than this sunshine. The sky was a bright blue, so intense that she found herself lifting her hand to shield her eyes, accustomed as they had grown to the semi-darkness inside the dugout, to the greyness of the dripping heavens. The sky now had the polished look of fine lacquer, shining, without hardness.

"It doesn't look quite real," Bethany said.

"We'll just hope it is," Wade told her. "It's going to be a sight easier to do this work if the good weather holds—"

It held, but even so, the work was not easy. He had spoken as if it would be done in no time. Actually, it was the work of days. He worked as quickly as he could, using the stuff he had at hand.

First, he took the fence posts—those precious ones he had placed in the earth last summer. Along the wire inclosure now there were gaps at intervals, where the wire sagged low, even as the side of the dugout had sagged.

"Can you spare them?" Bethany asked.

"I'll get more," he told her. "The house has to be finished in a hurry, while the weather lasts."

He placed the posts at intervals against the side where the wall had caved in, setting them in to fence out the crumbling earth as he had earlier fenced out wandering cattle. Between them he filled in with some of the wood he had brought in for fuel, although this was not so satisfactory, being of uneven sizes and shapes. When he had finished, it was a crude, solid wall.

"My goodness," Bethany said, "it looks like a picture of a stockade."

Behind this wall he piled in some of the precious maize— not the part set aside for seed, but the dry feed put aside in the shed against the days when snow would come. And then he put the dirt back of that, packing it in firmly. Finally he was finished, and when he put the carpet back on the floor, sure enough, you could scarcely tell that it had ever had a mud bath.

"Looks good as new," he said.

"It ought to. I scrubbed it hard enough."

She still was not satisfied with the way the wall looked. She almost expected to look up and see an Indian peering through it. She got one of her patchwork quilts and hung it up, but that extended only from one edge to the window. By contrast, the bare portion looked even harsher.

"It looks sort of—grim—" she complained.

"I'll nail some boards over those posts," Wade said. "Break up those boxes canned goods come in and use them—"

The boxes, too, went into the work of reconstruction, the signs "tomatoes" and "peaches" turned inward. Still it was not quite the effect she wanted.

"I know," she cried, "I'll do what Milly did. I'll paper the boards with newspapers—"

She made paste out of some of their scant supply of flour, and together she and Wade pasted the paper on the wall. When they were finished, they stood back to look at their work.

"It looks wonderful!" Bethany exulted.

"Sure does," Wade agreed.

Now that things were back in order, he was himself once more. He hadn't fooled her a bit though, Bethany thought. For a while he had been as scared as she, and as lost about what to do, for all his pretending to be so sure. That was his way— uncertainty made him stiff and blunt and impatient.

Anyway, they had things fixed up now. They had been able to do it with what they had on hand.

"I'm glad we put all those papers on right-side-up," she said. "Now when I get lonesome I'll just walk over to the wall and start reading."

She wondered if he noticed that there wasn't a *Star Hill Gazette* on the wall. Or if, noticing, he knew the reason for it.

She wasn't going to have him living in a house whose walls were covered with news concerning the affairs of Mrs. Brad Bishop. Not if she could help it, she wasn't.

CHAPTER TWELVE

With the coming of December, Bethany began to think about Christmas. Whatever they had, she knew they must make for themselves. For, even if there had been a store at the corner of the dugout, loaded with gifts, there was no money to buy them. She had thought, earlier in the fall, that she would drop an indirect hint about a lamp like Mrs. Newsome's. That was before she had to tell Wade they needed more supplies.

"We're about out of flour, Wade, and coffee, and sugar. With Christmas coming, I thought I'd do a little baking—"

He said, "Make a list—"

She had not yet become accustomed to the way she must order groceries here, looking ahead for months, trying to estimate how much flour and sugar and all the rest of the staples one would need. More than that—trying to figure how little one could get along on. They were luckier than most because of Wade's friendship with Hud Johnson, the freighter. He was willing to bring them things; if Wade could estimate the time Hud's wagon would be heading for Mobeetie, he could drive across to meet it.

She worked on the list until she felt she had reduced it to

the barest necessities before she handed it to Wade. He took it and began to figure up the cost, slowly, using a stub of a pencil. When he was finished, he went to the bed and pulled out the box in which they kept their valuables—the papers for the claim, and the little bag of money. From the money bag he counted out what he thought would be necessary. So intent was he that he did not know Bethany saw how little money was left.

But she did see, and after that she did not even think about a lamp like Mrs. Newsome's.

The preparations she made bore the stamp of the country, of their own needs, and her own ingenuity. She secretly unraveled a sweater, steamed the yarn over the spout of the tea kettle, and rewound it. Then, secretly again, she knitted it into a muffler and gloves for Wade.

She sent him out hunting for a deer or an antelope. "I don't care which," she said. "Just so it's meat—" When he came back with an antelope, she made a part of it into mincemeat, using molasses for sugar and plum preserves for raisins.

Wade, too, was busy with his own preparations. He rode into the breaks and found a cedar tree. It was small and greenish brown, the trunk twisted by the wind. About the tree there was a sturdy, enduring look; in some indefinable way it made Bethany think of Lizzie Dillon. It had bowed to the winds passing over it and, in acquiescence, had found strength to endure.

The smell of cedar brought back Star Hill, and home, and the tree that always stood in the parlor. She had only to shut her eyes and see it all, plain as if it were here in this room with her—the sheen of tinsel, the glittering ornaments, the strings of popcorn and the paper chains. And among all this brightness the candles gleamed, winking bright eyes as if they, too, could not believe the magnitude of the beauty which surrounded them.

Here there were no popcorn strings, no bright ornaments. Here there was nothing.

She made paper chains, those decorations beloved in her childhood, from newspapers. Old Kansas City *Stars* fell beneath her scissors, and the finished effect was not too much unlike a popcorn string. She used, too, the colored pages of the mail order catalog.

"We won't be ordering any work shoes," she said, looking at Wade's boots, "or any yard goods or dress bonnets. Here—hand me the scissors—"

She snipped away, remembering how she and Rosemary used to make paper chains together each year. And, as always, she pushed the thought of her cousin away from her.

Yesterday a box and a letter had come through from her mother.

"I've tried to put in some things I think you can use," the letter said. "A few dress lengths, and so on. And a warm shawl. I am afraid you will get cold this winter."

She launched into the news of the town, painstakingly, item by item.

"Your cousin Rosemary is well. She gave me some things to put into your box, but I did not send them. They are mostly to wear to parties. I did not think you would need them, but if you do, write me and I will send them."

Bethany could well imagine the sort of things Rosemary wanted to send—the utter uselessness of them, the complete unsuitability. She could hear Aunt Clara's words, "I know about homesteaders—I've helped pack a-many a barrel for them.—"

Rosemary had not wanted to send those things as one sent a missionary barrel. Her purpose was not that kindly.

"We'll miss you at Christmas," her mother said. "But we are glad that you are happy in a home of your own. We'll think of you. And you must think of us and know that we will be trying hard to make Christmas just the way we used to do when you were here."

Bethany looked at the date on the letter. It had been a month on the road. For a moment she felt very much alone, very far from home. Here she was in a prairie dugout, making meager preparations for a strange and alien Christmas with scarcely anything about it to remind her of Christmases in Star Hill. The sun shone, warm as spring, over the dun flatness of the land. Maybe Wade had marked the calendar wrong—maybe this wasn't Christmas at all. In all the country around them there was no trace of it.

Oh, yes there was. Christmas was here in this very dugout —in the little tree she had trimmed, in the preparations she was making. She wasn't going to spoil this Christmas of her own making by thinking too much of the ones she had known back in Missouri.

By mid-afternoon on Christmas Eve everything was finished. Wade went that morning for water and was gone so long that almost she began to worry about him. Just as her concern threatened to have a sharp bite to it, he drove in.

"M-mm—" he said as he came into the dugout. "Something smells mighty good." He went to the stove, lifted the lid of a pan. "Think I wasn't coming back?" he asked.

"No—I wasn't worried. You knew I was going to have mince pie for supper."

"I guess that's why you dressed up—because you knew I was coming?"

She had put on her best dress. She had set the table with the best dishes, and made a center piece out of the brownish-green cedar. The dugout was warm and cheerful; it smelled of roast antelope and dried beans cooking and mince pie. In the corner, the Christmas tree shone bright and gay.

"Sure looks like Christmas in here," Wade said contentedly.

"Now you just hold supper back a minute while I dress up."

They sat down to eat in great elegance. Almost like Mrs. Newsome, Wade said. He made her sit still while he waited on the table, and afterwards he offered to wash the dishes. This she did not allow. She didn't tell him the real reason for her refusal, that she was afraid he would use too much water.

When the dishes were put away, he got out the harmonica and began to play. He played "Jingle Bells" and Bethany said it was funny to be playing that when there wasn't any snow at all and the weather was as warm as spring. Then he played "Old Zip Coon" and she tapped her foot, keeping time. He swung into a dance tune and she got up and began to twirl around by herself, lifting her skirt and going through the figures of the dance. He came to her, held the harmonica in one hand and her with the other, and played while he led her through a dance of sorts. The tune came out all wheezy, partly because he was moving while he played and partly because by this time they were both laughing a great deal. He took his harmonica out of his mouth long enough to ask her if he might have the honor of the next dance with her. And she said she thought she'd rather have a look at the moon.

Together they went to the door of the dugout, opened it.

"Did you ever see such a moon?" Wade asked.

Actually, Bethany never had. It shone as bright as day on the vast silver surface of the prairie, seeming to draw light from it as well as to give light to it. So still it was, so bright and calm, it might have been the first Christmas night the world had ever seen. Bethany, feeling this, spoke uncertainly,

"It's—it's the way I've always thought that first night might have been—"

Wade, too, was moved by the beauty of it. He began to sing softly,

"Silent night, Holy night—"

She joined him.

"All is calm, all is bright—"

Together they sang, their hands linked, and it was as though they sang of their own world—this silent quietness, this moon-washed peace. Perhaps even now, she thought, her mother and father were singing the same words back in Star Hill—singing with friends and kin. She could see the people in the church, hear the sound of voices raised in song, smell the great tree. She could see and hear and smell these things, so real was their memory, but she did not regret being away from them. They were a part of her childhood, and far behind her. She was a woman now, and she was making Christmas in her own home, in her own way.

She and Wade were making it together.

Next morning dawned bright and clear. Wade was up before her, making a fire in the little stove. He turned, caught her eyes on him.

"Huh, spying on me, eh?"

"Merry Christmas, Wade," she cried. "Oh, merry, merry Christmas—"

She jumped out of bed, ran to him.

"Merry Christmas," he said, kissing her. "Hey, you stop running around in your bare feet. You'll take your death of cold—"

He lifted her, carried her over to the bed and set her down on it. He kissed her again.

"M-mm—" he said. "I can't stand here all day, wishing you a merry Christmas—"

But he seemed in no real hurry to leave.

"You go take care of the stock," she told him. "When you come back, I'll have breakfast ready."

She did. Breakfast was on the table and her gift to him was

lying by his plate. He pulled on the mittens, tied the scarf around his neck. He went to the mirror and preened before it.

"Now I'm the fine one." He kissed her again, rubbed the mittens against her cheek until she made him stop.

"And won't these come in handy before the winter is over," he said. "Here—wait a minute now; turn your back until I tell you to look."

He went outside and presently came back with a great bumping and thumping.

"Now—" he said.

His gift was ingenuity itself. Somewhere he had got a small keg—Bethany knew the preciousness of the find; water containers of any kind were so valuable that they were cherished next to the possession of water itself. He had made a removable cover for this keg and a spigot arrangement at the bottom, so that once the keg was filled with water all she needed to do in order to draw a bucketful was to turn the spigot.

"Why, Wade—" she cried.

She went to the keg, ran her hands over it, turned the spigot to see how it worked.

"Why, Wade—darling—" She ran back to him, threw her arms around him, kissed him several times. "Oh, thank you—thank you, darling—"

"My gosh," he said. But he was proud, grinning like a small boy filled with pride at his accomplishment. "The way you carry on! You women—lose your minds at the sight of water—stampede like a thirsty cow—"

"You try washing wishes in a cupful of water some time, and you'll understand," she told him.

"I know—" he admitted. "I kept remembering what you said about the pump in your Ma's kitchen, and I got to wondering what I could do about it. Now you can just write her and tell her you have water in the house—"

She cooked Christmas dinner, wishing they might have company to share it. Company went with Christmas. She had asked Butch and Slats, but they refused. Whether it was because they had something else to do, or because they felt that she and Wade should be left alone that day, she did not know. So she was greatly surprised to see Slats ride up, alone, just as she was ready to put dinner on the table.

"Merry Christmas," she said, letting him in. "You got here for dinner, after all. Where's Butch?"

"Merry Christmas," he said, but there was no merriment on his face now. "I can't wait to eat, unless it's ready. Butch has gone riding for Doc. Milly's baby is mighty sick."

"The baby—" She said it with no surprise. The baby had always been sick.

"Yes, Ma'am, that's right. Butch has gone to Mobeetie for Doc."

He looked at Bethany uncertainly, seeing the best dress she was wearing, the tree, the table with its decorations.

"I hate to break up your Christmas, and all," he apologized. "But me and Butch—well, we just thought maybe it might help Milly to have you. If you could go, that is—"

"Of course I'll go," Bethany said. "But let's eat something first, for it's a long ride."

They turned toward the table, but for once Slats showed no interest in food.

"Is she—is the baby very sick?" Bethany asked, knowing even as she said the words the graveness of the illness. She had been out here long enough to know that, in this country of far distances, one did not send lightly for the doctor. You went to him, if you were able to travel at all.

"Yes, Ma'am," Slats said. "I'm afraid she is. I think—well, I think it's about the end, Miz Cameron."

"How is Milly? Does she know?"

"Sure—she knows. I kind of think she's known all along—"

Yes, Bethany was thinking as they rode along, Milly knew the baby would never be really well. That was why she handled it softly, as one handles old lace. Anyone could see that she was not like other babies, kicking and cooing and wanting to be taken up. If she did these things at all, her attempts were so feeble that they were more pitiful than lack of effort. Tom had urged her to get the baby out in the sun more, but Milly knew that would not help. She would not thrive in sunshine, being more like one of those delicate little woods flowers that grow only in the shade, hidden under great trees. In a house protected by trees and growing things, she might have done better. Here, she had no vitality. This Milly knew, feeling a great helplessness in the knowledge, forty miles from a doctor, and farther than that if he were out on the edge of nowhere, making another call. If you were sick, you couldn't ride that far. If you were really sick, you couldn't wait for a doctor to ride to you.

Anyway, what was the use of having him with the baby? There was nothing he could do but say that she did not seem well. Milly knew that herself. She knew, as no doctor could, that each day the baby was a little weaker than it had been the day before, that the sum of all her days added up to weakness that could not be overcome.

"Did the baby get worse suddenly?" Bethany asked Slats.

"Well—no. It just looked like Milly admitted it all of a sudden. Butch and me, we went over with some things for Christmas—"

He told Bethany how it happened. Milly had tried to make Christmas for the baby. She had Tom bring a little cedar tree from the breaks and she trimmed it, keeping it covered while the baby was awake, working while she was asleep, planning to surprise her Christmas morning. She hung a home-made rag doll on it and all sorts of bright things—pictures cut out of the catalog and card board stars covered with tin foil. She put one of Baby's stockings on it.

Slats and Butch had Hud Johnson bring down a doll and some oranges. "A kid's got to have oranges for Christmas," Slats explained. This morning, early, they rode over with them. Milly set the doll under the tree and put an orange in the stocking, she took the cover off the tree, and picked the baby up so that she could look at it.

"And then is when it happened," Slats said, a great look of pain on his face, and also great uncertainty as if he were trying hard to understand something. "I mean—the baby just looked at the tree and smiled a little. Sort of tired-like; it wasn't a bit the way kids act when they see a tree. Milly went white and turned to us. She said, 'Butch, will you go for Dr. Kilgore?' Looked like she gave up, like she knew it wasn't any use. So Butch rode off for Doc, and I came for you—"

"Poor Milly," Bethany said. "I'm glad the doctor is coming. He can't do anything, but it helps to have him—"

"Oh, sure," Slats said. "I don't know how we'd get along without Doc—"

He told the story of Doc and his coming to Mobeetie. Partly it was to keep Bethany's mind off Milly, she felt, and partly because he felt a need to talk—to keep words coming from him, no matter what they were.

Doc had come from Boston. He wasn't much shakes as a doctor back there—just didn't seem to have the knack for it. And then he got sick. He knew what was the matter. He was a "lunger," and he gave himself six months. He had always wanted to see the West, so now he decided to go there for those six months that were left to him. He traveled as far as Dodge City by train and then bought himself a couple of horses and a camping outfit. He rode off into space, not much caring where he went so long as he was on the move.

At first he could travel only a few miles without resting. Then he began to feel stronger. He could ride farther in a day. He did not lie awake at night, looking at the stars. He slept, and the next morning he got up and rode again.

Where first he had ridden aimlessly, wanting only a sense of movement and a feeling of getting away, now he began to have some purpose to his journey. He came upon the freighters headed west and south. He fell in behind them and they let him follow, asking no questions, but giving them the benefit of their knowledge concerning camping sites as well as protection from the Indians. And so, following them, he came at last to Mobeetie.

"I was there the day he rode in," Slats said. "A little pint-sized man without a gun and setting his horse like a tenderfoot."

Slats shook his head at the memory of it.

"And just when he got opposite Mike Cassidy's saloon, Hank came staggering out, sort of holding himself together. He had got into a—well, a right bad fight with a man, and they both of them started shooting. Only Hank got the worst of it —he was like a sieve, he was so full of holes. And he fell right at Doc's feet."

They did not know this little newcomer was a doctor. He certainly did not look like one. But he was off his horse, quicker than you could say scat to a dog.

"I'll take care of him," he said. "I'm a doctor."

"—and the way he said it," Slats marveled, "you had a feeling that maybe, for the first time in his life, he was proud to be one."

Doc stayed at Mobeetie. At first he had to piece Hank together, and then he had to look after him until he got well. By that time he seemed to like the place. Now he was as much a part of the country as anybody. He stayed in the saddle most of the time, for he wouldn't refuse to go anywhere, no matter how tired he was. He rode as well as a cowboy, and was as handy with a six shooter.

"And he's as well as I am," Slats marveled. "Sure is a different looking man from that little sick looking fellow that rode up here the day Hank got shot."

They came to the dugout at almost the same time—Butch and the Doctor, Bethany and Wade and Slats. Bethany saw a small man, with the stamp of the country bitten into him. He looked dark and weathered, like a piece of good leather. His spareness was not emaciation, but a quality that came of self-discipline and life in the open. She had a feeling that it had been a long time since he had thought of death in relation to himself.

Somebody introduced Bethany, and the Doctor spoke to her absently. He looked at the dugout swiftly, and with that look Bethany knew that he had sensed the thing that had already happened inside.

They went in and there sat Milly in a low chair, the baby in her lap. Tom was standing behind her. The baby lay so still, it might have been sleeping. But they all knew better.

"How long?" the Doctor asked.

"I don't know—" Milly whispered.

"Only a little while," Tom told them. "Fifteen minutes, maybe. She—she wanted to hold it, and I let her—"

"Yes," said the Doctor. "That was right. Here—Milly, girl. Let me have her—"

He took the baby gently as if she were really asleep. He carried her to the window, looked at her a long moment. Bethany moved over to Milly, put her hand on the girl's shoulder. The Doctor, finished with his examination, started to lay the child back into the box Tom had made for her. But Milly would not have it so. She reached out her arms, and he placed the little form back in them.

"There was nothing I could have done," he told her, knowing that was what she wanted to hear, knowing she did not believe him. "You know that, don't you, Milly?"

"Yes—" she said numbly.

There was silence in the room. Bethany stood by Milly, and Tom was at her other side, looking at her helplessly, his face baffled and uncertain. He did not speak, but they all sensed his thoughts. The baby had never been quite real to him, and now he could not feel real grief at her passing. Had she been a healthy baby, bouncing and ready to come into his arms and play, he would have learned to love her. But in the presence of this frail daughter he felt only unease. He was concerned about Milly now, and wanted to help her—and did not know how.

Butch and Slats, with Wade, sat on the other side of the small room. Something else must happen, and it was for this they waited.

Finally the doctor said, "Wouldn't you like us to dress it now—to—to make it ready—?"

Milly knew what he meant. She drew the baby closer in her arms.

"I won't have her buried here," she said, strong purpose in her voice.

"She wants to take it to Mobeetie, to the cemetery there," Tom explained.

"I won't have her buried here," Milly repeated. "There isn't even a preacher, or a church. If there are any prayers said— or any words—we'd have to do it ourselves. We'd put her out here, and she'd be all alone. And afterwards, we'd pile rocks over the mound to—to keep the coyotes away—"

She stopped a moment.

"I won't have it," she said.

Those who listened to her knew she was using her last shred of sanity to say the words, that what came after them would be ragged and uneven, like a cloud blown into shreds after a storm.

The doctor looked at her. "There's no reason you can't," he told her. "The river's all right for fording now."

He turned to Bethany. "I think you'd better go with her," he said. "Can you?"

"I can," Bethany said.

"It's a lone ride to Mobeetie," he reminded them, as if they did not know it. "We ought to—well, we ought to move fast. Can your horses do it, Tom? You'll have to go in the spring wagon, you know."

"I've got two we use mostly for riding," Tom said. "They won't like pulling a wagon—but we'll manage."

Butch and Slats got to their feet in a single motion. Wade followed them.

"We'll get the horses ready," they said, and were out of the house, glad of a chance for action.

Things went very fast after that. It was only a short time before Tom came out, carrying the little box. It was so light—almost nothing in his big arms. Milly followed him, wearing the warm dress and the coat Bethany insisted she wear. She looked very young—young as new motherhood; and she looked very old—old as sorrow. They helped her into the back seat of the light wagon, and when she sat down she said:

"Give her to me."

Tom hesitated. "Won't it be—too heavy—?"

"Give her to me—"

Tom did not protest, but set the box across her knees. He got in beside her. Bethany got into the front seat with Butch, who was going to drive. The doctor was already on his horse, and Wade and Slats stood holding the team, their other arms hooked through the bridles of their own mounts.

"We'll change horses at the Triple T," the doctor said. "I have an extra one there—left it the other day when I had to change in the middle of a trip."

"Let her go—" Butch said, and Slats and Wade stepped back.

For one electric moment the team stood still—they who were used only to the feel of man on their backs—and knew the galling shame of harness, the ignoble fact of a weight behind them. Then they sprang forward, wanting only to shake loose their badge of degradation.

There was little of a road to follow, and less desire to follow one had it been there. It was quicker to go by dead reckoning. Butch held the lines, his face strong and intent on the way ahead. Milly held the box and Tom held Milly. Bethany held to the seat, swaying with the motion of the wagon as it lurched along. The three horsemen followed.

The day was mild and bright. There was not even a wind. The very land itself seemed to stand hushed, finger on lips, to watch this macabre dash across it.

They scarcely spoke. When they came to the ranch headquarters, they stopped. The doctor took his own horse, and the cowboys unhooked Tom's panting team, put other horses in their place. Slats and Wade, too, changed mounts.

"I hate to take your horses," Tom said. "We—we are planning to drive pretty fast—"

The Boss was a huge man, white-haired and beetle-browed. He had come to the Panhandle when there were only a few of his kind there. The Indians were still a menace, but everywhere there was grass for the taking. No fences then, and no nesters. Nothing to bother the cattle but wolves and cattle thieves.

"I've been out here a long time," he said, "and I've had a lot of horses. But I never saw one yet that was more important than a man—or a woman. Come in and get something to eat before you go on."

They ate. All except Milly; she tried, but her throat would not close over the food. Bethany, seeing this, did not urge her further. When they had eaten, they were off again.

It was late when they got to Mobeetie. On their way in,

they passed the cemetery—the few dead lying decently to-gether, as dead are meant to lie. At their graves stood markers, straight and proper.

Kindly people took the box from Milly, and she let it go.

"Her name?" One of them asked, wanting to make a record of the burial.

Milly sat still, not speaking. How could she tell the man the truth. Not that the baby had no name, but the reason for it. From the first, she had felt the transiency of the child, had known death must be her young destiny. She knew for sure what she never admitted—that she had no right to presume upon the little one's immortality to anchor her to earth with a name. It was as if, even from the first, she knew that afterwards they would refer to this child as "Our baby—the one that died."

"We—she had no name," Milly said. "We hadn't named her yet."

The man put the pencil down on the paper. Across it he wrote,

"Baby Finch. Age, eleven months."

CHAPTER THIRTEEN

T HE GOOD weather held. It grew even warmer.

"It doesn't seem possible that this is January," Bethany marveled.

She wondered if spring had really started, if perhaps it was time to plant a little garden. She mentioned this to Wade, and he thought that was mighty funny.

"Go on and plant it," he told her, "if you want to grow a bunch of icicles."

Well, maybe that had been silly. But she would like to ride over to see Milly, if the good weather lasted. She had been thinking of her a great deal since the baby's death.

"That we can do," Wade agreed. "Not tomorrow, though. I'm going to haul water, and bring back some wood. Don't trust Panhandle weather too much, Bethany. It can change pretty quick, especially this time of year."

He was evidently not too distrustful of it himself, however, for when he went for water the next day he wore a light coat. And even that he put on the seat beside him.

After he was gone she busied herself about the house. Long since she had reconciled herself to the fact that the meeting of each day's needs was a thing sufficient to fill each day's hours. It was late afternoon before she noticed the cloud in the north. At first glance she thought it must be smoke, so dark and wild it seemed. Perhaps another grass fire had started. That was unlikely, though. Besides, it did not really look like smoke. She went to the door in order to see more clearly, and there she felt the warning chill.

It hit with unbelievable swiftness, that blizzard. And with unbelievable force. A wind came first, and after it the snow—great flakes, filling the air. The cold was hard upon the heels of the wind and snow. They were all a part of the whole—wind, and snow, and cold. The crazy droning sound of the wind was the worst of all—like a fiend let loose.

She thought first of Wade, somewhere on his way back from the spring. How close he was would depend entirely on how long he had spent gathering wood. She thought of him, remembering all the stories she had heard of men who froze to death in sight of home. She thought, too, of the women who walked the floor, waiting for their return. She wasn't going to waste any energy walking floors—there was work to be done, and quickly.

She wrapped up and began to carry in wood from the store beside the dugout, piling it neatly behind the little stove. She could only hope Wade had got more, for she was carrying the last of the supply. But if the getting of it delayed his return! She wasn't sure what she did hope for.

She led Rex and the cow into the shed and closed the door. The cow was richness to be guarded; she was going to have a calf in March. Then she went inside and watched the direction from which Wade would come.

He came at last. Above the whine of the wind she heard the sound of the wagon; through swirls of snow she saw him unhitch the horses, put them in the shed. When she opened the dugout door to let him in, a great rush of wind and cold came in with him so that for a moment the little room itself was a part of the storm.

She threw her arms around him. "Thank God," she cried. "You're home— Oh, Wade— I was so worried—"

She had not known the wind could blow so hard. The sound of it was a scream and a rush and a wild surge of fury. The force of it was a thing that shook the wooden top of the dug-out until she thought it must give way. This was no part of nature; it was a diabolical evil let loose in the land, screaming in baffled rage because a frail prairie dugout should stand be-tween it and its kill.

Compared to the whine of the wind, their own voices sounded eerie and unreal. It was all they could do to under-stand each other, especially if one turned his back while speak-ing, or talked from across the room. She found herself raising her voice, partly from a desire to make herself heard, partly from nervous tension. Her throat began to ache with the strain.

She cooked supper, but when she got it on the table Wade ate almost nothing.

"What's the matter?" she asked sharply. "Aren't things right?"

"I'm not hungry," he told her.

But he picked up his fork and tried to eat. He seemed to have difficulty in swallowing.

"My throat's a little sore," he said.

"You got too cold," she worried. "You were chilled to the bone when you came in—"

"Now, Bethany," he said crossly, "You stop your worry-ing. I'm all right—I'm just not hungry, that's all."

He put down his fork, gave up all pretense of eating. Oh, dear—she should have known better than to nag at him when he was like this. And yet, a demon of perverseness pushed her on to ask her next question.

"Wade, what about—well, what about those other cattle, out on the range?"

"They'll just have to take their chances," he said. "They'll manage. Cattle are smart; they drift toward shelter. If this doesn't last too long, they'll be all right."

How long was "too long"? She had to know.

"How long do you think it will last?" she asked, knowing she was silly and childish to press him so.

"Good Lord, Bethany—how would I know?"

He was worried, too. Mentally she began checking their supplies. Flour? Coffee? Meat? Beans? Yes, they had enough. Thank heavens that, out here, you bought for a long time ahead.

The room grew chilly. The cold closed in on them, tightened like a vise. Wade put wood into the stove, a little at a time, but the warmth it made was a feeble thing, scarcely going beyond the body of the stove itself. The pile of wood she had thought so adequate began to look very small indeed, entirely incapable of meeting the demands that were being made upon it. Might as well try to dam up the Missouri River with a fallen leaf.

Wade must have read her thoughts.

"I got a wagon full of wood," he said. "I'll bring it in tomorrow." He shivered a little, drew nearer the stove. He *had* got too cold out there in the storm. This time she was wise enough not to mention it to him. Instead, she went for the red shawl Mama had sent her for Christmas, put it around her shoulders. When she came back she brought his coat.

"I'm not cold," he said. But he put it on.

It was only a little past six o'clock. She would have to find something to do, something to make them forget a little the sound of the wind, screaming like a demented thing around the corner of the house. She got out her mending.

"Why don't you play your harmonica?" she suggested.

He got it and began to play half-heartedly. She wished she

had not even suggested that he play. The wail of it was too much like the wail of the wind. He stopped and coughed. And then he shivered again.

"I think I'll go to bed," he said.

"Go ahead," she tried to speak casually. "You've had a hard day."

He *was* sick. What if he came down with a really bad cold, pneumonia, even. Out here it would be almost like condemning him to certain death. There was no possible way to get the doctor in weather like this. All the medicine she had was carbolic acid and castor oil, neither one of which would be of any use now. But even if she had boxes full of drugs she would scarcely know how to go about using them. Her mother had been "good with the sick," but Bethany herself had picked up none of her lore.

"As soon as the mail goes through again," she promised herself, "I'm going to send for a doctor book and memorize it!"

She awakened from an uneasy sleep with the consciousness that something was wrong with Wade, and that he was trying to conceal the fact from her.

"Wade," she asked, reaching toward him, "are you sick?"

"I'm—I'm sort of cold," he told her. He was shaking; and his teeth chattered, although she could tell he was making an effort to prevent it. "I think maybe I've got a chill. Now, don't you worry—it's nothing."

He began to shake again.

She got up, wrapped the red shawl around her, began kindling a fire.

"Now you just stay in bed," he protested. "I'll be all right—"

She did not even answer that.

She fought the thing out, alone, sixty miles from the nearest doctor. She fought with stark terror in her heart and few weapons to draw upon. By now Wade was making no effort to stop shaking. She piled on him all the bedclothes she had. She took down the piecework quilt from where it hung on the mended side of the dugout, thinking how really little it mattered now that the posts showed.

She recalled that her mother used coal oil and lard for croup. How well she remembered waking in the night with that strange, eerie sort of cough which, to a mother, could mean only one thing. It would not be long until Mama was bending over her, applying the concoction whose healing odors would stay with one for days—in the smell of one's body, the taste of one's food.

"I don't want it," she would croak hoarsely.

Her mother would not even answer, going about her business of healing with a quiet single-minded purpose that was not to be diverted.

Bethany worked now, as she remembered her mother working—with coal oil and lard and strips torn from her own flannel petticoat. She wrapped hot stove lids in old cloths and put them in the bed beside Wade. She kept this up all through the dark hours of the night. She was not conscious that her prayers had words; they were made up, rather, of actions, of deep hopes. Everything she did was a prayer, was the strong essence of prayer.

Where at first Wade had been shaking with cold, now he complained of being hot, kept trying to push the covers back. He seemed scarcely aware of her there ministering to him. He moved restlessly back and forth, and sometimes he muttered hoarsely—words about working cattle, and things like that. Man-talk; range-talk.

She kept the covers over him as best she could, bathed his face, brought him water. Because he would not stay covered, she tried to keep the room warm, poking wood into the little stove. Even so, she was cold. She put on her overshoes, tied

Wade's muffler around her head. She kept the coffee pot boiling, both because the hot liquid put warmth in her body and because it helped her fight off sleep.

Morning came at last. She knew it by the light that was not quite light, that was different only in the degree which it missed being the whiteness of a snow-filled night.

The wind was still blowing. It sent the snow ahead of it—a cruel, white blinding cloud that engulfed all of earth and sky. Bethany, trying to peer beyond the little window, could see nothing but a vast whiteness.

Wade was restless, the sound of his breathing labored. Hearing it, she forgot about the wind. She went to the stove to put in more wood. And then she saw what she had been too busy to notice during the night.

There were only a few pieces left.

The stories she had heard of people who burned their furniture for fuel came back to her now. Stick by stick they burned it—a chair rocker here, a table leg there, a bit of a bed. They watched the pieces go up in flames, knowing the relief was temporary at best. Did they ever think, those desperate people, that it might be just as well to burn it all in one great blaze, making themselves warm and comfortable for a little while, and then give up to the cold entirely, rather than to stave it off, inch by icy inch?

She shook herself free of the notion, put on another stick of wood. A single piece. Then she turned the damper so the fire would burn more slowly.

The room was growing colder. The nails on the boards had turned white with frost. Her fingers felt numb and stiff. She put on another piece of wood. There were only a few sticks left. She counted them, facing the thing. Four small pieces. That was all.

Wade was muttering to himself. She bent forward to catch the words.

"—so cold—" he whispered.

That settled it. She would go for wood—to the wagon by the shed. Already she had on overshoes and a shawl; she put on coat and mittens. Wade was lying still in something that passed for sleep; she could only hope it would last until she had made her trip out into that screaming world of white, and got safely back once more. She lifted the latch, pushed the door to open it. It did not open easily; the snow had piled up against it. But finally she got it open, and then stepped out into a world gone mad.

There are some parts of your life—moments, hours, years—that you go through and when you are finished with them you do not believe you did those things you must have done. You couldn't; memory is playing you false when she insists you did. Such was Bethany Cameron, going to the wagon for wood.

After it was over, how was she to know how much of the horror that followed was real, how much dreamed of—dreamed in some dark nightmare no one would believe if she did nothing but repeat the story until the day of her death. The howling wild madness of the wind. The way the cold stung her face and hands and body. The way it bit through wraps to the very center of her bones, as if she stood up naked in it, like Eli during the fire. The way it sealed her eyes, so that she seemed to walk by instinct alone.

For a long time afterwards she did not try to tell about it. Later, much later, she learned to relate the story almost without emotion.

"Twice I didn't think I would make it," she would say. "But I did—"

The first time came when the full force of the wind struck her just after she stepped from the semi-protection of the dug-out. No one could stand up in this, she thought. It's crazy to try. She turned to go back. Wade's voice seemed to come to her. "—cold—" he had said.

She righted herself, pushed on. Inch by inch she fought her way toward the wagon. The wind would lift the snow in fitful blasts so that she could see ahead of her, dimly, a little at a time. Then the snow would close down again, leaving her only the memory of the wagon's position. Finally there came a rush of wind, stronger than any she had yet felt. It sent her to her knees, there in the snow.

She was conscious of pain—stinging, horrible. Her leg was broken. She knew it. She would perish here, helpless in the snow, while Wade lay dying in the house. She struggled, but the wind beat her back to the ground.

She was an atom, matched against a giant evil which was devoid of heart and soul. Against it no human being had a chance. She might as well give up. It was very comfortable here—like lying on a sunny slope back home. She felt herself drifting away into slumber.

And then a sound came through to her. A horse was whinnying. Nervously. Urgently. Where? What?

She listened, knowing it for what it was. Rex. He had sensed her presence with an instinct almost human. The whinnying came again. She roused still more, began to struggle to her feet. She stood up.

A gust of wind picked her up, pushed her along. She felt, rather than saw, the shape of solidness before her. She touched the side of the little shed.

She opened the door, went inside. For a moment she braced herself against the wall, held to it, as if here the wind still blew. Then she looked around. The work horses and the cow received her stolidly. Star was all delight. But Rex was almost hysterical. He jerked his head up and down several times; he reached out his nose to be stroked. She leaned up against him, holding to him, shaking with the joy of deliverance. Rex had saved her life. Had it not been for him, she would be lying out there in the snow drifting–drifting– She leaned her head against his neck.

Maybe she was nothing but an atom, she thought, fighting a vast and pitiless force. But she had something the storm could never have, for all its horror. She had a heart and a soul. She had love, and courage. She had the will to live. Those were things that endured; those were the things Rex could call to. They would last long after this storm had blown itself out.

She broke the ice on their water barrel. She got down feed from the rick and placed it before them. And as she worked, she felt Rex's eyes on her, questioning her as a human might.

"He's sick, old boy," she said, speaking as if he were a human who had asked. "But he's going to be well. See?"

It was the truth she spoke. Both she and the horse knew it.

She went outside. The wind had died down some; the snow was not quite so blinding. At the wagon she piled her arms full of wood. The trip back to the dugout was almost easy. When she went in, she thought Wade seemed a little better. She put the wood down, started back for another load. Just as she got to the door, she heard Wade's voice. It was weak, but almost natural.

"–where are you going–?"

"After wood," she told him.

"–snow too deep–" he whispered. And then he dropped off to sleep again.

She made two more trips for wood, piling it high behind the stove. She put in a few sticks. The blaze sprang up, beautiful and bright.

She heard Wade's voice again.

"–stubborn little thing, aren't you–"

He sounded like himself once more. She ran across the floor, knelt by the bed. "Oh, Wade darling," she cried, "how do you feel–?"

"Better—" he said. And dropped off to sleep once more. Easy sleep, natural sleep.

She put in more wood; she set the damper. Then she took off her wraps and shoes and, still wearing her house dress, got into bed beside him. She touched his face; his skin felt cool and natural. She had no more than put her head on the pillow until she too was asleep.

The stillness awakened her. After the noise that had beat upon her ears for so many hours, this stillness came as a thing more real than sound. She sat up straight in bed, listening.

The room was icy cold; she knew the fire had long since burned out. She jumped out of bed and kindled a blaze. She measured out coffee, the cold of the coffee pot making her fingers so numb it was all she could do to hold it. This done, she went back to bed to wait until the room warmed up a little. She was careful not to touch Wade lest she waken him.

The warmth from the fire reached her; she could feel the wonderful waves of it penetrating to the farthest corner. By and by the coffee began to boil, the smell of it filling the dugout. Beside her, Wade stirred.

"—M-mm—" he said, "—coffee sure does smell good—"

It was two weeks before they could get out to see the extent of the storm's damage. The first week Bethany cared for the stock, brought in wood, melted the snow for water. She did this over Wade's protest, pointing out that there was no sense in his risking a relapse. The second week, he took back his job.

"You did right good," he told her, after his first trip to the shed. "Say—you should have seen how glad Rex was to see me."

Some day she'd tell him about Rex. Some day—not now.

Finally he came in to tell her what she knew he'd say, sooner or later. "I think I'll ride out and look for the other cattle," he said.

"I'm going with you."

"It's still pretty cold," he objected. "The sun is bright, but it's cold."

She was not sure whether he wanted to protect her from the cold or from what they'd find out there on the range.

"I'll wrap up warm," she promised him.

It was good to be out in the open air once more, cold though it undeniably was. They turned their horses toward the common grazing ground, which, because of the fire, was away from the breaks now; away from the breaks and thus farther from protection. Wade seemed to guide by instinct, for there were no landmarks left. Where once they might have picked out a tall clump of grass in the distance and ridden toward it, now there was no grass visible. There was nothing but a great white flatness with a vast blue dome closing down on it. The cold had fused earth and sky into a single piece, with not even the seam of the joining visible.

"Don't look at it too long at a time," Wade warned her. "Close your eyes every now and then—snow blindness—"

They rode a long time, and saw no living thing. And then, at last, they came upon the cattle. Not just their own, but others.

"There they are," Bethany cried, her first glad thought that they were found, that they were all right.

And then she knew better, even at this distance. For, even though they stood in the pose of life, there was a look of death upon them. Theirs was a grotesque caricature of life, more horrible in its realism than death could be. They were statues, figures carved in red marble. For marble they were, frozen and held fast in the snow, with the white veins of ice over faces and dark hides. Some lay on the ground, but these, too, lay as if they were asleep.

The sun shone upon them, illuminating every rigid contour, telling every pitiful syllable of the manner of their death—the ceaseless drifting back and forth, buffeted by winds, numbed by cold, blinded by snow, hunting their way to some haven of warmth and safety. She remembered Wade's words, "It's good to be close to the breaks."

These had not been close enough.

"They're—they're frozen," Bethany whispered.

"Yes—" Wade was white-lipped.

"Our cows—and they were going to have calves in the spring—"

Wade did not answer.

"Those ranch cows—" she said. "The ranchers will never miss them, they have so many. But that was all we had—"

"Don't be selfish—"

He spoke roughly, but she understood. This was a hard thing that had happened. He had to arm himself in roughness, if he stood it at all. She could see his throat working, and she turned her head. It would not do for her to see him cry. But he did not cry.

"Could be," she heard him say finally, "that a few found their way down to the breaks."

But they both knew that had not happened.

Now she could go to him. She rode close, put her hand on his arm. "Don't you worry, darling," she said. And as she spoke, she remembered the horror of that day she went for wood, and how easily things could have turned out differently. "We're both alive, and that's more important than all the cows that ever grazed on this range."

CHAPTER FOURTEEN

Much as Bethany wanted spring to come, she could not forget that it would mean another payment on the land. It would mean, too, the necessity for buying more supplies. When they stocked up before Christmas, Bethany thought they had more than they would ever eat. Now she was beginning to wonder if she had enough to last until May, the time they normally would expect to lay in a fresh supply. She had never thought she would live to see the day when six months would seem too soon to be going back for groceries.

Groceries and land payments and interest. Those things take money. You say, "We have thirty years to pay for the land," and it sounds easy. But what about those years when you have nothing to pay with?

For several days Wade was very quiet and Bethany did not say anything to intrude upon his silence. Finally he said he thought he'd just ride over to the Triple T. Maybe the Boss would have some work for him. Bethany knew he didn't want to go. All the time he was so quiet these last few days he had been turning the idea over in his mind, rejecting it, considering it. To go to the Boss for work would be a sort of admission that he was as wrong in this farming idea as everybody said he was. But he went anyway.

The Boss regarded him from under beetling brows in a way he had of seeming to see right through men. In his look was a mixture of grudging admiration and puzzled wonder. He could understand Tom Finch, trying to start a herd of his own. That was a natural thing, like a small shoot breaking off from a parent plant. He could even understand Tobe Dillon, a dreamer too lazy to work for his dream. But this fellow, this Wade Cameron, flying into the face of things as they were, defying every natural way of the land.

Or was he? Maybe not. The Boss was silent, thinking. It was as if he looked farther into the future than man could see and caught the vision of hordes of Wade Camerons descending upon the land. There would be no stopping them. You could try he thought, as others had tried, would continue to try: branding their stock pretending to think it mavericks; accusing them (on trumped-up charges) of cattle stealing; bringing subtle terrorism to bear against them—even, as some hinted darkly, burning them out.

He would stoop to none of these. The nesters had enough with the wind, the drought, the blizzards and the loneliness. If they faced these, they deserved to win. In this country—maybe in any country—a man mostly made his own fortune.

This Wade Cameron, now—he had a sort of stubborn courage a man couldn't help admiring. He believed in the land, so he was as patient as the land and as strong. He was all for putting something into the land, instead of taking it out. Maybe he had something there. Anyway, if you got rid of this one individual nester, his kind would still come. It was like the human race; man, the individual might perish, but mankind, the race, went on. He liked this fellow. He wished he could help him. But hell, he couldn't give him a job. After the big die up, it was all he could do to find work for his own men.

"I'm sorry, Cameron," he said, coming out of his reverie. "I don't have work enough for my own boys. But I'd buy some feed, if you had it to spare."

"I didn't much think you'd have anything," Wade said. "But I thought I'd try. And I'm sorry I don't have any feed. Now that the grass is burned, I'll have to feed my crop to my own stock."

Wade went home to report failure to Bethany.

"Do you suppose he told you that because he—well, because he doesn't want us out here?" she asked.

"Oh, Lord no," Wade said, laughing a little shortly. "He minds me about like a horse does a fly. And sometimes I think he could switch me off about as easy—"

He was silent a moment, and then went on.

"No," he continued, "he doesn't mind me, individually. Funny, I could almost feel what he was thinking today when I asked him for a job. He just sees me as the first of a crowd who'll come later. I can see his side of it. He came out here when things were pretty wild. You think we have it hard now, but it's nothing to compare with what he found. And he sort of tamed the country down to where it looks good enough so we homesteaders want to come in and take a slice."

"Yes," Bethany agreed, "I can see his side."

"He's being pretty decent about it," Wade said. "A lot of the ranchers have made things tough for the nesters. We're having things easier here in the Panhandle than nesters in a lot of places. He shouldn't mind us, though. What he doesn't seem to realize is there may come the day when he'll be plenty glad to have a railroad to ship his cattle over. And when enough of people come, the railroad will come, too."

He talked as if a sort of instinct guided him, a knowledge only felt, without being fully understood.

"They're bound to have a railroad," she said, not so sure of it herself, trying only to encourage him.

"Sure, that's why we have to hold on to this land. No matter what happens, we've got to hold on—"

The days marched on, each one coming a little closer to the

time when the payment was due. There was, as well, the inexorable need for food and the equally inexorable diminishing of the stores which met that need. Each day there was a little less flour, less coffee, less sugar. It was almost as if these things went down at night, of themselves, as waters recede. Bethany was tempted to put a mark on the coffee sack each night to see if the contents stayed at that same place the next morning. She had long since given up taking sugar in her coffee.

Quite by accident she came upon an unexpected source of money. It was only a few days after they had found the dead cattle. The cold and the snow was still on the land, but the bright sun was beginning to nibble away at the edges of both of them. She was mending a torn place in one of Wade's gloves while he sat dozing in his chair when a knock came at the door. She got up, saw Butch and Slats on the threshold.

"Why, hello," she said. "Come in—"

"Hello. We thought you might have been frozen solid here in the dugout," Slats said. And then he saw Wade. "Well, you old good for nothing son-of-a-gun. Marry you a good wife so as you can sit around and do nothing the rest of your life."

"Oh, shut up and sit down," Wade said lazily. "I've been sick. Tell Doc he might as well go out of business because I've brought a real doctor out here."

"I've got some real medicine for you," Slats said. "Piece of beef. Want me to bring it in?"

"Oh, yes—bring it in," Bethany cried. She hoped she didn't sound like a starving person. Meat. That was real food. She hadn't let Wade know how little they had, fearing that he would insist on going out to hunt for some.

"Bring it in," she repeated. "I'll cook us all some—"

She set about cooking the meal, happier than she had been in days. After weeks of isolation, it would have been good to see anyone. But between them and these cowboys there was a special tie. Together the four of them had taken a wild ride to minister to a neighbor's need. Anywhere that was a bond; here, it was a hoop of steel.

"Have you seen Milly?" she asked. "I had planned to ride over, but the storm came."

"Yes, ma'am, we were over yesterday, Butch and me."

"Is she—how was she?" Bethany asked, not quite sure what it was she wanted them to tell her.

"She's a right brave little thing," Slats said. Butch said nothing. He stood there opening and closing his hands, looking down at the process as if it were a phenomenon he had never seen before.

"Tom lose any cattle?" Wade asked.

"Most of his herd. I reckon everybody lost some."

"Now you just sit down and visit," Bethany said, changing the subject quickly, "I'll have something ready pretty soon."

They sat down. Slats picked up the glove she had been working on. He turned it over in his hands.

"I sure would be right proud to have some like this," he said.

"I'll knit you a pair," Bethany offered.

"I'll pay you good."

"I don't want pay from you, Slats," she protested.

"I said, I'd pay you. And Butch here, he would, too. Only he's too scared to tell you so. Butch, you ought to have your hands froze right off your arms if you're too scared to tell the lady you want some mittens—"

Bethany could not be sure whether it was their own need that he expressed, or hers he felt. She would not inquire into that too closely.

"I'll make your mittens," she promised.

She raveled up the red shawl her mother had sent her. She did it with no regrets. A shawl was nice to have, and pretty. But when you weighed it against some good hard cash, the money was bound to win. Not for the sake of the money alone, but for the things it would buy. Her mother would feel that way, too.

When Slats came back for his pair, he was delighted. He held up his mittened hands, looking at them admiringly. "Now ain't we fancy!" he said. He slipped a dollar into her hand.

"That's too much, Slats," she protested.

"For mittens like this? You don't know what you're talking about. When the other boys see them, they'll all want them. Will you make them some?"

"Send them over, Slats," she said. "And maybe you'd better take Butch's to him, too."

"He'd a-come himself," Slats said, "but he rode over toward the Finches."

For once there was no laughter on Slats' face.

"That's good," she told him.

She took the two dollars he gave her, looked at them a long time. Then she pulled out the box from under the bed and put them there. It was mighty little company they had. But she thought she had never seen pieces of money that looked as big, shone as bright, as did those mitten dollars.

With Slats advertising her work, she did a thriving business among the other cowboys until the last bit of the Christmas shawl had been used up. She threatened to unravel Wade's sweater and convert that yarn, as well. But Wade said he'd have no Indian giver in his house; and, besides, did she want to have to nurse him through another bad cold?

The snow melted, the sun shone. The air was crisp and clear. She sat down and wrote her mother.

"We had a bad spell of weather," she told her. "But it is beautiful now. Wade had a cold, but I haven't been sick a minute. We had a nice Christmas. Wade fixed up a sort of affair so that now I have water in the kitchen. Your shawl was lovely. I can't tell you how much I have used it." (Indeed she couldn't, and that was the truth!) "We stayed in close during the bad weather."

On and on she went, filling pages with the small talk she

knew her mother wanted to hear—all the tremendous trifles families tell each other. But there was no word of the frozen cattle, or of the seriousness of Wade's illness. She could not yet bring herself to think too much about the night she had held back the shadow of death from their dugout walls.

She started to add something else—a request for yarn, so that she might knit more mittens for the cowboys. She had written the first words when she stopped, put her pen down. She sat staring into space for long moments.

That would be asking for help, a thing which she would never do. Aunt Clara said it would be like that—the missionary society would have to pack a barrel for her, as they did for the other homesteaders. When you took things, even from your own folks or from kind souls like the missionary ladies, it was charity. And charity was not for Wade and her, ever. They'd work things out some way, and by their own efforts. What was it Wade had told Tobe Dillon?

"I'll feel more like it's mine, if I pay for it," he said.

She looked down at her hands, red and chapped from snow and cold and housework. She looked at her broken shoes, at her dress, faded from much wear and many launderings. She got up and went to the mirror hanging over the tin wash basin. She looked at herself a long time. And then she came back and finished her letter.

"I wish you'd send me some pictures of the latest styles," she said. "I want to make up those dress lengths you sent me for Christmas."

When she had finished she made herself extra tidy and neat, and cooked a good supper before Wade came.

When he did, he brought news.

"Saw a cowboy today," he told her. "Said Tom's talking about going up to Kansas to work on the railroad."

"And take Milly with him—?"

She thought she could not bear to see Milly leave.

217

"I don't know. He said she might stay here, and hold the claim. But he didn't know for sure—"

"Milly—here alone—" Bethany protested. Milly's presence, under those conditions, would be far worse than her going away. Milly, so timid she could not even face a prairie dog—how could she stand up to the terrifying vastness of solitude?

"Well—they have to get some cash money—" He stated a simple fact, and she understood.

"Would you like to go work on the railroad?" she asked.

She could stay here and hold the claim. If Milly could, so could she.

He said, no, he wouldn't. He had heard of another way to make money. Newsome had told him about it—would like to try it himself, but his wife carried on something terrible when he mentioned it to her; said it was the most horrible thing she ever heard of—sounded like a ghoul.

"Say, what is a ghoul, Bethany?" he asked.

"Well," she said uncertainly, "I think it's one who preys on the dead—"

"The old gal is mighty close to right, then. It's gathering bones."

"Gathering bones—"

She remembered how her first sight of them had disturbed her. Now she noticed them no more than she did any other thing which was natural to the land.

"What would anybody want with bones?" she marveled.

"Oh—for fertilizer, and other things. The freighters take them up when they go for supplies. Glad not to have empty wagons. Say they sell good, once you get them to a railroad."

"You—you want to gather bones?"

"Sure—I'll haul them out to the road, and Hud will pick them up when he goes north."

So they set about gathering bones. Wade hitched the team to the wagon, and he and Bethany drove out on the prairie, searching for their strange treasure. At first Bethany thought she could not bring herself even to look at them. She drove the team while Wade loaded. He broke up the skeletons methodically, piling them as if they were so many pieces of wood. Bethany kept her eyes averted from the grinning specters of death which formed her cargo. After a while that feeling wore off. Here was just another example of nature's use of things. About these bones there was a kind of immortality. The buffalo got his life from the land, and he left something behind him that would make life possible for others. As Wade said, "You can't take and take, without giving something."

The buffalo had taken, and now they gave. She must remember that. You must give more than you take, and the gift must be no transient one, but something that may be harvested long after you are gone. She wrapped the lines around the brake, and got down off the wagon.

"Let me help load," she said.

"There's no need, unless you want to," he told her.

"I want to."

She touched one of the bones. It seemed warm, almost alive. The sun had shone upon it so that it held none of death's chill. She remembered the time Wade had made her touch the chips. How much she had to learn then—how ignorant she was of all the things that lay ahead of her. She thought of these things without regret, wondering if the buffalo, too, might not have been proud had he known the destiny that was to be his.

"Don't get yourself all worn out," Wade advised her. "Stop and rest if you get tired."

"I'm not tired," she said. "This isn't hard."

(It was as if she knew that in after years those who followed them would say, "My—you had it hard. I don't see how you stood it!"; that she would answer them, "We didn't notice it was hard. We did what we had to"; and that afterwards she would say in her heart, "It was our happy time.")

They got a load and Wade drove it off to pile by the side of the road where the freighters could pick it up when they went north. Then they set about collecting more.

"Don't you think we had better trade the first load for supplies?" Wade asked.

"Yes," she agreed, trying not to let him feel the relief in her voice, as she had tried not to let him know how little of everything was left.

Finally the supplies came—coffee, sugar, molasses, beans, flour, tomatoes. She gloated over the richness of them.

"We'll have a real meal tonight," she said. They did. She cooked with reckless abandon. It seemed to her that food had never tasted so good.

They got money for the next loads. Not much, but it was real. They ran their fingers through it, gloated over it like misers. Wade put it into the box with Bethany's mitten dollars. It made a good comforting click as he dropped it in.

And then he went outside and came back with a package.

"It's for you—" he said diffidently.

She stood holding it, making no effort to break the string.

"Open it—" he told her.

She opened it. In the box was a pair of pumps—black kid, soft as gloves. They had high heels and pointed toes and huge cut-steel buckles. They were utterly lovely, utterly useless. Where, in all this country, would she have a place to wear them? Mrs. Newsome's, perhaps, if she ever gave another party. Nowhere else.

But she *would* wear them: to church meeting in the spring, when the traveling preacher came back, as he had promised he would do; on Sundays, when she dressed up at home; when she went calling on Mrs. Newsome, as she would make occasion to do now that she had something special to show her.

"Try them on," Wade told her.

She put them on over her coarse stockings, lifted her calico dress and cotton underskirt so that she might have a better look.

"They fit perfectly," she said in amazed wonder. "How did you know my size!"

"Remember the day we spilled the water?" he asked. "Remember—you stepped in the mud—and got mad at me for laughing—"

How could she ever forget that day!

"—the print dried, and it was hard as a rock. I came by and saw it and, well—I just thought you had a cute little foot, and never had any pretty shoes or anything. And, well—I just wanted you to have some, so I measured the track and said to myself I'd get you some with the first money I had. And—well—I sent the print up by Hud, and he got the shoes—"

He was a bashful stripling, apologizing for the valentine he had sent, his uncertainty more moving than eloquence ever could have been.

The day she spilled the water! Now it was set in permanence; in Wade's mind and in hers, a link between them. She would keep the shoes as memory of their marriage rather than the wedding dress most women cherished.

She cried, "Oh, Wade—they are beautiful—" and ran toward him, the little shoes making soft thudding noises on the rag carpet stretched across the dirt floor of the dugout.

CHAPTER FIFTEEN

Spring came early that year.

Out of the dead brown of fall, out of the washed whiteness of winter, it came edging its confident way into a world of whose welcome it was sure. At first it was a feel in the air, a promise. The grass began to grow green around the cow chips, and, seeing this greenness, Bethany thought it the most beautiful sight she had ever beheld—more moving than Missouri wild flowers, than trees and leafy shrubs.

The maiden blush rose at the side of the dugout was not far behind the grass.

"You darling," Bethany cried. "You're going to grow—"

She dug around the roots, poured on water. She felt almost as if the rose understood her, was grateful for the praise no less than for the drink.

The calf came. It was a lively little animal, a mixture of both its gentle Missouri mother and its sturdy range father. It was not quite Jersey and it was not quite Durham, but it was strong and frisky, and much at home. It was a heifer, and that in itself was cause for rejoicing.

"—and think of all the milk and butter," Bethany exulted. "We'll have to get word to Slats and Butch."

"Uh—huh—," Wade agreed absently, his eyes on the sky.

"You know," he went on, "we sure could use a rain. Things are getting pretty dry."

And so they were. Come to think of it, there had been no moisture since the big snow.

"We'll have one before long," she consoled him.

But no rain came. One sunny beautiful day followed another. The wind blew a great deal more than she felt was normal for April, and sometimes it bore dust with it. The hot sun shone through the dust so that there was a kind of smoky brightness in the air. She was glad to stay inside the dugout. But even so, remembering her worry concerning supplies last winter, she was all for planting a garden. Wade told her to wait. It would do better after a rain. Besides, they were not out of danger of frost yet.

"Frost, as hot as it is!" She scoffed at the idea.

"Don't you get upset by a few warm days," he warned. "Remember—we're better than three thousand feet high here. Besides that, we're right in the path of any storm that decides to blow in from the Rockies. We'll wait awhile—"

They waited, and finally a rain came. Almost it seemed to make an entrance, conscious of its own importance. There was a big build-up, with wind and thunder and lightning. The land was bathed in golden fire, filled with awesome sound. But for all the fuss it was really a very small rain, not much more than a sprinkle. Although Wade had hoped for more, he did not complain. Instead, he set about plowing for maize.

"I'm going to plant a larger piece this year," he told Bethany. He put the seed saved from last year's crop, dead and brown now, back into the earth that had nourished it, there to await the recurring miracle of resurrection. Once that was done, he started fencing the newly planted field. He brought back posts from the breaks. Bethany did not ask him what she wanted most to know—where he would get the necessary wire. Presently she found out.

It would come as most of their things had come, from his own contriving. She saw him busy at the first fence, and it dawned on her what he was doing. He was taking from it one of the wires, leaving only two of the original three strands. This single wire he fitted carefully to the newly set posts.

"I'm just trying this," he told her. "It may not work. But I'll try. We'll sort of have to keep watching if the cattle get too close."

For the first fence he had thought three strands of wire were none too much. Now he would try to make out with one, and his own vigilance. That was the way things had to go out here—you made out with what you had. Maybe that was the way things went everywhere. It was what Mama used to call "Cutting your coat according to your cloth." You didn't give up, like Tobe Dillon, and say it was no use. You didn't think somebody ought to step in and make things easy for you. The ones who felt like that moved on. Only the managing ones stayed.

She and Wade meant to stay.

Bethany started her garden. She brought out the seeds saved from last year. By now she knew the ones that did best. The squash was good when fresh—she would dry some of the beans and peas for winter's use. She would dry meat, too— Wade knew how to do it, and he would teach her. And, of course, there were always the plums. She knew the country now for an adversary whose powers must not be underestimated. She must learn to fight it on its own grounds; last winter had taught her that.

Once the seeds were in, she and Wade again waited for rain. There was some promise—clouds rolling up and thunder and lightning.

"Wade," she asked, "doesn't it seem like the lightning is *brighter* out here?"

"Well," he said, teasingly, "maybe you're right. After all, we're nearly a mile closer to it."

Whatever the reason, she knew she was right. It played upon the prairie like an eerie light from another world. It flashed and the thunder crashed together, so that they seemed to explode all around her. She had never been afraid of storms, nor was she afraid now. Rather, she was awed. Even the storms out here took on a fierce, untamed air.

In spite of all this, there was next to no rain. May brought a few sprinkles, enough to bring up the maize and the garden, enough to nourish their hopes. June came in, very hot and dry. The sunny days marched by, one after another, and there was no measuring the difference in their heat. Butch and Slats rode over. They were mopping their faces, and looked hot and flushed. Bethany saw them stop with Wade, who was out looking at the maize. Presently the three of them came toward the house.

"Come in," she called, "I'll give you something to drink."

They filed in.

"Mighty nice and cool in here," Slats said, looking around him appreciatively.

"It's more than you can say for the outside," Bethany told them.

"June's the hottest month," Slats reminded her. "It will cool off later."

"You make me tired," she said. She took down three glasses, turned on the spigot and let water run into them. "You are always looking forward to something good that's going to happen. Can't you ever find anything good going on *now?* You men are all alike about this country."

She stirred in some molasses and vinegar and a pinch of soda. Then she handed each man a glass. Slats took a taste.

"Yes, Ma'am," he said. "This here stuff I'm drinking right now is good."

He drained his glass, set it down.

"The other day I heard about something else that's going

225

to happen," he told Wade, "but I don't know as I dare tell it, before *her*—"

"Oh, don't mind her," Wade grinned. "It's just the weather. She'll cool down after awhile—"

"I hear they've started surveying for a railroad," Butch said.

"The railroad—" Wade repeated. "The railroad—"

Here was his long dream, at last on the eve of fulfillment. He almost could see the road inching its way along. The ring of the picks was a song in itself, a song whose nuances were penetrating each day deeper into new territory. The road was a needle, pushing its way through new material, and the thread it drew after it was newness, too—new people, new ways, new hopes.

"Where's it coming?" Wade asked.

"No way of telling, yet. You know how them railroad boys are. They'll put it where they please. All I know for sure is, it's coming down the Panhandle, somewhere."

"Who told you?"

"The Boss—"

"I guess he doesn't like it much."

"He likes it about as much as he would the toothache. Get those tracks, and you'll have a country all cluttered up with people and fences. And then is when us old ranch boys will have about as much chance as a stump-tailed bull in fly time."

"Time may come when you'll be right glad to see that railroad," Wade said.

"Could be, but this isn't it. Oh, yes—something else. Tom sure enough has gone off to work with the construction gang."

"And Milly—?" Bethany asked, hoping the answer was not the one she feared.

"She stayed so no one can jump the claim. Leastways, that's what she *says*—"

"Milly—alone—" Bethany cried.

"We look in on her often," Butch said. It was the first time he had spoken. "Don't we, Slats?"

"Yeah, we do. When we saw she was bound and determined to stay, we told Tom we'd look after her. Otherwise, he never would have left her. But they sure needed the money, and she made him go."

Butch stood up restlessly, and Slats too got to his feet.

"Well, so long. I guess we better be going," he said. "Thanks for the drink, Miz Cameron."

They rode off into the shimmering heat.

The drought continued. By the end of July the earth was packed almost as hard as the dugout floor. Still no rain came. All day long the sun blazed across a copper sky, sinking at evening into a horizon mottled with reds and golds and ambers. There was no escaping the light of this sun. In a hilly country, or in a tree-filled one, there could always be the hope that behind that hill, or that grove, was a cloud which promised rain tomorrow. But here there were no illusions. You saw what was there—a bright and cloudless sky, with no hope in it.

Long since Bethany had known there would be no garden. She did not let herself worry about it, for she had promised Wade she would not. Anyway, they knew a graver worry than that which might be felt for a few vegetables, even though those were meant to supply part of the winter's food. Their concern was for the maize crop.

By August, they both faced the fact that this, too, was gone. The earth began to crack around sickly, dead stalks on which there was not even the promise of feed. When the wind blew, as it did much of the time, it kicked up dust from the plowed field, blew it toward the house. The wind made the dust and the heat even more unbearable.

"I could bear the heat of it if it weren't for the wind," Bethany complained to Wade.

"That's where you are wrong," he told her, an edge of sharpness in his voice. "It's like I always tell you—we couldn't stand the heat if it weren't for the wind."

Sure—she knew about the wind. It made the heat bearable; it was going to pump the water, once they got wells. It was a thing one could turn to his advantage, the way early settlers in Missouri turned to trees. Before long, he'd probably be trying to tell her that these broad flat stretches of nothingness were an advantage too.

That might all be true. But she still did not like the wind, never would like it. Today she didn't feel like pretending she did, either.

She kept the rosebush alive. It was all she could attempt, and even in this she was not sure she would be successful. She gave it all the water she dared, which was not overmuch. In weather like this the spring could dry up. Every cupful of water was something to be cherished. Still she watered the rosebush. Wade knew this, and did not forbid it. Perhaps for him too the bush was a symbol of their will to live in this land.

She wondered much about Milly.

"I should ride over to see her," Bethany said, "but it's so hot—"

Because of the heat she stayed at home, getting word through Butch and Slats concerning Milly.

"We look in on her right frequent," Slats said. "She's lonesome, but she's making out all right. Always tells us there's nothing she needs, but we must be sure to come again."

"I wish she'd come over here and stay with me awhile," Bethany said. "Tell her I want her—"

"We've already told her," Slats said. "Didn't we, Butch? We said she ought to come over, that you'd like to have her."

"I'll tell her again," Butch promised. "Next time I go—"

"She won't come," Slats prophesied. "Looks like she is just sort of glued to that place. We took her a cat," he finished.

"A cat?"

"Yes—found one close to the road the other day. Figured somebody riding through on the stage had lost it, or somebody coming out to Mobeetie to live. Good thing we found him when we did—coyotes would have finished him off before long."

"That's company for her," Bethany said.

"Sure—that's what she says."

"Does she hear from Tom?"

"Yes—he's got a job on the railroad, and he hopes he can get home before winter sets in. That way they can sort of see things through."

Bethany was thoughtful after the cowboys were gone. Tom was making money on the railroad, enough to "see them through." She stood it as long as she could, and then asked Wade the question that had been on her lips for days.

"Wade—what are we going to do?"

"You mean for money?"

"Yes."

She did not need to add that it wasn't money for its own sake, but for food, and land payments, for life itself—for the things that would make it possible to stay there.

"If you mean, are we going to give up this place and go back to Missouri, just because we don't have any money in sight, the answer is *no*."

He said it louder than was necessary, and banged the table with his fist as he spoke. The dishes rattled like castanets. "I'm sticking it out," he said.

She did not ask "How?" although she wanted to. The word beat at her lips; its urgency constricted her throat.

"Do you think I'd give up now?" he asked more calmly. "Now—with the railroad coming through—"

"But that won't be for months," she told him. "Maybe for years. I remember Papa talking about how it was at Star Hill.

They talked about it and they talked about it. Then the surveyors came. And after that, it was months before the crews began to work. It was two years before the trains ran, and people talked about how fast they got things done!"

She wanted to add, "You know we can't hold out two years. We'll do well to make it for two months." But this she did not say.

"I know," he said. "The road won't be here tomorrow, just because they've decided to start one. But it will be here."

"It may miss us by miles—"

"It may. But it will be somewhere in the Panhandle. Wherever it comes, it will be closer than we have one now. And when it comes, others will follow. It will take time, but it will come. And when it does, our land will be worth something. This is no time to turn loose."

"Wade," she asked timidly, for she could not bring herself to question his judgment easily, "Wade—you still are sure this is farming country—? Maybe Tobe was right when he said it was just for cattle."

She was thinking of the dead maize when she said it, and he knew she was—knew she feared the things she did not see, which is the most cruel fear of all.

"Tobe *was* right. It is good for cattle. We'll always raise them out here, I think. And maize is right. And—and other things—"

"But what if it—if it doesn't rain—like this—for years—?"

"It hasn't rained this year, but that's no sign it won't next year. That's no reason to give up. I can't ask the weather to guarantee that it will be good. A man has to take his chances. More times than not, things will work out for him. And if they don't—well, I still have to take my chances."

He sat still a moment. Bethany said nothing; she did not feel he expected her to.

"I sort of like it better that way," he finished, grinning at her shyly, wishing she could understand, fearing she would not. Women were different. They liked things to be sure-like. It was because of them, as much as anything else, that men had to work toward a measure of security. It was only the Tobe Dillons of the world who overlooked that. Still, a man couldn't give up his self-respect just because a woman wasn't willing to take a few chances. Therein lay Clyde Newsome's weakness. Bethany was better about this than most women. She knew a man was free only so long as he had fight left in him, only so long as he did not give up, as Tobe had done, and expect other people to hand him things he had not earned. She knew that a man who was not free was less than a man. Maybe she understood better than he thought she did.

"Tobe was right about cattle," Wade went on. "We nesters know that; we'll probably always try to have them. But if we don't try something else, we'll be nothing but little ranchers. Same way with raising maize—that's just another way of feeding cattle. We've got to add something of our own, something different—"

"What is it?"

"Wheat," he told her. "As long as we were so far from the railroad, it wasn't practical. But now that's going to be changed—"

"Oh, wheat—"

"It ought to do well here," he said. "Wheat, and maize, and a few cattle—they'll work out fine."

"I guess so," she said, trying to rise to his enthusiasm.

"I know it's hard now, Bethany. All we have is a law saying we can file on a claim. And the country doesn't seem to have heard about the law—or maybe doesn't mean to mind it, even if it's heard. If we can just hold on till the railroad comes, things will be better—"

"Yes—" Bethany agreed. Even she could see that a railroad helped. It sort of whittled down a country, made it man-sized.

"Looks like maybe we got here at the wrong time," he told .her. "Too late to start ranching, too early for farming. Right now we're sitting smack dab on the edge of time. It may be a little while before anyone can tell which way things are going to go."

He straightened up, brushed back his hair.

"But I'm going to stay here and see," he said.

"Sure," Bethany agreed. "Sure we are."

CHAPTER SIXTEEN

No MATTER what Bethany did, Milly's face was always before her. She was a part of the sighing of the wind; she was in the heart of the silence; she was the symbol of goodness that had been overcome by evil.

Bethany felt she could have borne it better if only she could fix the blame for Milly's going. Certainly Tom could not be blamed, for he had not wanted to leave her alone. Everybody knew that. He tried to get her to go back to his folks, or even to Mobeetie, or to make Bethany a visit. But she refused even to consider any of these suggestions. She gave as her reason the fact, which certainly no one could dispute, that somebody might jump their claim if she too went away. Bethany thought she wanted to stay because here she felt closer to the little dead baby.

Tom would never have left her except they had to have money. He made everything ready, doing all he could in order that it would be easier for her to manage in his absence. He stocked up with needful supplies, he hauled a great quantity of wood. He insisted on her learning to shoot a gun. She was mortally afraid of it, but she tried hard to learn. He set up tin cans for targets, and was provoked with her because she invariably shut her eyes when the gun went off.

233

"Oh, well," he said resignedly, "you won't have to use it for anything except maybe to scare off a coyote now and then, or shoot you a jack rabbit for supper—"

"Don't you worry about me. I'll be all right."

"I wouldn't leave you, Milly, if I didn't think I had to." He was very sober about it. "It will be mighty lonesome—"

"I know you wouldn't, Tom. And you aren't to give me a thought. Butch and Slats will look after me."

"I know that. I wouldn't go a step if I didn't."

Butch and Slats, indeed, did come as often as they could. Sometimes they merely dropped by to say hello. Sometimes they brought her gifts of fresh meat, for, although she tried, she had little success with the gun Tom had taught her to shoot. The minute she took it up her hands began to shake so that she couldn't hit any target, no matter how big it might be or how obligingly still it might stand. They brought her a letter from Tom. He was working on the railroad which was edging its way across the continent. From the first it was a thread of certainty; even before it got to the land itself, it reached out to the men who lived in it, giving them work. The history of homesteading was often written in the stories of men who paid for their claims with money earned while they worked on the railroad—and in the stories of the women who stayed at home to hold the claim while the men were gone. They brought her the cat.

Bethany saw him when she rode over to see Milly. He was short haired, squarely built. He settled down in Tom's chair as if he belonged there.

"I named him Tom," Milly told Bethany, smiling faintly. "He's really like him—sort of calm about everything. And you wouldn't believe how much company he is. I couldn't stand it here without him."

The cat had some sort of a bronchial difficulty so that his meow was a deep bass and even his purr sounded as if it were being pulled across a rough file. When she talked to him he would answer. She told Bethany she had got so that she could understand him—he had one way of asking for food, another to be let out, and a third impatient monosyllable which she interpreted as "Leave me alone, can't you!"

"Why don't you bundle him up in a basket and come home with me for a visit? I can't tell you how much I want you," Bethany urged.

"Bethany," Milly said slowly, hunting for words with which to say what she meant, "I can't leave. I mean, I *mustn't* leave—"

There was a sort of desperate resolve in her words. Then she smiled a little, and went on.

"I know everybody wondered why I married Tom—they just as good as asked me. I didn't tell them it was because he wasn't afraid of things. I was afraid of everything and he was afraid of nothing. I thought maybe if I married him I'd learn not to be afraid."

She was quiet for a moment, stroking the cat's grey sides. He arched his back and began to purr hoarsely.

"And sure enough, I learned a little. Not much, but a little. And then the baby came."

She was silent, for such a long time that Bethany thought she wasn't going to speak again. And then she did.

"I've thought so many times," Milly went on, scarcely above a whisper, "that it was my fault. About the baby being so delicate, I mean. Maybe I was so weak and scared, I passed it on to her—"

"Oh, Milly," Bethany protested. "You mustn't feel that way. You mustn't. That didn't have anything to do with the baby's death."

"I know I'm foolish," Milly said, "but I've had that on my mind. And because I did, I wouldn't leave when Tom went to work on the railroad. I told myself I was going to stay right here and learn not to be afraid. I guess you don't understand," she tapered off uncertainly.

"Oh, but I do!" Bethany assured her earnestly. "It's this country. I'm afraid of it myself. I've never told anybody this, not even Wade. But when I'm by myself I can't look at it. It's so big, I get dizzy, as if I were looking down into some great depth. Now that's real silliness for you."

After that, Bethany did not again urge Milly to leave, even for a short visit. She got news of her through Butch and Slats. She meant to go and see her again, but the heat was too intense. Besides, there was another menace now. The coyotes were infected with rabies, and it was wise to stay inside and to keep the horses in the corral as much as possible. Any sort of a coyote bothered Bethany. She had long thought they uttered their mournful howl, not so much because of their own loneliness as to drive home to her the fact of her own. The quirk of their mouths bore the stamp of ironical laughter, sardonic and unquenchable. Wade shot any that came near the house or the corral, taking no chances on whether they were infected. Even in death they bore this sly look, as if they knew a good joke they did not chose to tell.

It was Slats who came to tell her about Milly. But it was a Slats she had never seen before. His face was old and haggard. He might have been a stranger bringing news, so flat and cold and distant his voice sounded.

"It's Milly. I've brought news of Milly—"

"She's sick?" Bethany asked, looking at his stricken face.

"She's dead—"

"Oh, no—" Bethany whispered. "Oh, Slats, no—"

"It was the cat," he went on tonelessly. "We thought we was doing such a fine thing, taking it to her—"

Butch had been a witness to her death, coming in sight just in time to see what happened, but not soon enough to prevent it. In fact, at first he thought Milly and the cat were playing some sort of game. He saw Tom, slithering across the grass, headed toward her. She was backing toward the dugout, slowly, watching something. And then he saw she had a gun, and knew it was no game. Tom's back was arched, his tail straight in the air. He and Milly were both rigid with fear and horror. And then Butch saw the reason for it.

A coyote was headed toward them, the face of the animal a mask of horror itself. Its jaws were dripping, and it came straight ahead, straight as vengeance itself. Seeing this, Butch started riding very fast, his six shooter ready. He called to Milly he was coming, but either she did not hear him or thought she must not wait. She raised her gun, and as she did, the cat jumped. He knew her for his friend, his refuge against this horror that pursued him. He flung his body against her, his forelegs around her neck, clinging as a child might cling. He knocked the gun from her hands, and it fell with a dull roar. And Milly, too, fell, with Tom still clinging to her.

"But Butch, he got that—well, he got that coyote," Slats said with fierce rejoicing.

"Poor Butch—" Bethany said softly.

"Yes, Ma'am, we both feel bad. We keep thinking if he hadn't stopped somewhere up the trail to light a cigarette, maybe, he would have got there in time. Or if we hadn't ever given her that cat. It was the cat's fault, and ours for giving it to her. It was the cat that made the gun go off and—and kill her."

"Slats," Bethany said urgently, "don't you and Butch feel bad. Don't blame the cat, or yourselves. That cat meant everything to her. She couldn't have stood being alone without him. Milly just wasn't meant to live out here. Some people aren't. She tried, but she couldn't make a go of it."

Slats regarded her somberly.

"Maybe you are right," he said at last. "It's true of men, all

237

right. Maybe it's true of women, too. There were four of you women out here, and now only you are left. You can't count Mrs. Newsome, because she's going to take off the first chance she has—"

"Where's Butch?" she asked.

"He's at Mobeetie. Went over to see that Milly got put beside the baby. And now he's going to go hunt Tom and tell him. And if you don't mind, now, I'll be going, too—"

He did not say "To Mobeetie." He did not need to. She saw him riding off into the silent distances. And as she watched she thought of Milly—gentle Milly, who would never be afraid again.

Bethany was busy about the house that morning when the Newsomes drove up in the buckboard. They drove slowly; one horse was limping badly. Mr. Newsome went directly to the corral, but Eva Newsome came to the dugout. She looked tawdry and bedraggled—her gloves shabby, her shoes dusty. Besides that, she had been crying and had taken no pains to cover up the traces of her tears.

"Oh, do come in," Bethany urged her. "I'll make some coffee, and even fry some flapjacks, if you'll eat them. You must be hungry from your long ride."

She did not care for Eva Newsome, but she was a woman, and Bethany had not seen a woman since—since Milly was here. So she made the caller welcome now, pressed food upon her.

"Oh, no—I couldn't possibly eat a bite," Mrs. Newsome protested. The way she said it reminded Bethany of her own actions on the day she called on Lizzie Dillon for the first time.

The woman looked around her, and a shudder of distaste seemed to reach out and gather her up, shake her in its jaws as a cat would shake a mouse. No voluntary movement, this,

but something that rose up from within her through no voli-
tion of her own.

"We're leaving this country—" she said. "I—I can't stand it
any longer."

The words burst from her and, after they were out, she
seemed more in possession of herself. Having emptied herself
of a great truth, she was relieved.

"I—after what happened to poor little Milly Finch, I
couldn't stay. I haven't slept—I haven't had a night's sleep
since I heard about it. Think of her, lying dead and alone
there on the ground. If Butch hadn't come just at the moment,
and shot that coyote, it would have—it would have—"

She could not bring herself to say it.

"But he came," Bethany said.

Although she could not yet talk about Milly's death, it
did not make her feel she must leave the country. It was not
the fault of the land that Milly could not learn to live there,
or that the Dillons had left, or that the Newsomes were now
leaving. You could not blame a land for the weaknesses of the
people who for some reason, perhaps through no fault of
their own, could not remain upon it.

"And now this drought," Mrs. Newsome went on. "And
last winter, with the blizzard freezing the cattle. Much as I
disliked Tobe Dillon, I sometimes think he was the smart one,
pulling out when he did."

Bethany had nothing to say to that.

"But now we're going back," she continued. "Back to East
Texas. Papa has a store there. Really, it's the biggest store in
that part of the country. Clyde is going to work for him."

She said it nervously, yet with a certain pride.

"When I think of all we have gone through out here when
all the time we could have been at home, having things easy
with pleasant work to do—well, when I think of that, I get mad
at myself for standing it as long as I have."

Her eyes moved restlessly toward the window, as if she were wondering how something was progressing out there—something she knew about, something maybe everybody knew about, except Bethany. Bethany sensed this in the quick, furtive glances of the woman, as if Eva Newsome had delegated herself to keeping her occupied until the thing—whatever it might be—was accomplished. Was Clyde Newsome trying to persuade Wade to go back to East Texas with him, even as Tobe Dillon had tried to take him to New Mexico? She felt sure that was not it, but she knew something was afoot.

"The things I've had to put up with," Eva Newsome went on. "After the way I grew up—in town, with nice people around me. Not miles from anyone, with only cowboys and nesters for company—people nobody could possibly want to associate with."

She saw she had gone too far.

"I mean, except you," she added hastily. "I've enjoyed knowing you so much."

Her nervous, simpering formality made Bethany feel she did not need to express gratitude for the exception made in her own case.

"And to think—I lived in a dugout. Like a prairie dog. Or—or a snake. I have never let my folks know how I was living. Lots of times I'd wake up in the night, thinking I heard a noise—thinking maybe a snake had mistaken the dugout for an abandoned prairie dog hole and moved in. I'm mortally afraid of snakes."

Milly had put it differently, Bethany remembered.

"I keep thinking what if a snake should bite the baby," Milly had said. It was as if, in these two speeches, Bethany saw the difference in the women.

Milly had been thinking of the baby and Mrs. Newsome was thinking of herself. That was the difference; first, last, and always, Eva Newsome would think of herself.

"And the sort of makeshift furniture we have in these—these holes in the ground," she went on. "I hate to say it, but we wouldn't use them in a nigger house back home."

And then she saw she had erred again.

"I didn't mean your house," she said. "You've made more out of this place than any of the rest of us did—"

Her voice trailed off uncertainly, implying that the thing which had been made was still far short of what was needed.

Bethany looked around, seeing her own dugout through Mrs. Newsome's eyes. The makeshift bed in the corner. The quilt and the newspapers covering one side of the wall. The rag carpet over a dirt floor. True, the floor was almost as hard as rock and the carpet was cheerful and bright; but the floor was still dirt, the carpet rag.

"We have a Brussels carpet in the parlor back home," Mrs. Newsome went on. "And lace curtains. They come to the floor. And we have five windows in the parlor. Imagine that—five—"

Bethany, grateful for her two small ones with real glass panes, tried obediently to imagine the richness of five.

"And what a job it is to wash and iron the curtains. Good thing we have niggers to do it for us. I had never, never in all my life, washed a piece of clothes until I came out here."

Before we wash here, Bethany was thinking, we must first haul the water. That is a day's job. The next day we wash. The main thing is not how clean we get the clothes, but how little water we use while we are doing it. And afterwards, we don't waste a drop of the washing water. Out here, water must be used more than once, if we can work things that way.

"You must have hated to leave that lovely house," Bethany said. "Did you sell it, or rent it?"

"Well," Mrs. Newsome admitted, as if the truth were coming from her involuntarily, as the shudder had done, "we didn't do either, really. It—it's my mother's house."

Then she caught herself, and her next words were light chatter.

"But it is just like ours. We have never felt but what it was."

They lived in her parents' house; they worked in her father's business. Those curtains, that Brussels carpet, those windows—all were her mother's. Bethany looked at her own rag carpet and her own small windows, and was glad for them. She would not have traded them for all the grandeur Mrs. Newsome would find—in another woman's house.

She tried to say primly, not letting her own joy show through, "I know your mother will be glad to have you back."

"To be sure." Eva Newsome's nose had that pinched look again. "I know she will."

Just then Wade and Clyde Newsome came walking around the corner of the dugout. Wade was walking a little behind Mr. Newsome, who was leading a horse.

It was Rex. The horse Wade had ridden to Texas. The one Bethany had steered the wagon by. Was Wade planning to go with the Newsomes? For one crazy moment Bethany's world lurched unsteadily. She stepped out of the door with Eva Newsome. Wade saw her, came to her.

"Bethany," he said, so abruptly that she knew he found the telling hard. "I've sold Rex."

"Sold Rex!" she could only echo his words stupidly.

He couldn't do this. Out here, a horse was not just a horse. He was a man's pride, his prestige, his livelihood. He stood between him and danger; he made conquest of the country possible. He was a symbol of manhood itself. A man on foot was less than a man; he was a thing to be mistrusted and feared.

"Aren't you—are you ever afraid of, well—strangers?" Bethany once asked Lizzie Dillon. What she had meant was strange men, of course.

"At first I was, a little," Lizzie told her. "And then I

242

learned better. Except one time. I seen a man a-walkin', and I got the young'uns and we went in the house and hid. Turned out to be Tobe, but when I first seen him he was too far away to tell. No need to be afraid of a man on horse—most likely he's a cowboy. They are always nice to women and young'uns. But if you see a man a-walkin', you git inside the dugout and stay there till you make sure who it is."

And here was Wade selling Rex, putting himself voluntarily into the class of men who were not to be trusted. But that was not the worst of it, bad though that might be. Rex was more than a horse. He had saved their lives the day she went out into the blizzard. She hadn't told Wade about this episode yet, thinking she would do so some day when all their troubles were past—when they, and Rex, were fat and safe and comfortable, growing old together. Now she could never tell him.

"Oh, no—" she started to protest. And then she stopped. Something told her that there was more to the transaction than just the sale of Rex. For no ordinary reason would he part with the horse. He was having a great struggle with himself; it showed in his face. He didn't want to sell Rex—every bit of him was crying out against it. But something was pushing him on.

Rex sensed that a strange thing was happening. He arched his neck and gave a short, nervous whinny.

"Easy, old boy," Wade said. He touched the horse's flank, and the animal grew quiet.

"I appreciate this, Wade," Clyde Newsome said, his voice a dead thing, without spirit or feeling. "I hope you don't ever regret it. Things look bad now, but it's good land. You'll make off it, if you can just wait—"

"I won't regret it," Wade assured him. "I can wait—"

And then, Bethany knew what had happened. Wade had traded Rex for Newsome's section of land. Even back in Missouri he had talked of wanting it.

"I've got my eye on that section with the spring," he had said. Now he had it.

"Do you want to ride over to Mobeetie with us now?" Clyde Newsome asked.

Mobeetie! They would sign papers there. That would make the transaction legal and right. That's the way the nester did things—with law and order backing him. He had to. Being so little himself, he must have a secure thing to back him up.

"No—I'll come over by myself. I'll have to get back, you know, and if I went with you I'd be stranded."

There was a quiet satisfaction in his voice.

I have to get back, he said.

He had to get back to his land—to his two sections. Two sections to make payments on, and they weren't sure how they could handle one! Wade had doubled a burden which already seemed impossible to carry.

For a moment a wave of hot resentment flashed over her. He had no right—no right at all—to do this thing without first asking her how she stood in the matter. She too would have to meet this burden. She had helped with everything they had done up until now—hauling water, searching for the cattle after the blizzard, gathering buffalo bones. She had kept house in this land where housekeeping was a thing of contrivings and deprivations. She had fought loneliness—oh, how she had fought loneliness, that greatest enemy of all. Now when she heard his proposition to heap yet more of these burdens upon her, she wanted to cry out, "Oh, no—"

But before she could open her mouth, she saw Eva Newsome, her nose pinched in a gesture of triumph. And she knew that here was a woman who had said, "Oh, no," to all her husband's plans and dreams. Bethany shut her lips fast.

Clyde Newsome unhitched his own horse, and led the limping animal to the corral. He hitched Rex to the buckboard, while Wade watched, his young lips set tight, making no move to help. Rex looked around at him, as if to ask what manner of foolishness this was. Harness he knew only slightly; a saddle was his beloved burden. Surely his master did not mean to ask him to wear these trappings that were being fastened upon him now. Wade walked over, put his hand on the horse's sleek neck.

"It's all right, Rex," he said. "That's a good boy—"

Bethany turned her head quickly. She did not want Eva Newsome to see the tears in her eyes.

"Well, I guess we are ready," Newsome said at last.

He helped his wife into the buckboard, and slapped the lines over the backs of the horses.

"Get up—" he said. The team moved off, Rex stepping skittishly, but giving no real difficulty.

"Good-by," Clyde Newsome said, his voice a little gruff for a man ready to return to the opulence his wife had pictured.

Eva Newsome sat very straight beside her husband, the rigid triumph in her own stiff, erect figure making her husband's shoulders look all the more stooped. She turned to wave good-by, but he did not even look back.

It was not until the woman waved that Wade turned to Bethany.

"I know you think I am a fool," he said.

She did not answer, did not deny the charge.

"I'm not, really. Listen, Bethany. He wanted to trade his section with the spring on it—the one I've always wanted—for a horse to drive back to East Texas. They couldn't travel with their horse limping like that. And his wife was bound to go."

"You didn't have to trade Rex. You rode him out here—"

"I couldn't let him take one of the others. I had to keep Star and the other two because they'll work to the plow. Rex won't —besides, I rode Rex out here for land. I'd be foolish not to let him go if I thought I could get more land for him."

Still she did not answer.

"It's good land we are getting. Even without the spring, it's good. But just think of it. We have a spring of our own now—we are independent. If we ever want to sell, there is no telling how much more we can get for the land. And with the railroad coming through—"

He stopped, intent upon the magnificence of the dream he had. The grass beneath his feet was dry and parched. His best horse was gone; in its place was a limping wreck that might never be of any use. He now had two sections of land, where only an hour before he had been wondering how he would meet the payments on one. His cattle had frozen in last winter's blizzard and his crop had died in this summer's drought. But still he dreamed a dream.

"How are you going to make the payments—and the interest—?" she asked.

"I should have asked you before I did it, Bethany," Wade said slowly. "All the time Newsome was trying to talk me into doing it, I knew I should come to the house and see what you said. But I just—well, I just couldn't tell him—"

He stood, contrite and ashamed. He knew that she should have been asked, that it was cowardly not to have asked her. She it was who must bear the hardship as much, even more, than ever he would have to do.

Bethany looked out across the prairie, saw the buckboard silhouetted against the nothingness of the landscape. It was headed east, the track it made pointing like an arrow toward failure and despair. The men who had no courage headed east; the men of vision came west. Men of courage did not go back, no matter how much their wives wanted to leave. Better than that—maybe the men stayed because of their women, not in spite of them. Maybe such men had the sense to pick out women who would stay.

Suddenly she was glad, exultantly glad, that he had not

246

asked her first. She took one more look at the Newsomes, now a speck on the horizon. She turned to Wade.

"You did exactly right," she said firmly. "You know I wouldn't have wanted you to come trailing in to ask me. What would Mr. Newsome have thought of you?"

"I knew you'd feel that way," Wade said. "I knew it, or I never would have traded."

CHAPTER SEVENTEEN

Just she and Wade were left now—and the ranches. The ranches were like time itself—making no move yet, with the inexorable patience of nature, seeming to close in on them. She and Wade had two sections. Beside the ranches, their holdings were as a drop in a bucket. But the sections of the Newsomes and the Finches—and Tobe Dillon, had he owned land and stayed with it—added together would have meant something. As it was, she and Wade were no more than two castaways on a pinpoint island.

She was more than ever conscious of terrific loneliness. Even though she had seen her neighbors only infrequently, it had helped to know that they were just over the horizon, no distance at all, as distances went in this country. If only they had a dog it would be company. She had mentioned this to Wade when they first came out, but he had said no.

"Nine out of ten will chase cattle," he had explained. "And if they don't, they'll still bark like crazy and scare the calves. Before long some cowboy would have to shoot it. The ranchers are tolerating us; there's no need to do anything we don't have to, just to stir up trouble."

It was all mixed up. Wade could be dead set about putting up a fence and plowing the land, no matter how the ranchers

felt about these things. And yet he would refuse to have a dog because it might antagonize them needlessly. It didn't make sense to her. It was like Poco, ready to shoot a man without blinking but tipping his hat to a lady and riding off without hurting anyone; like Slats drinking buttermilk while he laughed at them for keeping a cow. She tried to tell this to Wade.

"Oh, but fences and plowing are different," he explained. "The law says we can do that—you see, don't you?"

Maybe she did, just a little. She supposed it was the things which went beyond the law that made it possible for people to live together. Because there was no law saying you couldn't keep a dog, Wade had to be all the more careful about doing it. That was the thing the nesters represented—the way of living together.

Butch and Slats came by. They looked at Bethany's clean dress and smooth hair appreciatively.

"You look mighty nice, Miz Cameron, I must say," Slats said. "Wade about somewhere?"

"He's right here in the house, wanting me to make him a cup of coffee. Come on in and have some, too."

"Still thinks we don't come for nothing but food," Slats grumbled. The two of them edged into the dugout carrying their hats, grinning at Bethany with relaxed and friendly ease.

"Hello, Wade," Slats said. He did not joke, as he was wont to do, when they came in and found Wade not working. He did not call him a lazy loafer. His attitude was polite, almost formal.

"How are things with you?" he asked.

"Oh—so-so—"

"Heard you bought Newsome's section of land—"

"Yes—sort of traded, really."

"That's what I heard. The Boss would have bought that from Newsome, if he had known it was for sale."

Newsome must have known that, Bethany was thinking. He could have got more money, and a horse, too. Why didn't he go to the Boss? Suddenly she knew. This was Clyde Newsome's defiant gesture against his wife. He would leave, since she made it impossible for him to do otherwise, but he would arrange the leaving to his own liking. The section he had loved he would put into the hands of the man to whom it would mean most, a man who would do with it as he himself would have liked to do. Bethany sensed it, sensed the defiant courage with which he must have worked out the deal. This was his last satisfaction, his last gift to the country he had been forced to reject.

"The Boss will buy it now," Slats said. "Fact is—he sent me to ask if you'd sell. Said he'd get one of the cowboys to buy it, if you know what I mean—"

"Did he want you to buy it?" Wade asked, his voice sharp and quick.

"No, sir, I told him I wasn't hankering to get hitched up to no land," Slats answered.

He had wanted Slats to do it, and Slats had refused! The air in the little dugout became friendly and right once more. Slats had brought the message because he thought Wade might be glad to have it; because, maybe, in bringing it, he would do his friend a service. But he would not be a party to the sale. Not Slats! He knew what the land meant to Wade.

"I just told him I'd tell you," the cowboy said, the edge of formality gone from his voice. He was the old Slats once more.

Across the table Wade's eyes met Bethany's. In them there was a question, one she understood. He wanted an answer. She knew what he hoped that answer would be; it was one she could not bring herself to give.

It was only sensible to sell the section, now that they had the chance. It would give them money to pay interest and the part due on the other land they had. They could buy supplies. Not

many, but some. With food on hand, they would not have to live in fear of want this winter. Already it was September. A person had to think of things like that. Because of the drought, she had put up nothing from the garden. There was scarcely any money left in the box. They couldn't go through the winter living off jack rabbits, like the coyotes. One could face wind and stillness and soul-chilling loneliness better if one had food in the cupboard, money hidden in a safe place. But to face these things with nothing—nothing—

Wade's eyes held hers. He could not come to her when Newsome wanted to trade, but now he could. This time he was asking her what she wanted to do.

It was right to sell. Selling wouldn't mean they had to leave. The Boss knew that. He wasn't trying to get rid of them; this was his way of being kind. It really wouldn't look like failure if they sold.

"Well, Wade, what do you want me to tell him?" Slats asked finally.

This time Wade's look had to be answered. As certainly as she sat there, Bethany meant to nod her head, to signal: "Yes— yes—, Wade, sell." Every frantic yearning, all her fears of the land and the things it could do to them welled up in her eyes. Wade saw this. He turned slowly to Butch. He opened his mouth to speak. And then Bethany did what she had no intention whatever of doing. She shook her head.

Wade squared his shoulders.

"No, Slats," he said, "I guess we'll just hang on—"

"I'll put the food on the table," Bethany said, jumping up. She told herself she ought to feel scared and maybe a little mad at herself for acting so silly. Here had been the chance to make things easy for themselves, and she had turned it down. She couldn't complain now, no matter what happened. But she remembered the look in Wade's eyes, the way he squared his shoulders when he told Slats no. She guessed maybe it was worth it; anyway, she hadn't felt so light and free in weeks.

"Well," Slats said slowly, "I don't know but what you are right. The railroad is certainly a-pushing through. We were down south about a hundred miles or so not long ago. Bunch of men down there, surveying and digging around, and that sort of thing."

"Guess we'll be shipping cattle over that railroad some of these days," Butch said slowly.

"Well, that won't hurt you any," Wade told him.

Now that the business had been disposed of, the talk was easy and right once more. Bethany put the food on the table.

"Pull up your chairs," she said. "It's ready."

They sat down at the table, but Slats for some reason did not seem hungry. His mind went back to Wade's words.

"No," he said slowly, "I guess you're right, Wade. It won't hurt us any, as you say. But it's been sort of fun, driving cattle up the trail—" He paused a moment, his eyes faraway and remote. "It had to come I guess," he went on finally. "You can't drive cattle up a trail that's all spotted with fences. The danged cows go every which way but the one you want to head 'em. You're lucky to hold your own, anyway. We have to have railroads, the way things are going, if we are to get the critters to market."

"You're right," Wade agreed. "Because, once this railroad comes through, there'll be a lot of people coming in, most of them getting land and wanting to fence it—"

"Yep, that's the trouble with a railroad. It's like discovering gold. A lot of people you don't want are bound to rush in, once it comes."

"And a lot of people you do want," Wade reminded him.

"You may be right," Slats agreed. "Anyway, that reminds me I heard some news about your friend Poco." He grinned at Bethany.

"He's no friend of mine," she protested quickly. "What did you hear?"

"He went and got himself killed—"

"Killed!" she remembered the courtly little bandit, bowing and riding away into the breaks.

"I reckon you can blame the railroad, really," Slats went on. "He tried to hold up the payroll. The paymaster was a big Irishman who had never heard of Poco, and he said no little— well, excuse me, Ma'am," Slats was having a hard time with the story, "anyway, he said no little person like the one that stood before him was going to take money away from him. So he just ups and whams him with a pick handle—"

"I reckon the hardest part for Poco was that the man didn't know him," Butch put in. It seemed to Bethany that, since Milly's death, the boy spoke even less than he used to do. "You're right, Slats—the railroad is changing things—"

Sure it was changing things. It did not stop for Poco any more than it did for the ranches, Bethany was thinking. It was not afraid of them. It did not even know there were things that some people held in fear.

"It's going to change us more than that, I'm thinking," Slats said. "As I was saying, Butch and me were down south about a hundred miles a week or so ago. Talked to some men while we were there—hunters camped on the creek. They said the railroad was fixing to come right along where they were. Said there was no telling how this country would boom once the railroad come through. They said right where they were sitting would be a fine place to ship cattle from, on account of the creek."

They were silent, turning over Slats's words in their minds. It was as if they were peering around the corner of time, looking at the shape of things to come—as if, by their very wishing, they were invoking a mirage which mirrored the image of their desires.

A bunch of men living together in five tents of buffalo hide. A blob of inconsequential nothingness on the great face of nothingness itself. Close by ran a yellow creek, bearing the soft Spanish name the intonations of which rolled gently off the various tongues of the men. Around the creek were growing acres of small yellow flowers. But already the men knew the seeds of the town were there; the four in the dugout felt it too.

The town was not yet born, save in their minds. But it would be born—a new nucleus of a new frontier. Even now they realized, without quite knowing how, that it would be shaped out of the needs and desires of the people who came to build it—the people who did not know as yet that they were even going to build. It would be all the things they planned for—and none of these. It would be itself—a place shaped out of the hopes and dreams and wishes of thousands of people, most of them as yet unborn.

All these things the four of them felt. What they could not know, of course, was that the town would be named Amarillo.

"Well," Slats said, "I guess we'd better be loping along. Thanks for the chow."

"Oh, you're welcome," Bethany told him. "I wouldn't feel you'd been here if I didn't feed you."

"Neither would we," Butch said, grinning at her.

They rode off. They rode a long way, and neither said a word. Occasionally Butch would look at his companion's face, recognizing the thing that was spreading over it—gradually at first, and then more rapidly, until at last it was a stranger who rode beside him. Finally Slats spoke.

"I reckon I'll be taking out," he said. Even his voice was not his own.

"Mobeetie—?"

"Yes—"

"Think you're bound to go—"

"Think I am." Slats put his hand into his pocket, drew out a few bills. "Want to keep 'em for me?" he asked, not even looking to see how much it was.

"Yep—I'll keep it. But, Slats—"

Slats did not even seem to hear.

"Slats—" Butch tried again, this time putting his hand on the other man's arm. "Slats—would you let me go with you this time?"

For a moment Slats came back, regarded Butch with measuring eyes.

"I could, kid," he said finally. "But I don't want to—"

"Oh, that's all right—forget it."

"It ain't as if you wanted to go for yourself," Slats explained, pondering the matter.

They rode on again, the silence of the land one with their own silence. At last Slats spoke.

"Tell you what, kid," he said, "this time I won't be gone so long—I promise—"

"Bethany," Wade was saying, back in the dugout, "I was —well, I was glad you didn't want to sell."

"Oh, I wanted to, all right," she admitted honestly. "But somehow, I couldn't bring myself to tell you so—"

"Same here," Wade said. "I wanted to, in a way. I almost said yes. And then I remembered how much we had at stake. Besides, that would have seemed like trading Rex off for—well, for stuff to eat this winter. I couldn't have done that. Land was different—"

It was the first time he had mentioned Rex since the trade. But it was not the first time he had thought of him, Bethany well knew.

"As I said, we have a lot at stake."

They had two sections of land covered with brown grass.

They had a patch of dead maize, inclosed with a makeshift fence that even the ranch cattle, grazing near, seemed to find incongruous. Guarding nothing, it was, like a poor old faithful dog standing by his master's grave, unwilling or unable to accept the fact of death. They had three work horses and a limping no-good one. They had a cow and a calf. That was all.

No—that was not all. On one section they had a spring, and in this country that was everything. They had the knowledge that the railroad was coming through.

"I'll think of something, Bethany," he promised her. "I'd cut lake hay, if I could manage for a mower and a rake. But it's too far to go to ranch headquarters for one, and there's no other to get."

There was, indeed, the lake hay. Nature, as if trying to make amends to her children, seemed to see that it was best in dry years. Wade could, and did, cut this for his own stock—slowly, with infinite pains, as his fathers had cut grain. But he did not get enough to sell. What he cut he stored safely away for winter's use.

In fact, everything he did had an air of preparation about it. He brought back wood from the breaks, piling it against the side of the dugout. He went to the prairie for a load of chips. These too he piled away for future use.

"My goodness, Wade," she said. "You act as if you were expecting another blizzard tomorrow."

"You never can tell," he replied.

When he spoke that way, it was just as well to give up trying to talk to him. Anyway, she didn't feel much like talking herself. It was the heat. Summer had no right to hold on this long. She was worn down with it. She felt dried out and dead, like the tall center stalks of the bear grass. She could not sleep, and she had scarcely any appetite. That was just as well, with supplies as low as they were. Wade shot some quail, brought them in for her to cook. Although he did not comment, she knew that he had noticed the way she picked at her food and had thought the game would taste good to her. She tried hard to eat them, so hard that Wade was aware of her effort.

"Good Lord, Bethany," he said stiffly, "you don't have to make yourself sick just to keep from hurting my feelings. *I* don't care whether you eat them or not—"

He was worried. She ought to be able to say something, to do something, to relieve this worry of his, this deep concern. She had stepped in between him and Poco. That was an easy thing, something done instinctively, as one closes his eyes when an object passes too close to them. Now she was powerless. Action, even action involving danger, would be a relief. Doing nothing was hard on a person. Like silence, it ate into the brain.

There were two kinds of silence, she thought. There was the comforting kind she and Wade used to have—just sitting in each other's presence, feeling no need to speak but still being glad the other one was there. There was that different kind they knew now—a thing too wide to bridge, too great to ignore.

The days went on.

"Bethany," Wade asked at last, "how are we—when will we need supplies—?" He was polite, almost formal.

"I think we can last until October," she said. "I'm being very careful—"

"I know." It was almost as if he were impatient with her for answering. Time was when she would have been deeply hurt by this impatience, even resentful of it. Now she felt only a great lassitude, a great weariness. Maybe the country had worn her down after all. Maybe she was like Lizzie Dillon—had just stopped caring.

She could not tell Wade these things; now they talked scarcely at all. Often she looked at him, knowing his quietness had some purpose behind it. What this might be she did not even bring herself to wonder.

And then, without warning, she knew.

"Bethany," he said, speaking suddenly, as if he had only just made up his mind, "Bethany—I'm going to have to leave—"

"You—you mean to—stay for good?" she asked.

"No—just for awhile. I've got to get hold of some money."

She knew that, but she waited for him to go on.

"I've been thinking about it. I need more than I can make gathering bones, although, come winter, I may do that, too. You know I can't get work on the ranches, burnt out and frozen out and dried out the way they are. They've had a hard time, too."

Yes, she thought, everybody had had a hard time. Maybe that was all this country was good for—hard times.

"I thought I'd ride up north a ways—maybe as far as Dodge City—and see what I could find."

"You mean working on the railroad?"

"Maybe. I don't know for sure until I get there. But I'll do something. I've thought it all out—"

"I guess you're right," she agreed.

"Well," he said, "that's settled. Now we'll just go over to Mobeetie and catch the stage. I'll ride Star, and Newsome's horse will get you there. And once we're there, I'll sell the horses. They won't bring much, but it will be enough to get you back to Missouri. You can wait there until I can make some money—"

Back to Missouri. Back to Star Hill. Bethany Fulton Cameron, coming back home to stay while her husband looked for work. All too well she knew the things Star Hill would say to that.

("Have you heard," the neighbors would ask, "have you

heard! Wade Cameron got burned out on that Texas claim of his, and Bethany's come home to her mother."

"It's as I always told you," Aunt Clara would remind her. "Homesteaders starve to death, unless someone helps them."

"So—you've come home to stay, Bethany," Rosemary would drawl. "Dear me—I guess Wade wasn't such a catch after all. It's as Mother said, the Cameron men never amount to anything.")

Home to Missouri! Once the words would have been sweet to her ear. Now they smacked only of defeat and failure. She remembered the ruined crops, and the dead stock—those things on which their hopes had been built. She remembered the bones they had gathered, and the mittens, and the scant rations. Those were little things—those were as nothing at all compared to this new price she would have to pay, if she went to Missouri now.

She said, "I'm not going, Wade."

"Not going?" he did not believe her. "Of course you are going!"

"No," she said it so quietly that he knew she must mean it. He tried another tactic.

"You can't stay here alone. I won't let you. Remember—remember Milly—"

"I'm not like Milly. I'll be all right—"

"I won't hear to it—"

"I won't go. You know as well as I do that someone has to stay here to look after the claim and the stock."

In the end she wore him down.

It did not take him long to get ready. Most of the preparations had already been made during those weeks in which his decision was growing in him. The day came to leave, and, having got his things ready, he saddled Star. He came to stand awkwardly before Bethany, speaking almost as if he were a stranger.

"I'll write you as soon as I get settled," he told her. "But maybe I won't be gone too long—"

"Don't hurry. Take your time to do whatever you need to do."

All along she had felt he had something else in his mind—something he was so unsure about that he did not quite know what it was himself. Of course, he couldn't tell her if he didn't know himself.

"Butch and Slats will look after you. They promised me."

They had made that same promise to Tom when he left Milly, but Bethany would not let herself think of that now. She hoped Wade was not remembering either.

"I've got a lot of plans for when I get back," he told her, thus hoping to make his leaving sound like a casual, ordinary thing—something of short duration, like a trip for water or a ride out on the range to look after the cattle. "By that time maybe it will have rained, and I can make us a real fence. I'll try to pick up a few cattle up in the Territory. Ought to be able to get them cheap, after the drought and all. I may even try to dig a well—"

If his plans were visionary, they at least had confidence and purpose back of them.

"I'm going to make something out of our land," he said. "With the railroad coming through, I can do it. I'm going to plow up another piece, and fence it. I'm going to try to get some wheat seed—the kind that will grow here—"

"That would be good," she said.

"Well, I must be going. Good-by, Bethany."

He took her in his arms and kissed her, gently, as if he meant to be gone only a little while. Then his arms tightened around her, and he kissed her several times—roughly, so that she knew that if she said one little word, maybe, or let one tear slip down her face, he might not leave her at all.

She did not say the word, shed the tear.

"Good-by," she said. "Don't worry—I'll get along fine."

She drew back just a little, but enough so that he remembered it was time to go.

He left her there, beside the dugout door. She watched him ride away; she continued to watch him, waving to him each time he turned to look back. And when he had at last disappeared into the vast reaches of the plains, she went back inside. She threw herself down across the bed and cried for a long time. After that she felt better. She got up and looked at herself in the mirror; then she combed her hair and made herself neat.

She had held herself straight and strong until he was gone. She had been brave, and she should be proud of herself. She had not broken down in front of him.

She had not told him she was going to have a baby.

CHAPTER EIGHTEEN

SHE was alone.

Loneliness was a strong taste in her mouth, a swirling surge in her heart. There were times when she reminded herself that she need not have endured this—if she had told him about the baby, Wade would have stayed, would have found some way to work out things here at home. No matter how he felt about it, a man would have to stay then. But always she was glad she had not told him. Once she had taken advantage of him. She was a girl then—young, foolish, thinking only of what she wanted. Now she was a woman and she must try to make up for that other time.

She thought much of Milly. Gentle Milly, who had never done harm to anyone, and yet had met a strange and cruel fate. It was not fair that Milly should have had to suffer so. She wondered if maybe the world wasn't made up mostly of unfair things.

Now here were she and Wade, who had come out wanting nothing but a chance to work, to make their own way. They had not asked for anyone to give them anything—the land they worked, or seed for the land, or money, or supplies. All they asked was that fate, or the weather, or the country give them a chance. And what had come to them? Prairie fires and drought and blizzards and deprivation. And separation and loneliness.

Maybe Tobe Dillon had been right. Maybe the country did resent them. Maybe there was a force, subtle and cruel, that worked against them. You can't fight fate; it's too much to ask of anyone.

It was the stillness. That was what was wrong with her. It came in waves, more terrifying than any noise could be. She braced herself to meet it, restrained herself to keep from running out into the night to meet it. Once, long ago, she had flung herself into Wade's arms, sobbing fearfully at the menace of silence. Now he was not here for her to turn to. And she was even more afraid now than she had been then. Whatever she saw wore the face of fear. And finally she knew fear for what it was, saw grinning madness peering through its eyes.

She knew she must find work for her hands to do, so she took to making things. Shelves. A footstool. A table. She used the boxes canned goods had come in; she used some of the wood Wade had piled beside the dugout. She could touch a piece of this and feel a certain strength and comfort coming to her, almost as if he were here himself.

It did not matter what she made, what the things looked like when she was finished. That was not the core of the matter. Her real business was the conquering of fear. Housed in the blessed actuality of noise, she could hold fast to sanity. She worked far into the night until finally she was so exhausted that once she went to bed she could almost sleep.

She had been free for a long time of thoughts of Rosemary, but now they began to move in on her again. How did she know that Wade had forgotten about Rosemary? How did she know he hadn't gone to her now? She saw the image of Rosemary, and it was the face of silence itself—inscrutable, waiting.

She must stop thinking things like that. She made herself go through the regular routine of living. She cooked, and tried to eat. And then one day she found she could not swallow at all. The muscles of her throat refused to work. She was really frightened. There was no telling what she might have done had Butch and Slats not come that afternoon. It was as if they sensed her need, knew it was almost as urgent as Milly's last one had been. So great was her emotion at seeing them that she could not speak at all. Any sound she made would have ended only in hysterical laughter.

"Howdy," Slats said. "Brought you something—"

It was a couple of prairie chickens, dressed and ready for cooking.

"Wondered if you'd cook us a bite," he said. "We can't eat that stuff the cook puts out. He's in love with a town gal, and he don't know any more than a spook what he's putting in the chuck. Like as not to find a lobo wolf stewed up if we don't watch him—"

He was making the story up, out of whole cloth.

"Sure—" she said, the sound of her voice coming like the sound of a rusty hinge on a gate.

She cooked the meat for them, and together they sat down and ate. The muscles of her throat worked once more, and she could swallow. The food tasted delicious—she wanted to cry at the wonderful, glorious taste of food. She wanted to hold every bite in her mouth a long time, savoring the taste of it. She wanted also to swallow in a great hurry, lest by some evil magic she should once more lose the power to do so.

"Sure is good chow," Slats said. "Reckon we could get you to come over and take cook's place? He's liable to leave any minute—"

She laughed at that. She had not laughed since Wade left— or for a long time before. She remembered now. She had not laughed since he told her he must leave. Since he left she had talked to the horses and to the cow and calf, but she had not laughed. A lone person can talk to animals, or to herself, she thought. But she cannot laugh to herself. That action holds a taint of madness.

It was after she laughed that they told her, waiting as though they knew she could not have borne to hear Wade's name mentioned before that.

"Oh, yes," Slats said, "we were supposed to tell you that Wade left his horse at the ranch and caught a ride up on the stage. He had the chance, and he said it was too slow, riding a lone horse up to look for work—"

She wondered why the boys had not brought Star back with them. The next moment Slats explained that.

"He said he'd pick up the horse on his way back—that way, it wouldn't take him so long."

Wade had told her he wasn't going to be gone any longer than was necessary. He meant it. Still, she was surprised that he would take the stage.

"Thank you," she said. "Thank you for telling me."

"Got anything we can do?" they asked. "We got the day off, and we're ready to work."

"No," she said, not taking advantage of the opportunity they offered.

"We figured to haul some water, and that's just what we are a-going to do. Want to go with us?"

"No—I believe not."

She could not bear to go to the spring. That would make Wade too unbearably near.

They hauled the water. They checked her supply of wood and chips. They gave some hay to the stock. And then they came to tell her good-by.

"So long," Slats said. "We'll be going along. We'll watch the mail when it comes through and get your letter to you. May have to send it by someone else, but we'll see that you get it—"

"Oh, thank you—" she said.

Butch hung back. After Slats was gone, he stood before Bethany, twisting his hat between his hands, shifting from one foot to the other.

"I reckon you ought to know," he said finally, "we think you are a right brave person—"

He fled. It is doubtful that he heard her as she cried after him, "Oh, thank you, Butch! Thank you—"

She knew she had just received the Accolade.

After their visit things went better. She had a grip on herself, and she held fast to her gain. She mended her clothes, setting fine, neat patches on cloth almost too frail to hold them. She re-read "Pilgrim's Progress," was surprised how much more meaningful it was to her now that she herself had come through the slough of despair. She read much from the Bible, setting herself to memorizing a certain number of verses each day. She found Mr. Longfellow rather thin brew, set beside those other two. He was all right, she guessed, if you wanted something to read aloud in a front parlor to well-bred, genteel people. But the others were something to hold to, something you could set your teeth in.

She went out to care for the stock, keeping her eyes fixed straight ahead of her, not looking around at all. She walked as a child walks in the dark—afraid to look behind him lest the thing he sees may be a thousand times more fearful than that which he fears. It was foolish for her to feel that way—by and by she would get over it. She had already conquered much; she would wait awhile before she made herself face the real enemy, before she made herself stare into the terrifying face of infinity.

She was doing pretty well—better than she had hoped for. She wouldn't push herself too far.

Finally a young cowboy came riding up to bring her a letter.

"Slats and Butch, Ma'am, they couldn't get off to come," he told her shyly, "but they said for me to bring you this letter, and to see if there was anything I could do for you."

"Thank you," she said, reaching out for the letter, her hands trembling so that she could scarcely take it when he handed it to her. "No—I mean, there's nothing you can do—"

She saw Wade's writing on the envelope—strange, she had never had a letter from him before. She had known him all her life, had been his wife for more than a year, was carrying his child. But this was his first letter to her.

"Are you sure?" the boy persisted. He had his orders, and evidently was bound on carrying them out.

"No" she said, knowing that she sounded impatient, if not ungrateful. The boy had ridden miles to bring her this letter. She should ask him in, offer him something to eat. But she could bring herself to do neither of these. All she wanted was for him to be on his way, leaving her alone with her letter. Wade's letter.

"Well, if you are sure there's nothing—"

"Nothing—and thank you, so much—"

He did not persist, but rode away and left her.

She went into the dugout and sat down in the little rocking chair. She had begun to tremble again, so that she could scarcely tear open the letter. At last she had it open, saw the words.

"My dear Bethany," (the letter began) "I take this chance to write you, hoping the letter will not be too long in going through. I am well, and hope the same of you.

"I suppose by now Butch and Slats have told you that I took the stage to Dodge City. Hud Johnson is driving now, so I helped him out and got to ride free.

"I must tell you, my dear wife, that I did not get work on the railroad. I could have had it, but when I found out how long I would have to work in order to get the money I needed,

I knew I could not spare so much time. I need to be back home."

Bethany liked that, re-read the words.

"I decided I would come on to Dodge City, and try something I had in mind. But that did not work, either. So—"

The page fell from her hand. She turned to the next one.

"—so, I have decided to go on to Missouri. I am going to try to borrow money there to keep us going. I tried in Dodge City, but I know no one there and they will not let me have it without security, which I could not give—"

He had gone back to Missouri. To Missouri, to borrow money!

"—I would not have done this, my dear wife, if I had not thought it was the only way. I will come back home as soon as I can get the matter attended to. I hope you are getting along all right. I think of you a great deal.

                              "Your loving husband,
                                    Wade Cameron."

The letter dropped to the floor.

Wade had gone back to Missouri to borrow money! Already debt had cast its long shadow across the years ahead. Now he was preparing to deepen that shadow, to make it longer. That he should go back to Missouri to do this made it a thing not to be borne—a thousand times worse than taking a missionary barrel, the ultimate disgrace she had yet been able to picture. It was defeat and failure, more visible and sure than wagon tongues pointed East.

She cried, "Oh, no—no—"

She picked up the letter, re-read the words. Yes, that's what they said. She hadn't misread them.

"Oh, no—Wade—" she said aloud once more. "Oh, you can't —you mustn't!"

He might have been standing there before her, so urgent was her plea. And then she knew how foolish she was. Wade had gone. He was there by now, and everyone in town knew he had failed in Texas, had come back begging for help, as they all said he would.

"I told you so," Aunt Clara would say. "I tried to tell you, but you wouldn't listen. Just like all the Cameron men."

By now, Brad Bishop, smug and complacent, knew that the boy who had refused a job in his bank had failed in the work of his own choosing. By now they all knew—everyone in Star Hill.

Rosemary knew.

That was the real trouble. She might as well face it. Much as she hated the thought of his borrowing money, she hated far more the other thoughts that came crowding in on her now.

How was she to know that borrowing money wasn't just an excuse for him to go back and see Rosemary? Maybe he had meant to do it from the first, had never intended to look for work on the road, to try to borrow money in Dodge City. He couldn't get them because he didn't really want them. Why else would he have left Star at the ranch instead of riding him on up the line, looking for work as he went?

If she had been distressed before, now she was distraught. She walked back and forth, back and forth, across the rag carpet. She squeezed her hands together until she felt pain in them; she looked down at them stupidly, not knowing the reason for the pain. Then she unclasped them slowly, walked over to the little keg to get a drink.

With the touch of the spigot under her fingers, reason and sanity returned. Here was a visible manifestation of Wade's thoughtfulness for her. She let her hand rest upon the damp coolness of the keg, felt healing shame in her heart. How *could* she think such things of Wade? She drank some water, put the glass down. Then she went weakly across the floor and sat in a chair, feeling as if she had escaped some great, though nameless, danger.

From the first, Rosemary had cast a shadow across her marriage. Although she had not been here at all, every day Bethany had fought her. And now, suddenly, she did not want to fight any more. Maybe it was best that Wade go back and see Rosemary. That wasn't the thing that took him back, but, even so, it was good that he would see her. Maybe the sight of her would settle things, once and for all. Whatever happened would be better than the way things were now. You can't live with fear and uncertainty every day of your life. Better to know a hard thing for sure than to crouch in fear and terror beneath its shadow, never seeing the real shape of it.

She had thought in her heart that Rosemary was like the silence itself—she had seen her face as the image of silence. She had to stop letting ideas like that get hold of her. She had someone besides herself to think of now. She couldn't be forever like Eva Newsome, concerned only for herself. She had faced the problem of Rosemary. Now she would face the silence. She would make herself look at those wide spaces, the place where silence dwelt.

Where at first she had gone to the corral, keeping her eyes fixed straight on the path she travelled, now she made herself look around a little. Not much at first, for when she looked she dropped her eyes involuntarily at the wide nothingness around her. The first day she looked as far as the plowed field. The next, she let her eyes range farther. It was the end of the week before she could bring herself to stand still and look— on and on—to the farthest edge of the horizon's rim.

Again it was Indian summer, with a soft and benign gentleness wrapped around the land. The grass might be dry, but there was a brightness upon it, a golden wash of light. The sky was very blue; the clouds shaped themselves into endless patterns of majesty, ever-changing, ever-lovely. Below them, the earth seemed more comfortably small, more a thing she could understand. Looking at the clouds somehow gave her a sense of proportion.

And then one morning a strange thing happened to her. She found that she could look at the level and limitless land with no sense of pain at all. She thought, "Of course, this isn't like Missouri. All the time I've been trying to compare the two of them. They aren't supposed to be alike. This country is like nothing but itself."

She stood facing the knowledge, letting it flow through her. There was a sort of rhythm to the silence, a feeling of purpose. If you were still and quiet yourself, you could feel it, get into the spirit of it. Maybe that was what Wade saw in it. Maybe that's what all the Cameron men had been looking for—a country they could believe in. His grandfather had thought it would be California; his father must have been sure it would be Kansas. For Wade it was Texas, and for Wade things were going to be different. He had married a woman who, at long last, could see his country the way he did.

"It's—it's like infinity," she thought, gazing across the miles of space, "it's like life everlasting—"

The country seemed to reach out, to renew itself so that each mile added more miles; so that each new mile was, in turn, the seed for other uncounted miles as yet unborn.

"It's like creation," she thought. "It's like my baby—"

The next day Wade came home.

He came just at sunset. Bethany saw him a long way off. At first she would not let herself believe it was he, but presently he was so close that she knew she could not be mistaken. She began to tremble a little, but she did not rush outside to wait for his coming. She combed her hair carefully, although her hands shook so it was hard to pull the comb through it. But she did not change her dress. This one she had on was clean. She mustn't rush at things. She had held in so long, now was not the time to give way.

He dropped the reins and came to the door and she went

there to meet him. Even as he came, she knew that his were not the actions of a defeated man. He had got what he wanted from the trip. She must make herself wait for him to tell her what this was.

He said, "I'm home, Bethany," and he took her in his arms, kissed her.

"Yes," she said. "You're home—"

"It's good to be back," he said. "I've worried so about you. I worried all the time. I didn't tell your mother you were alone, but I didn't sleep nights, thinking about you—"

"How is Mama—"

"She's fine. You must go back for a visit soon, Bethany. She and your father are lonesome for you."

"I'll go back. How's Papa?"

"He's fine, too—"

They were talking little things, holding themselves back from what they really wanted to say. They were feeling around the edges of the matter, carefully, not yet trusting themselves to come to the heart of it.

"The dugout is still the same," he said, looking around him. He still held her hand, scarcely seeming to know he was doing it. "Once I woke up at night, and for a minute I couldn't remember what it looked like. It scared me. I was ready to start back next morning, before I got the money—"

She asked, her voice strangely thick, "Oh—you got the money—?"

"Yes," he said, and now he was down to the core of the thing. "Yes—I got it."

He had got it from Papa, she guessed. That was all right, maybe, and the way things ought to be—all in the family. But she wished they hadn't been forced to take money from her folks. It was—well, it was sort of like the Newsomes, only in a different way, of course. But if Wade thought that was all right, she'd have to trust his judgment. After all, she was all

Mama and Papa had. If they wanted to help her, why shouldn't they?

"I got it from the bank—" he told her.

From the bank. The words jumped out at her, writhed before her. The bank! That meant Brad Bishop. That meant he had to go crawling back to the man who had watched him go to Texas with a sort of amused condescension in his smooth face. He had to humble himself to Brad Bishop, to Rosemary's husband.

He went to Brad Bishop, which was in a way taking something from Rosemary.

"Oh—not from the bank," she cried out, wishing she could stop the words, powerless to do so.

"Don't think I wanted to do this, Bethany," he told her. "Don't think it was easy—"

"I know—" she said stiffly.

"But listen, Bethany—it was like I told you. There was just no other way. I had to do it—"

She could understand that. You did what you had to.

"I couldn't take it from your folks," he told her. "They would have given it to me, I know. But it had to be a loan—"

No—he couldn't take it from Mama and Papa. Hard as things were, she was glad he felt that way.

"So I went to Brad Bishop."

"He—he let you have it?"

"Not at first. He wouldn't even listen to me at first. But I kept on. I guess, if you keep on saying the same thing long enough, people will finally listen."

Of course, it wasn't easy. She knew that, just as she knew he wouldn't tell her all of the hardships for a long time, maybe never. Afterwhile the soreness would wear off, but not soon. He could stand it now because he had got what he wanted. But he couldn't talk about it overmuch.

273

"What did you tell him?" she asked, thinking this was a safe question.

"I told him I wanted money to buy cattle, and seed, and wire. I even told him I'd have to use some for interest and land payments."

"And what did he say?"

"He asked me what security I could offer."

That's what she wanted to know, too.

"I told him I didn't have a darned thing but my faith in the country."

So that was how he got the money. He asked for it in confidence and faith. That wasn't like begging at all; that bore scarcely any resemblance to failure. You couldn't give things to a man who believed in himself and in the venture he represented. You made him a loan. That was different. Brad Bishop was a business man; he knew what he was doing.

"I told him," Wade said, "that if I wasn't able to pay him in five years, I'd come back to the bank and work it out. I signed a personal note, and he handed me the money."

"You told him that?" she marveled.

"I was that sure I wouldn't have to," Wade said.

"You won't—oh, Wade!—I know you won't!"

She was as sure of it as she had ever been of anything in her life. Because she was sure, she could ask him the next question.

"Did you see Rosemary?"

As soon as she said the name, she felt better. She had been an idiot to stand cowering in fear of it all these months. Whatever his answer was, she would always be glad she asked the question before he brought it up himself.

"Yes—I saw her."

"How did she look?"

"Like she always did—maybe even a little prettier. Except—well, sort of hard-like. I understand she and Brad don't get along too well."

"Did she—did she know about the money?"

Ah, that was what rankled; that was the hard thing.

"I don't know," he said. "Maybe. Come to think of it, Brad probably told her. But who cares if she does know? Who gives a hoot about what Rosemary thinks?"

Bethany faced him, not saying a word. But what she was thinking came through to him. He looked at her slowly, searchingly. He put his arms around her.

"Bethany," he said, holding her so that she really had no choice, "look at me—"

She raised her amber-flecked eyes, very dark and intense now, to his face.

"Bethany," he asked, "you haven't been thinking—all this time—that I—well, that I still wanted Rosemary?"

She could not answer. She could only stand there in his arms, trembling a little, a pulse hammering in her throat.

"Oh, Bethany—Bethany—darling –" he whispered. "I didn't. Oh, I don't—"

He bent to kiss her, and then stopped, as if there was something else he knew he must say.

"I guess I never wanted her, really," he said. "I think I stopped wanting her the minute you said you'd come to Texas with me."

He kissed her.

"—I thought you knew," he whispered. "All along, I thought you knew—that it was you I loved—"

Bethany rested in his arms, savoring this moment of joy, tasting the exquisite sweetness of it. In a little while she'd tell him about the baby. There was no hurry. They had a lifetime before them. It stretched out, far-reaching and bright, like the country they lived in.